Roberta Latow ha~~s~~ .... ~~dealer~~ with galleries
in Springfield, Massachussetts and New York City.
She has also been an international interior designer
in the USA, Europe, Africa and the Middle East,
travelling extensively to acquire arts, artefacts and
handicrafts. Her sense of adventure and her experiences on her travels have enriched her writing; her
fascination with heroic men and women; how and
why they create the lives they do for themselves;
the romantic and erotic core within – all these
themes are endlessly interesting to her, and form
the subjects and backgrounds of her novels.

'Latow's writing is vibrant and vital. Her characters
are much more than caricatures and she describes
them in such a distinctive, dynamic way that you
can't help but be swept along by them. Latow is a
pleasure to read . . . she's a popular writer for the
Nineties' *Books* magazine

The Pleasure Seekers

Roberta Latow

HEADLINE

First published in 1996
by HEADLINE BOOK PUBLISHING

First published in paperback in 1996
by HEADLINE BOOK PUBLISHING

10 9 8 7 6 5 4 3

ISBN 0 7472 5305 6

Typeset by Palimpsest Book Production Limited,
Polmont, Stirlingshire

Printed and bound in Great Britain by
Cox & Wyman Ltd, Reading, Berkshire

HEADLINE BOOK PUBLISHING
A division of Hodder Headline PLC
338 Euston Road
London NW1 3BH

For
the friends we have all made
on the islands of our dreams

Neptune's song, his perfume,
I am seduced, enthralled.
The sea, the sea,
How bright the sun,
its heat, it burns my flesh,
sears my heart, and melts my soul.
I sat and waited for him in the sun.

— *The Epic of Artimadon*

LIVAKIA, CRETE

Chapter 1

The comments were always the same when D'Arcy was driving in a cloud of heat and dust through the mountain villages in her cherished 2CV: 'Here comes the ugliest car on the road. A sardine tin on wheels. My donkey goes faster, Kiria D'Arcy.' Only some of the teasing was accompanied by broad Cretan smiles and enthusiastic arm waving from the tall, handsome men sitting on stone walls under the hot morning sun. She always waved back, often shouting out a cheeky reply in perfect Greek and giving one of her dazzling smiles. Sometimes she would stop and have a coffee and a chat with the men; at other times they would wave down the Deux Chevaux to hitch a ride.

Laugh as they might at the beautiful American's small bright aquamarine-coloured car with its fold-down coral canvas roof, they had the greatest respect for the way it took the twisting and turning narrow dirt roads and climbed the tracks carved out of the mountains. The way it clung to the stony ground on the breathtakingly steep descents never ceased to impress either.

D'Arcy Montesque and her car were a familiar sight to most in this still remote area of Crete. She smiled as she saw an old man dressed in traditional male dress: white leather boots, black embroidered vest, billowing trousers and a fringed black sash. He raised his arm and rotated his wrist. She could almost hear the clicking of his tongue: a Greek expression of wonderment, and admiration, especially when accompanied by a near toothless smile.

D'Arcy was on her way to her village, Livakia, ten miles on at the end of this sometimes impassable road. It was somewhat like going through a pass. The car clattered round a tight bend and the terrain opened up into a spectacular vista: rugged, arid and stony mountains on either side of a crescent-shaped valley that crashed steeply down to a bay of luscious blue sea, rolling out to meet the sky on the horizon. The beauty of the place took D'Arcy's breath away, as always. The light like no other, the heat, the sea an eternity sparkling silver under the sun. It was a place of magic – where the ancient gods might have lived; where D'Arcy did live.

She sat in a clearing next to the road with the motor still running, looking straight out across the Aegean. Taking a deep breath, she was filled with wonder and joy. She never took Livakia for granted. A sigh, a smile for the gods, and D'Arcy pulled up the handbrake, cut the motor, and hopped from the car. It had been a bone-rattling ride once she had left the main road but she never tired of the drive, respected it. It did after all afford her and everyone else living in Livakia privacy, kept it a kind of Shangri-La. D'Arcy pulled off her hat, slapped it against her thigh to loosen the dust, and tossed it on to the seat before she walked several yards to the edge of the clearing and looked down: Livakia, an amphitheatre of houses, whiter than white, hugged the side of the mountain and its small natural harbour.

There had always been a village there, even in ancient times. It was not unusual to find fragments from different civilisations when rebuilding an old ruin as most everyone who lived there had to have done at one time or another. Livakia was one of those island villages that had flourished and then died several times throughout its history. The last forty years had seen the near abandoned and crumbling village rise slowly to flourish again. D'Arcy felt very much a part of its recent history.

She saw the donkeys and the donkey boys making the steep zigzag climb up through the village towards the clearing. The clip-clop of hooves on stones and the nagging of the animals' handlers prodding them on – familiar sounds of home. She smiled, called down to them and waved. Donkeys were the primary mode of transportation in Livakia, their handlers a Mafia all their own who were treated with respect and care. Everything that came into Livakia, either by boat or overland through the Lefka Ori range, had to be manhandled for the last stage and loaded on to paniers. Transport was by foot, water or beast in Livakia.

D'Arcy returned to the car and began unloading it. She had been to Chania and the post office to pick up parcels from London: books from Heywood Hill for Laurence, tea and coffee from Fortnum's, chocolates from Rococo for her. Cheese and olive oil for Arnold, figs and peaches for Edgar and Bill, ink for Rachel purchased in Chania. A shopping trip out of Livakia was never for oneself alone.

By the time the donkeys had arrived she had pulled up the roof of the 2CV, locked it in place, and backed the car several hundred yards round a bend and into the cave where she kept it.

One of the five donkeys was loaded with her things. A donkey handler was sitting on the stone wall that ran along the edge of the clearing, smoking a cigarette, while another was squatting with his back against the wall, running a string of worry beads through his fingers. D'Arcy exchanged pleasantries with the donkey men and delivered a carton of cigarettes and a pair of sunglasses they had asked for. She declined the offer of a ride down the hill in favour of a leisurely walk down the cobblestone paths. It would be several hours before she would see her parcels again; the donkeys were waiting for a delivery of period roof tiles for Mark. One of the donkey men, a strapping, handsome and proud-looking hunk with a reputation for womanising and for prowess in sex with the young and beautiful foreigners who found their way to Livakia, could not resist a clicking of his tongue, a husky whisper of admiration in Greek and the announcement: 'All the girls want to fuck with me, D'Arcy. You are missing something special. I really want you, Kiria D'Arcy. Give in. I can make you very happy.'

'And I want you so much, Petros, but I want you more as a friend. We can't be both. Once I had had you, to see you with another woman would make me crazy with jealousy.'

One never hurt the pride of a Cretan man. This was an island famous for its vendettas. D'Arcy spoke with a straight face and a hurt expression, and watched him pull himself up with pride, lust still simmering in his eyes. He rubbed the swell in his trousers, and shrugged his shoulders. That was D'Arcy's cue. She smiled and shrugged hers, and started down the steep path. They played this scene about twice a year. He never gave up.

D'Arcy had to go all the way down to the port and walk around one side of it before she started climbing up again to her house. She always marvelled at the peace and quiet of Livakia. One hardly ever heard a sound coming from the houses and that was something because there was a great deal of living going on behind those walls: couples and families, children, and lovers, passion and love. But there were unwritten laws here: a respect for privacy, the Livakians as well as the foreign colony in residence supporting each other. That did not, of course, stop the petty jealousies nor the Cretans' favourite pastime, gossip.

D'Arcy was smiling to herself, thinking about the gossip. How no one minded it, how everyone looked forward to it. It was one of the pleasures of life in Livakia, like the sun and the sea, time, sex and love. It made everyone's life seem in some remote way a part of one's own, and most especially so between the foreign residents. There was an undeclared co-dependence upon one another, like a group of castaways. Only they had not arrived by chance. Each of them had come to settle in Livakia because he or she was a pleasure seeker who had found paradise.

She was thinking that as she passed one of the ruined houses – no roof, just crumbling walls on several levels, with a very old fig tree in what must once have been its courtyard. There was a splendid view down across the white houses and other walled courtyards, other ruins yet to be restored. Splashes of magenta and coral and bright yellow: flowering potted plants and climbing Bougain-villaea, the odd weather-beaten palm tree poking high above the white walls and stony ground. It was a different view than the one from her house but one that afforded a clear impression of the magnificent amphitheatre of the village with the Aegean Sea as its stage, just as hers did. There was the scent of wild thyme, the heat of the sun, ripe fruit on the fig tree, and Mark Obermann sitting on a broken stone bench in the shade of its branches. D'Arcy felt compelled to pick her way over the ruins and join him.

He seemed lost in thought and unaware of her approach. There was something irresistible about Mark's boyish looks: the slender but strong body, the sandy-coloured hair and piercing blue eyes, lips that should have been sensuous but were not. A charisma of intelligence and suffering, depths yet to be discovered. Women didn't so much fall in love with Mark as want to rub up against him, excite him into making love to them. It was his promise of genius, his vulnerability, the way he made you feel you were missing something by not being an essential part of his life. He made you believe he was the writer, the poet of genius everyone would have liked to have been – and he was, and that was his power. He was what other people aspired to be, and men and women, the famous and the infamous, his peers and the most simple of Cretans, respected him for that. Everyone liked him, some even loved him, though most saw his flaws and ignored them. That was the way in Livakia.

Their affair had been brief and intense and for a short time D'Arcy had actually thought she might be in love with him. That had been more a passion of the head than the heart or the loins, she realised. In fact it had been the sex that had made her understand there was something fundamental missing in Mark. He calculated all, every emotion of his life. He fucked the way he wrote a book, and had no idea what love was really about. Although he talked a good game of it, he was not a player. D'Arcy could afford to like him because she understood him now. Their affair had ended just as it should have, with no drama, just a running out of steam. They were friends, though they often sparred and disagreed about most things with the exception of their mutual passion for Crete, the Cretan people, and Livakia in particular.

She sat down on the bench next to Mark. He did not turn his head to greet her, merely placed an arm round her shoulders. They remained that way in silence for some time, enjoying the shade, just taking in the view. Mark finally rose from the bench to stand on it and reach into the leaves to pluck from the tree two purple figs bursting through their skin. He hopped down and offered one to D'Arcy.

'You didn't happen to see a van loaded with roof tiles on the road, did you?' he asked as he sat down and split open the fruit to suck out its succulent flesh.

'No, but I did see the donkeys up in the clearing waiting for it.'

'Come to dinner tonight, it's a long time since we've had a quiet evening together. I'd like to read you something from my new book. I'll cook for you the way I used to – your favourite fish stew if the men come in with a catch.'

'It's a long time since you've asked me.'

'But it's thanks but no thanks, is that it?' he asked before she could continue.

'Another time. Laurence is cooking.'

'His cooking's a joke.'

'Well, I know it, and you know it, even Laurence knows it. But he's cooking for me tonight.'

Conversation between them was over. They returned silently to enjoying the view. Periodically when they were alone D'Arcy sensed there was unfinished sex between them and that always made her feel uneasy. Since their brief affair there had been many women who had come and gone in Mark's life. He made each one of them believe she was the woman he wanted to settle down with. It was all stars in the eyes and gallant gestures, open affection and declaring the woman in question beautiful and clever and talented, the most amorous and sweet in the world. All his friends would believe it, even D'Arcy for a short time, until he would flaunt the chosen lady just that little too much in front of her.

It was at those times that she would remember she had been there just like them, and Mark would break their hearts as he had not broken hers. Those women fell for the dream, and the pleasure of being in love. They were under the spell of sex in the heat, of it all: Mark's pitch, and the place, not the man, the real man within, whom he so cleverly kept hidden. Maybe the bond they still had between them was that they had never been fooled by the trappings; they were hardened pleasure seekers who knew there was more to be had than they could give each other. It had saved them, kept them friends, not left them with broken hearts, nor bitter about each other. There was something else besides: they had been born on the same day of the same year in the same time zone. Significant? Maybe not, but difficult to discount.

D'Arcy rose from the bench, placed a kiss on Mark's cheek and left him as she had found him. It had been her plan to go directly home, bathe and change and then go to Laurence, but meeting Mark had changed all that. She was halfway down the village. She took a turn off the path, and another, and then climbed several steep stairs and let herself through Laurence's weatherworn gate. She called out, announcing her arrival, and was suddenly struck by how much she missed Laurence when she was not with him.

He appeared in the door, a smile on his lips. Whenever he heard her voice or saw D'Arcy she brought that particular smile to his lips, and he knew exactly why. He had never met a woman like her before. D'Arcy Montesque was pure pleasure. She had been born and bred to live for it and had no neuroses about it. She was the least complicated, the most sexy and loving woman he had ever been involved with. She wore her intelligence and talent like an invisible coat, but not her beauty. She wore that, like her mother before her the locals said, displayed proudly, merely to give them pleasure. And it was true: to see anyone as beautiful as D'Arcy was in itself a joy. Her kind of physical beauty lifted the spirits, brought people a moment of pure bliss.

He watched her now as she rushed up the last few

stairs to him, her auburn hair shining silk-like in the sun, violet eyes full of joy, face so young and fresh. Hers was a chiselled beauty: the high cheekbones and pointed chin; a perfect oval face, strong and sensuous yet somehow mysterious, and with an enchanting depth to it he had yet to fathom. Her long slender neck and collar-bones were exposed above the wide crescent-shaped neckline of the fine white linen dress she was wearing. The sun was behind her and he could see clearly the shape of her body: the extraordinarily long legs, slender hips, the heavy and succulent breasts that enticed with every step she took. Around her waist a belt of bright blue glass beads caught the sunlight. In her hand she carried the long linen jacket she would have worn in Chania or the mountain villages she might have stopped in on the way home. D'Arcy never dressed to offend or incite Cretan lust.

'I didn't expect you until much later.'

It was not what she had planned: sex, to be ravished by Laurence right then and there. But the moment he appeared in the doorway she was overcome with the desire to couple with him. D'Arcy had always found Laurence incredibly sexy. There was erotic attraction between them, that special sexual chemistry of something primitive, animalistic, when need and desire to die for a few seconds in the bliss of orgasm block out all else.

They suited each other physically, mentally, erotically. She found his English reserve exciting. And to see it crumble as he threw all sexual caution to the winds was thrilling. Sexual abandon and the quest for pleasure and

12

nothing more was what kept them together, enhanced life and their relationship while allowing them to remain their own independent selves.

D'Arcy said nothing. She didn't have to, she was speaking to him with her eyes, with every curve of her body. There was an aura of sex about her, a scent. She was luscious as ripe fruit, and she was offering herself. He plucked her from his doorstep like a warm peach, an offering from the gods.

He pulled her into the coolness of his house and his arms. She dropped her jacket and he heard her beaded belt clatter on the stone floor. He stopped kissing her only long enough to pull her dress over her head. Her body was warm and damp with perspiration and her skin had the faint scent of honeysuckle. It invaded his senses, she invaded his soul.

The roundness of her breasts, the weight of them in his hands, the pale pink of their nimbus, smooth and silky, cone-shaped and tipped with short slender nipples against the tan of her skin. They were breasts that tantalised and were to his eyes the most sensuous and beautiful he had ever seen. Naked she was like fire and ice. He seemed as if mesmerised by them as he stood back from her and slowly unbuttoned his shirt, climbed out of his jeans. With every move she made – to slip out of her panties, remove her shoes – she used her body to incite his lust, and it worked, he wanted her more. She was sexually loose, free, and incredibly elegant, but lewd in her lust. He could never get enough of her when he wanted her as he did now. Secretly he liked to think of her as the corrupting factor in his sex life, that she was the one responsible for their depravity. He used even that to excite himself.

He draped an arm round her waist and let his hand drop to caress her smooth clean-shaven mound, to slip his fingers between those most private of lips and fondle her as they walked through the house to his bedroom. Together they sat at the foot of the bed, looking not at the spectacular view from the window in front of them but at each other. How much she wanted him could be seen in her eyes; her body seemed to scream for sex, in any form, in every way. He could deprive her of nothing. Her desire had the ability to drive him to extremes, to do anything to bring on the long and strong orgasms she revelled in. He loved her and hated her for that and because she had possession of him. Laurence had not the will nor the desire to drive her out of his heart as he did all women he thought might change his life. He merely settled for secretly resenting their love affair while happily living with it.

Such mixed emotions overtook him now. He gently pushed D'Arcy back on the bed. Her luxuriant hair spread out across the rough white cotton sheets, she threw back her arms and smiled at him. Had ever a woman looked so wanton, so open and ready for a man, sex, the taste of come? He wanted to bathe her in it, drown her in pools of luscious sperm. D'Arcy always accepted orgasm as the elixir of life itself.

He lay on the bed next to her and rolled on his side to face her. She was on edge, bursting with pent up sexuality, sensuous, hungry for him and his sex. She lowered her gaze from his eyes to his phallus, so large and pulsating with desire for her, and then looked at him once more, deliberately licking her lips ever so slowly with pointed tongue.

There was lust and a huskiness in his voice. 'And so it begins. A voyage to oblivion,' he told her as he pressed a deep hungry kiss upon her mouth and continued other kisses down her body while he slipped over her, straddled her with his slim, wide-shouldered muscular body and draped his scrotum over her face, sliding the knob of his penis between her lips. The feel of her warm moist mouth, her tongue encircling him with caresses, made him close his eyes for a moment with a shiver of pleasure and push a little bit deeper, wanting more as he slid his arms under her knees and raised her legs off the floor to spread them wide apart on the edge of the mattress. With deft fingers he searched out those most intimate of lips and sucked on them, nibbled at them, licked them as nobly as she was tending to him. He found her small, ever so sensitive bud, the clitoris, that can deliver as strong and pleasurable an orgasm as exquisite penetration. He excited it and was rewarded with a taste of honey as she came on his tongue.

He immediately slid off her body to stand at the foot of the bed between her legs. Laurence gazed at her for one brief moment before he raised her legs and none too gently pulled her bottom up off the bed. He held her that way by the waist and in one forceful thrust sank himself as far as he could into D'Arcy.

To be penetrated by a man at the right moment in the right way was for D'Arcy one of the great joys of life. She had not moved since the moment Laurence had pushed her down on the bed. Now she closed her eyes and raised her arms as if to heaven and called out in a voice filled with passion and that special moan that comes only with sexual ecstasy: 'Oh, yes, yes! Laurence, it's wonderful. You're wonderful.'

She came and came again. Her orgasms drove him wild, they always did. The more she came and the stronger her orgasms, the more out of control she was in her submission to him, the better the sex was for him. He gave in to his own lust; he was ready now to deal with sexual depravity, all things carnal. Until D'Arcy such desire had only been possible in his fantasies. He penetrated her again and again in that position then changing his rhythm, the pattern of his thrusts, rolled her over on to her knees and took her from behind. The excitement of being riven again and again in these two positions was sublime for D'Arcy, and the thrill of sex with her like this no less so for Laurence. Then the moment arrived for them. They came together in an explosion of lust which they rode out on for a few seconds into oblivion. He had been right when he had told her: 'And so it begins.' For indeed that was only the beginning of sex for them that morning.

The post and the newspapers arrived by boat – how often was dependent on the weather, the boatman and what else he had to carry to Livakia, if indeed he felt like making the trip down the coast at all. The delivery was the first highlight of the day for D'Arcy and every resident of Livakia. Like everything here it was a casual arrangement, though since it was the boatman's livelihood and he lived in Livakia, the post at least was more or less reliable.

The port was where the Livakians did all their living when they weren't in their own houses; there, and in the narrow streets off the port, climbing up the side of the amphitheatre-like hill. There was a well-stocked grocer's shop, Mr Katzakis's, selling the best of the Cretan cheeses and honeys and olives, all sorts of foodstuffs native to the island and Greece. It smelled strongly of rosemary, lemons and Retsina. Amid the open bags of beans and flour, barrels and kegs and shelves of tinned goods, were upturned boxes where you could sit down and drink Retsina run off from a barrel into old-fashioned copper measure cups, smacked down on the makeshift tables with chunky, stubby glasses.

It was always cool, dark and relaxing when one stepped out of the sun and into Katzakis's emporium. You could read the paper or your post, having picked it up at the post office, drink a glass of Retsina so strong it could strip the paint off walls while nibbling at slivers of cheese, slices of salami, a dish of black olives. You had to bring your own bread. There you could pass the time of day with whoever else was in the shop and catch up with the latest news coming in from the boat people who arrived daily with the deliveries.

If there was a catch there was fish for sale off the boats, and bread and cakes from the baker who also, for fifty pence, would put your roast in his oven. That was another morning sight in the village: large roasting tins filled with lumps of lamb surround by what seemed like a peck of potatoes, or huge round tins of stuffed peppers, moussaka, a pastichio, or anything else that needed an oven, being run down the steep steps from all over the village by little boys, mothers or grandmothers to the baker's oven to be cooked in time for the midday meal.

There was another grocer's shop, smaller, which carried the foodstuffs Mr Katzakis did not; they had an understanding. A barber's shop boasted one chair for cutting, three for waiting, and sold newspapers and Aspirin, shampoo and hair gel and spray, male and female unmentionables, and had the only pay telephone in the village. The barber was also the mayor. His was a minute shop squashed between one of the two best tavernas in the village, the Kavouria, and the carpenter and local boat builder's shop. Next to that was the greengrocer who only opened when he had something to sell, and above him was the police station run by Manoussos Stavrolakis and his assistant. The other restaurant was not on the port but just off it in a tiered garden overlooking the sea. Three small coffee shops where nothing but coffee, ouzo or Retsina was served and backgammon and dominoes were played on wobbly old wooden tables completed the commercial life of the old port. You drank wine in the tavernas and brought your own bottle of spirits with you if that was your tipple.

The largest of the three churches in the village was several houses behind Mr Katzakis's and boasted a very pretty bell tower containing six bells that rang all at the same time. A stone and white-washed plaster palace for God and the village and all the surrounding villages too poor to have a church of their own, it boasted magnificent icons that drew connoisseurs from all over the world, gold and silver altar pieces, as well as a great many silver votives and candlesticks of considerable weight and size to hold the tall fat beeswax candles. There was also a priest, a powerfully influential man in the community and on the island, big and black-robed and heavily bearded. Everyone respected him, including two visiting monks from Mount Athos who appeared to be studying with him on a rather indefinite basis. They floated in their flowing black robes and crosses through the village, sat in the port at the coffee houses – inside in bad weather, out in good – dined in the tavernas on occasion and enjoyed the company of the foreigners in residence, altogether very much a part of the life of Livakia.

The other two churches were small, modest and white, typical Greek Island churches with domed roofs. Twenty people would have packed them. They were dots on the landscape, hanging in precarious places high up on the cliffs above Livakia. There were breathtaking climbs to them, spectacular views from them. Someone made those climbs every sunrise and every sunset to ring each church's single bell, and at different times of the day if the church had been opened by a believer there to pray, or mourn for a lost one, or merely to look at the frescoes and place fresh flowers below the painted and gilded portrait of a saint. The Cretans loved their saints. Thousands of such small churches, some very poor, others mini-Byzantine museums, studded the island. Byzantium had flourished there and was respected still, if not by all. Much too often thieves robbed such remote churches for Western dealers and art collectors.

The sound of the church bells of Livakia was one of the

joys of living there. It had a special ethereal quality about it that had to do with the acoustics, the topography of the place. There was something unworldly, almost mythic, about the sound of those bells and the way it echoed over the village, resounded off the cliffs. Also the sound of the sea and the wind in Livakia had a deep and spiritual quality, as dramatic and eerie as the sound of the bells.

There were no hotels. There were however a few rooms to be had in the village. The mayor rented three above his shop, there were two over the taverna on the port, and several of the villagers rented rooms in their houses if a stranger was lucky enough to find that house and knock at the door. One such house was far less humble than the others. Very large and beautiful, it stood proudly against the hill and was the first house visible from the sea as one rounded the point and sailed into the port. That was Elefherakis Khalkiadakis's house where he took in the rich and the famous from all walks of life. A poet, a prince, a writer, painter, or any sort of scholar who found their way to Livakia, either by chance or at the recommendation of one of the residents, always stayed there. He or she had only to be one of those and a pleasure seeker, though it helped too if they were also a fantasist in search of the mythology of the place and had a love of the ancient Greek world. Elefherakis was passionate about his country and its mythology.

At Greek Easter and Christmas there was not a bed to be had in Livakia. Then Cretans who had moved away from the island returned from the mainland for a taste of home and the celebrations. In summer they came for their holidays, but only on short visits. Livakia was not a place for droves of foreign tourists – too quiet and unspoilt. The action was elsewhere on the island. Most of the time if tourists did come they were staying with friends and became briefly part of the community. At this time of year most of the rented rooms in Livakia were empty and the foreigners that were there were accommodated at Elefherakis Khalkiadakis's house. Everyone adored staying there. He was grand and generous, a charming and amusing host.

Elefherakis was one of the people sitting in Katzakis's store drinking ouzo and waiting for his order to be filled when Arnold Topper arrived looking just as he always did, neat and well pressed in his stone-coloured chinos and thin blue Brooks Brothers shirt, sleeves rolled up, collar open, a small red scarf tied round his neck, his shopping basket on his arm.

Elefherakis watched with wonder as Arnold greeted the grocer and gave his order in atrocious Greek with a Harvard accent. The wonder was how he could be so well put together so early in the day, having had to be picked up off the ground after slipping slowly from his chair in a drunken stupor at the Kavouria the night before. Elefherakis knew, as did everyone else in Livakia, that Arnold would not remember that or who had brought him home and put him to bed. Everyone had been caring for Arnold in that way for as long as he had been living in Livakia; few said anything about it. No one liked to embarrass Arnold because he was the nicest of men, sober or drunk, intelligent and very good company when sober. Few people except Mark Obermann that is. Arnold's bad Greek, even after living in Crete for more than ten years, and his drunkenness were bones of contention between the two men whose friendship had become uneasy. Mark found Arnold's weaknesses a burden on him and the community, and took every opportunity to embarrass the American about them with clever innuendoes, pointed remarks, even outright verbal attacks on Arnold's worthlessness.

People came to Arnold's defence but it was difficult. To shut Mark up was not easy. His command of English as well as Greek and German was impressive. There were few who could use language as he did; he was a joy to listen to, as natural an orator as he was a writer, knowing the power and pleasure of words and how to use them. But Mark Obermann was a Fascist in the worst sense of the word. One always had the feeling that he actually believed there was no room for the weak, that the world would be a better place without the crippled, only he was too clever to come straight out and say that.

'There's a boat coming in, I saw it from my house. May I join you?' Arnold politely asked Elefherakis. Then came his measure of Retsina. It slopped over the rim of the copper measure cup when placed on the table and slopped again as Arnold raised it with a trembling hand to pour some into his glass.

The Greeks were forever nibbling when they drank. They had the unshakeable belief that to eat while drinking would save the liver, the sanity, and the health. Mr Katzakis placed a chipped white plate covered with chunks of white feta cheese with dribbles of olive oil over them on the table in front of Arnold. 'You drink, you eat, Mr Arnold,' he emphasised.

Everyone knew how drink had taken over from food in Arnold's life, and both the Cretans and his fellow expatriates tried at every chance they were given to tempt his palate. But there was an unwritten law in the community: freedom was all. A man had the right to live his life as he wanted it, and that was respected.

Elefherakis and Arnold were laughing when Rachel al Hacq entered the grocer's. Arnold was being extremely amusing about the tourists invading Crete who never saw or understood the island or its people. The two men stopped talking to watch and listen to Rachel. She was an act: the perfect little flirt, the coquette supreme, who spoke with pursed lips and fluttering eyelashes, slinked like a cat, and dressed to accentuate her impressive cleavage, tiny waist, and provocative bottom. All five feet of her was packaged like a sex kitten and finished with the thickest, most sexy French accent whether she was speaking English or Greek.

And she was pretty, very pretty and very feminine, with short dark hair that framed an oval-shaped face with all the right features in the right places. Her act was the same whether it was with Mr Katzakis to wheedle down the price of a peach and get an extra lemon for nothing, or the butcher for a little less fat on her one lamb chop, or trying to seduce a man whom she wanted for a night of sex or to pay for her dinner, or just to secure an audience to listen to her bemoan the trials and tribulations of being a poet.

Over the years she had had a sex scene with most every available man in Livakia though she denied this to be true. She had an image of herself as the worldly virgin and wanted everyone else to have that same picture of her.

She had it in her mind that it was her unavailability that excited men's interest, that brought her the attention she sought, and the power to seduce and twist men round her little finger. Everyone rather liked playing her little game with her. The fact was that the men enjoyed her flirting; it did excite them into wanting her. They would gladly succumb to her charms and go along with the elaborate plans she would make to meet them for sex. She liked sneaking into their houses under cover of darkness, or if it were to be a daylight liaison, to walk boldly with them to their houses or a secluded beach, her books under her arm, issuing declarations to all she passed that she was going for a poetry reading, a lesson in Greek, to cook a French dish for the man in question.

Second only to her flirting was her passion for herself and her good looks; she worked on them both endlessly and with zeal. After that came her pride in being a Sephardic Jewess whose family had for centuries been Iraqi Jews of wealth and culture before her father had fled with his family from Baghdad. She had a conviction she was born to be beautiful and a poet, and flitted back and forth from Paris to Livakia to prove it. She was part of the Livakia scene, the entertainment and the fun.

The two men watching her now had both had her: Arnold a long time ago and never a second time, Elefherakis long ago and forever it seemed – or at least whenever the moment was right. They had an understanding. Periodically when her money had run out she would go to him and he would bankroll her until her mother sent money from France, when she would make an elaborate play of trying to repay him which he would gallantly refuse. Elefherakis was a very wealthy man and his generosity would never allow him to be a loan shark, he would much rather be a friend.

Finished with Mr Katzakis she turned to the two men and joined them. It was time to move to the taverna and a table under an awning in the sun.

Chapter 2

Laurence never threw anything away, and rarely bought anything. He disliked spending money on things, with the exception of books and recordings. He could not be bothered with the hassle of bringing anything into Greece and was too lazy to fetch and carry anything except the necessities of life: food, loo paper, malt whisky and wine, and then no further than from the port to his house. He was a man who liked to keep his life pared down to the essentials.

He disapproved of waste, his or anyone else's, so Laurence lived with the flotsam and jetsam of other people's lives. He was the only foreigner in Livakia who had furnished a house to overflowing by making no more of an effort than saying yes to every gift offered, to every bargain offered, anything being disposed of for one reason or another – someone's need for money, the closing of a house, a divorce, an exit when the dream of living on a Greek Island went bad or an even better life presented itself elsewhere. He was not a discriminating householder – in fact, he was a magpie, and his house a hodgepodge of things piled upon things.

With no effort at all in a Cretan setting he had managed

to create a '1930s English cottage in the Cotswolds' look that rambled on from room to room. Contributing factors were visits from his mother who had arrived with bolts of English flower-patterned fabric, mistakes she had made and stored away since the beginning of the Second World War; wild flowers, some near dead and dried out, others fresh, displayed among the bits and bobs he never looked at or cared anything about; books stacked high on every surface, even the floor; his snorkelling, fishing and climbing equipment; baskets and boxes of things shifted with the tide of his needs. Yet, amazingly, amid the clutter he could find within seconds anything he wanted.

The interior of the house was eccentric; it had great style without even trying, just like its owner, and seemed even more so because it was so incongruous with the two-hundred-year-old Cretan ruin he had haphazardly restored with the help of a Greek architect friend. Laurence loved his house, it was the centre of his life and he thrived there. D'Arcy did not. She only liked it for a few hours and then had the overwhelming desire to open all the windows and throw everything out. Laurence would sacrifice nothing for the woman he loved, least of all anything he thought of as part of himself. That was why they lived in his and her houses.

Yet in his own strange way he could be the most generous of men to his friends and neighbours, as long as they did not infringe on his privacy. He was reticent, even secretive, about the manner in which he lived, worked and loved. People respected that and him as a man and a scholar. One of the joys of living in a small community in a foreign country, and especially in a remote village on an island, was that the inhabitants did not pry into other people's lives. They might gossip about the way they lived, but they rarely interfered. They needed each other too much for the fun of life: good company, great banter, sex, pure pleasure.

One only had casually to say over lunch or dinner at the taverna where the foreign colony all gathered at least once a day, 'I wish I had brought a . . . back with me.' Or, 'Does anyone know where I can find a . . . ?' and Laurence or someone else was there with the suggestion that they pay a visit to his house where they could root it out for themselves. Invariably people would find what they were looking for or needed: a length of rope, a spool of the right coloured thread, tools, a piece of chain, a table, a lamp, a bulb or a chair. Lawrence would happily hand over said object, refusing to take any money.

His cluttered kitchen looked like every other room in the house but with a cooker, a wall oven, and an enormous stainless steel sink. His cooking was somewhat like his house. It had been Arnold who had labelled him one evening at the Kavouria when a dozen or so of the foreign colony and several of the local Greeks were dining together. He had come to Laurence's defence when Rachel had commented, 'Laurence, I love you, but please, never cook for me again. They would hang you in France for your cooking.'

Mark, who thought himself a gourmet and a great chef, picked up on it, declaring Rachel was being generous. It had been then that an already drunk Arnold had stuttered

29

and slurred, 'Eccentric. Laurence is an eccentric cook.'
And the label had stuck.

Now D'Arcy, replete with sex and love, was feeling
pangs of hunger – even an eccentric meal created by her
lover would do – but there was no scent of cooking in
the house. It was dusk and the heat of the day was at last
subsiding. She had come out of a deep dreamless sleep
and felt as fresh and happy as she did hungry. Opening
her eyes, she saw a naked Laurence sitting on the window
ledge, his back against the jamb, one knee on the floor,
the other bent and resting on the sill. How handsome he
looked, and how much she liked his long slim body, his
phallus flaccid and draped on his thigh, the bush of dark
pubic hair, the muscles in his thighs. Even his feet and
his toes, long and slender, were without a blemish and
very sexy, like his long arms and legs, the way he moved
and used them. The shock of thick hair he wore on the
long side, just touching the collar of his shirts, framing
an open face with lazy dark blue eyes and sensuous lips,
was sexy because it sent out signals that beneath that
cool English reserve was sexual fire ready to flare up. He
was smoking a cigar – his guests always brought Havana
cigars or malt whisky – and looking out across the roof
tops to the sea.

D'Arcy forgot about her hunger, too busy revelling in
the handsomeness of her man. Very quietly she raised
herself a little higher against the bed pillows and thought:
This is a man to have babies with. That was not something
that pleasure seekers such as D'Arcy often thought about,
and it took her rather by surprise. Especially since she was
aware that Laurence never gave himself wholly to her. He

was holding back on love. Strangely this was the very first time she realised just how much. The great sex, the love he did afford her, and all his other admirable qualities, had clouded her vision about that.

That English reserve! He was only as free as it would allow him to be. He had not the freedom D'Arcy possessed, something she was born with, that was innate in her and she had been brought up with, that allowed her to submit totally to a lover. That was what he had demanded of her and received from her in exchange for the love he could give her. Only for brief moments in their sex life did he fly free as a bird, soar to heights he had only dreamed of. She smiled to herself, thinking of those moments and of how marvellous they were, how much she loved him for at least being able to achieve those.

'I don't smell anything delicious coming out of the kitchen.'

'I think I've created enough delicious for you for one day.'

'Oh? And not for you?'

'There were benefits. Blissful ones actually,' he told her in one of his English understatements. They smiled at each other, the sort of smiles that come from love, contentment, a deep regard for one another.

'You're hungry and I'm famished, and there's no food in the house. Your fault not mine, you never let me out of bed long enough to do the shopping . . .' She was amused. Sex, most especially when he was out of control and lost in lust, had always to be seen as her fault. This time she had to admit he was right. 'So no eccentric meal for you tonight. Pity, because I was looking forward to cooking for you. Instead I will buy you the best meal we can find and a bottle of wine fit for the goddess of my bed.'

'I think I'll rush home, bathe and change, and meet you – where?'

'Pasiphae's.'

That was the restaurant with the best food and where one could sit in an enclosed courtyard to dine. Often the local musicians would go there to play. But the owner of Pasiphae's was temperamental; one never knew until one arrived there whether he had been in the mood to cook or not. If he had been, the place would be open. If he hadn't, he too, like Laurence and D'Arcy, would be dining at the Kavouria on the port overlooking the water.

'Pasiphae's then,' agreed D'Arcy.

Laurence smiled. He slid off the sill and walked towards the bed. Never taking his eyes from D'Arcy's, he said, 'Legend has it that Pasiphae was the wife of King Minos. She was said to have had a degenerate love for a white bull. Do you think you have a degenerate love for me?'

'Yes, if you think I'm a degenerate,' was her clever answer.

Still naked, and looking to him as luscious and lascivious as she had been since he had removed her dress hours ago, he watched her as she slid lazily across the bed to rise and dress. D'Arcy was not quick enough. He was on the bed next to her, pulling her back. 'One last look at you, one last lick, one last taste.'

She knew what he wanted. He adored looking at her genitals, fondling them, licking and sucking on them. She had never known a man as accomplished at the sexual act he was about to perform as he was. To be loved and adored like that was thrilling. Few men loved the sex of a woman as Laurence did. He knew how to make her flower, feel her worth in bed.

Another thing he loved nearly as much was to watch D'Arcy being penetrated by him with his own flesh or by one of his beautifully made sexual toys. She saw him reach for a pale lavender object, an elegant work of art shaped like a man's penis and studded with minute carved flowers, an object of pleasure from a collection of Japanese pornographic art of the Edo period. He used his tongue and his long slender fingers and then, when she was silky and moist with come, together they watched as he made the jade vanish, take possession of D'Arcy, and slowly reappear again as he drew it from her. Once, twice, and then he stopped, removed it, and lay on his side next to her to hold her in his arms and give her a tender kiss. To wield a wand of pleasure and power over D'Arcy in any form had become an important part of Laurence's life.

They used an array of such sexual toys to enhance their sex life, an extravagant gift from Max de Bonn, the libertine *par excellence* of all the foreigners living in Livakia. Before Laurence began a serious affair with D'Arcy, he and Max had reputations for being great studs and lovers, friends who shared their extravagant sex lives and women with each other. Some claimed they still did in very discreet orgies behind D'Arcy's back.

She watched her lover lick the jade. It was as if he didn't want to miss a drop of her. She was his honey, his elixir of life, his champagne. She was taken by surprise:

a vision of Max licking that piece of pornographic jade flashed before her and was gone. She knew that Laurence had wanted a sex scene for the three of them. In the heat of lust he had several times asked her if she would allow Max to join them some time. She had always rejected the idea, knowing there were no limits to what might happen if Max became involved in their sex life. He was much more of a devil with women, a greater adventurer, a true libertine down to the marrow of his bones. That flash of Max's handsome virile good looks prompted her to say, 'Laurence, are you not sure it isn't you who has a degenerate love for me?' With that she kissed him lightly on the cheek and slid from his arms and off the bed.

D'Arcy stopped to speak to half a dozen people in the lanes and along the port and corniche that led round to the narrow street and the climb to her house. She held the unique position among all the foreign women who lived in Livakia of being liked and respected by the Cretan women in the village. They had a special place in their hearts for her as they had done for her mother. They talked to D'Arcy about anything and everything, these women who still lived by the old Cretan ways and stayed in the background of family life, for the most part at home. It helped that she could speak with them in their own tongue, and that most of them had known her since she was a child.

She was talking to one such woman, Aliki, who had called to her from the small wooden balcony of her house, when Melina Philopopolos, a young Greek girl who had one day appeared in Livakia and never left, stopped to

34

ask D'Arcy if she could speak to her. Having been told she could walk along with her when D'Arcy had finished her chat, the girl leaned against the whitewashed wall and waited.

Immediately upon the girl's arrival, the tone of Aliki's voice changed. An atmosphere, a cloud of something unpleasant, seemed to darken their conversation. Not for long though. Aliki cut it short and abruptly walked from the balcony into her house, but only after warning: 'You never look the evil eye in the face, D'Arcy.' And raising the hem of her skirt and unpinning from her slip a blue glass bead in the shape of an eye, she tossed it down to her. The amulet was worn to ward off the evil eye in which the Greeks so fervently believed. Aliki's quite clear insinuation that D'Arcy needed protection from Melina caused the girl to shrug her shoulders and laugh.

The Livakians, like most Cretans, were suspicious and superstitious about strangers and had not taken well to a Cretan girl they knew nothing about landing in their village with a couple of ruffians from Iraklion. They had seen her as a tramp, without family, a loose creature with no money, nothing in fact save for the thin dress she wore on her back and shoes that would not last a winter. After Melina's friends left, to see her scrounging food from the tavernas and sleeping out in the open, actually begging money from the foreigners, had done nothing to endear her to the villagers. They were embarrassed by her – Cretan pride does not allow for such bad behaviour. Poverty should be worn with dignity if it had to be worn at all.

Short-legged and chunky-looking, she was dark-skinned

with black hair. Her features were common, almost crude, there was something slovenly, almost dirty about her that came from being rock bottom poor. And yet there was a certain animalistic raunchiness about her that was for some interesting and provocative. She was not literate, and there was a sort of inner darkness in her eyes. But whatever she was, she had been clever enough to find a deserted cave in which to take on the donkey men and several of the other young studs for a few drachma and never be found out. The men kept her secret among themselves because that sort of behaviour, once made public, would have had the women running her out of town, if not something much worse. But all that stopped when Mark Obermann found her, in rather bad shape, in one of the deserted ruins where she sometimes slept. D'Arcy knew about her sexual activities only because she had inadvertently discovered the cave and an incredibly sexy yet sordid scene while on one of the solitary walks she so enjoyed.

Melina taunting five, big, handsome, virile men, with her raunchy talk and a crude strip-tease; exposing one shoulder and then both her breasts, raising her skirt and tucking it into her belt to offer herself from the waist down with suggestive bumps and grinds. She ran her hands over her breasts, rendering them as a gift to one of the men. He lunged for them and sucked hard on the nipple of one while pulling roughly and slapping the other. Fired up by his hunger for her, her whole body took on a lustful glow.

Melina shoved the man away from her and shouted to them all, 'You can have me in ways you never dreamed of, but at my bidding. It has to be the way I want it, when I want it. I'm going to take you all on and we'll see if you really are as sexy as you claim to be.'

D'Arcy wanted to run away, leave them to it, but she was too mesmerised by the girl's performance.

The men seemed sexually enslaved by her even before she arched her back and shoved her pelvis forward, ran her fingers seductively through her own pubic hair and separated her most intimate lips with her fingers. 'Now, let me see who shall be the first to warm themselves in my fire,' she chided, her own lust echoing in her voice. Not one of the men answered.

They watched in silence as she then turned round, bent over and offered her bottom, spread the cheeks and gyrated seductively. Melina had the men in her power and she was playing with them for her own pleasure. She swung round and then went to one of the them and unzipped his jeans. He was fully erect and large, she was generous with praise for his sex as she fondled it and demanded the others expose themselves.

D'Arcy was amazed at how Melina controlled the men with her lust, ordering one man to suck on her breasts, another to caress her bottom, while another fondled her genitals and she gave oral sex to yet another. That didn't last long only because Melina didn't want it to. 'I want your cocks, and your come, now you do as I tell you,' she shouted at them. One of the men seemed too eager, tried to take over the orgy, she slapped him hard, he held her tight by the wrist but it was he who finally backed down from the confrontation when she kissed him wildly on the lips and used her hands and her mouth to convince him to stay in line.

D'Arcy watched Melina crawl on to a large boulder lying on the stony floor of the cave. She spread a sheepskin rug under her knees and leaning on her elbows raised her naked bottom. Laughingly, she called out her instructions.

It was a scene of several men taking her in turn, powerful men fucking for lust, and a young girl clearly lost in her own sexual pleasure, but remaining always in command. D'Arcy slipped away stunned by what she had seen and quite overwhelmed by the debauchery that Melina had so skilfully generated. D'Arcy had not been observed. She had kept the secret and had never told a soul.

Mark had taken Melina in, offered her room and board in exchange for cleaning his house, and proceeded to lobby for her acceptance into the community. He could be very convincing and knew well the Cretan mind and heart and how to win them over, at least enough for Melina to live in peace and try and make some sort of a life for herself. He began with the chief of police, Manoussos Stavrolakis, his friend, and by far the most influential man in Livakia after the priest whom Mark had then won over. The schoolmaster was his next target and the most difficult of the three because Melina had no desire to go to school and he had no desire to teach her. But few could say no to Mark Obermann when he went after something and used his all-American charm. The three men's tolerance was taken as example and the villagers fell into step and in time became civil to her.

That had been nearly a year ago, and now only a few of them were still leery of her. Most had grudgingly to admit that she had come a long way since Mark had taken her in. They admired him for that, and Melina for the visible changes in her life.

The foreigners all knew that Mark was playing Svengali, writing his own version of *Pygmalion* with her as the heroine, and each one of them was, in their own way, secretly worried about it. They could see vestiges of the old Melina just barely under the surface of her new life. However, whatever Mark was doing with Melina, she did at least appear to be a changed girl from the one who had first arrived in Livakia.

Mark had taken her into Iraklion and Chania and bought her jeans and shirts and shoes and a dress, had taken her to a hairdresser who had trimmed her long curly hair, and though she was no great beauty she was now attractive, and had a sensuous quality about her that both Mark and she kept as hidden from everyone as much as possible. *He* found this malleable young girl strangely exciting and was devoted to her, *she* was obsessed with pleasing him.

Since Mark could barely keep himself with what he earned, right from the outset he had hustled for her in the village, and still did, asking everyone to hire her for odd jobs so that she could have, at the very least, survival money and a degree of independence. He was dictating the work ethic as against the beg ethic. The foreigners had been reluctant at first; they disliked the tension she created with the Cretans who were less forthcoming with odd jobs for her. And they were concerned about the company she kept. Where did she vanish to when Mark was on a trip to the far end of the island or in Athens for long periods of time, and she was meant to stay in Livakia and care for his house? But Mark won his friends over and they and the other villagers, though still unsure of their feelings for her, now accepted Melina as part of the Livakian scene.

The changes in her were so evident, people had nearly forgotten how bad-tempered and crude she could be. They knew her now as diligent, devoted to Mark, listening to every word he said, believing it to be gospel. Her adoration of Mark, learning to read and write at his behest, working on speaking a more educated Greek, trying to speak English, all these things were impressive enough for people to forgive Melina her lapses: the occasional burst of rudeness, disrespect to her elders, embarrassing Arnold with little digs that might have come from Mark's mouth. People now made excuses for such behaviour, believing that for a poor, unfortunate child she had already come a long way in a short time.

She was living a more independent life but still under Mark's roof, following him like a shadow whenever he allowed it, aping his every word, every mannerism, his arrogance. Mark's opinions were now her opinions. When he was away she boasted to several of the delinquent boys she hung out with about her life with Mark. How he confided in her and she held this foreign genius's life together. And strangely she did have an influence on Mark, hard to define and which confused everyone who knew him.

D'Arcy was indifferent to Melina. She greeted her whenever their paths crossed and was always civil to the girl but never got involved with her, hired her for the odd job or offered her help in any form. There was no particular reason for that, and it was certainly not because D'Arcy had seen the sexual side of Melina's life and how much the girl enjoyed it. It was not in D'Arcy's character to be judgemental, and certainly never about another person's sex life. If anything she appreciated that the girl realised she had to be extremely discreet in her lust. And it had been lust that was going on in that cave. Melina may have taken money for her favours but she was not merely a whore, because she liked the sex and the power it gave her. The money was necessary; the sex probably gave her the only moments of happiness in a miserable life.

D'Arcy looked at the girl walking next to her and was grateful that Melina had no idea that she had been seen. Then the humiliation would have had to be dealt with, and such a humiliation in Crete could be dangerous. D'Arcy's silence had been instinctive and so was her behaviour towards the girl.

They had only gone a short distance from Aliki's house when Melina got directly to the point. 'Can I work for you?'

'But I have no work for you, Melina.'

'Mr Laurence, I could work for him?'

'You would have to ask him. But you already work for him when he needs the odd job done.'

'Mark says I need to have a steady job, he doesn't like to see me hanging round with my friends all day, but I like having fun all day. You do, and Rachel does, and Kiria Plum too.'

41

'We're in different circumstances from you.'

'That's it?'

D'Arcy did not like the look that quite suddenly appeared on the girl's face. Anger, the girl was brimming with it. But that didn't faze D'Arcy in the least, she put it down to Cretan temperament and she had been dealing with that all her life. 'That's it,' she repeated.

'I thought you would help me because your mother was a whore like mine was and you're a bastard like me.'

D'Arcy could not stop herself from laughing.

'Are you laughing at me?' asked an angry Melina.

'No! Oh, no, not at you. At my mother being called a whore, and me a bastard. You would have to know my mother to know how wrong you are about that, and meet my fathers to appreciate how much more than that my mother is, that I am. Though, mind you, I don't think she would be as offended as you think she or I should be at your calling us those names. Think, Melina, if we were no more than those things, would we have the affection and respect of the people here?'

D'Arcy walked away from the girl only to be chased after. Melina fell into step with her. 'Please, you won't tell Mark I called you those names?' she begged, genuine panic in her voice.

'Of course not, I've already forgotten it.'

'Really?'

'You have my word on that.' It was a little thing but D'Arcy noted that the girl did not apologise for the slurs.

They continued to walk in silence, several people stopping to speak to them. At the end of the corniche, before D'Arcy started the climb to her house, she turned to Melina and dismissed her with, 'I turn off here, see you around.' Thirty yards away she had already forgotten the girl and the incident.

The following morning was yet another glorious day of sun and sea and a leisurely breakfast on the terrace with Laurence. Arnold stopped by for a coffee and to pick up the things D'Arcy had brought for him from Chania, and to leave a loaf of bread, hot from the baker's oven. Edgar and Bill arrived for their parcels, bickering as usual, and Rachel for her ink. No one seemed anxious to leave and so the morning slipped away in laughter and amusing conversation. Coffee was exchanged for white wine and fried haloumi cheese produced to go with the fresh bread.

D'Arcy was sitting on the terrace wall looking down past the romantic gardens she had created in the old ruins separating her from the path that ran along the edge of the cliffs, plunging into the sea below her house. Year by year she had bought every parcel of land and crumbling ruin in the vicinity of her house, thereby managing to become one of the largest landowners in Livakia. Most everyone in the village guessed it was she who owned the land but she had been discreet when making her purchases and so few really knew the true extent of her holdings. The gardens were open to the public when she was not wanting to be alone or entertaining in them. The villagers were more proud than envious of what she owned because they knew she had not bought the land for greed or mere privacy, but to conserve it, restore it, make it a place of beauty for them all to appreciate. They had seen too much of their rugged and wild island eaten up by the disease of tourism: concrete hotels, busloads of transient drunks who never really saw the island or its people for what and who they were. If there was any envy it was among the foreign colony residing in Livakia and those who wanted to make their home there but had to leave. It was such a struggle to buy and restore anything in Greece that many who wanted to do so gave up in despair.

They were remarkable gardens that would never have thrived at all in that dry and stony terrain except that D'Arcy, against all odds, had drilled for a well and found water. Beautiful and in keeping with the terrain, there were architectural and walled gardens, within walled gardens, set one above the other on tiers of rock climbing both along and up the cliff. Hanging gardens, mysterious for their timelessness and the ethereal, indefinable aura they created that wrapped itself around a visitor walking through them.

The ground was mostly stony with a few patches of grass and wild flowers. Large fragments of mosaics from antique times, and dull and worn marble paving slabs, stood within the ruined, free-standing walls of roofless houses, cleaned down and looking like mystifying sculptures in the sun, caressed by the wind as they stared out across the sea.

Hundreds of terracotta pots of flowering shrubs indigenous to Crete and two palm trees of considerable height and age vied with a few cypress and fig, several olive trees, lemons, and a peach tree. Antique amphorae fished from the sea and encrusted with fossilised marine life stood on pedestals, and there were besides marvellous life-size sculptures from the Classical period, whole or fragmentary for the loss of a limb or a head, a face worn away by the centuries, wind and the rain. The huge stone head of a lion with a curly mane set in the cliffside gushed water which cascaded over rocks into a pool. There were marble chairs more like thrones for the gods, stone benches and the odd table of white marble, dulled from the sea spray and occasional mists. And above all, the glorious sun and light of Greece.

What work, what passion, what love of place it had taken to create such gardens. What madness, thought D'Arcy, as her mind drifted away from her friends and the sound of their laughter. A fishing boat in full sail rounded the point and she watched it lazily sail into the bay. The luxury of living in a timeless place, that was her life and had always been her life. Even during the years she had been away from Livakia, she had found ways to live for pleasure and play. People said of her that she was not her mother's child for nothing, but they said that about her sister and two brothers as well.

She saw him far below her on the path before he saw her. As D'Arcy watched him, he walked as if he owned not just the earth beneath his feet, which he did not, but the world. It was a walk with a swagger in it, a special kind of big man's walk, fearful of nothing. There was arrogance in his stride, the way he moved his limbs, used his whole body, even his shoulders when he walked. His walk was like that of the Cretan shepherds when they came down from the mountains into the villages and cities. Rugged men used to dealing with real life, ready if they must to cut down anything that crossed their path.

D'Arcy had always liked Max's walk. Her eyes following him, she smiled while remembering a ravishingly beautiful and amusing Italian girl who had been brought to the island by him. Max was addicted to adventures, most especially sexual ones with women he had never had before. After several weeks their scene was over. Sitting in the port having a coffee with D'Arcy one day and watching Max approaching their table, Gabriella had sighed, 'Ah, Max. He walks like he fucks.'

D'Arcy had always felt sexually attracted to Max, but was determined not to be another notch on his belt. They had always wanted each other; he never stopped asking, D'Arcy never stopped rejecting. These two very sexual beings, close friends for years, danced round each other with their sexuality. D'Arcy had always wondered about sex with him and what she was afraid of.

At last he looked up to see if anyone was on the terrace of her house. He always did when he passed her way. He waved and gave her one of his dazzling smiles. He had the looks of any and all of the great sculptures of the god Zeus with his shock of thick curly golden-brown hair, a magnificent well-cut beard framing a big and gloriously handsome face, sensuous lips, fantastic bone structure, a large and beautifully chiselled nose, and eyes of a dark, dark blue with fire and passion in them.

Today he wore no shirt, displaying a body he loved to show off for its perfect male figure of long shapely legs, muscular thighs, narrow hips and muscular rounded bottom. It was impossible not to admire the rock hard stomach, powerful arms, wide shoulders, broad chest; even his neck was thick with muscle. Strength and power seemed to emanate from him. To see him walk from the sea was to imagine Poseidon had come up from the depths to breathe life into the modern world. The Cretans adored Max, he made friends of them all over the island. They called him Max-Zeus. Men and women alike admired him for his looks and legendary sexual prowess. He was the epitome of courage and male virility, much admired traits to the Greeks and most particularly the Cretans.

'I'm going fishing, want to come?' he called up.

'Where?'

'Karinios.'

Karinios was a small rugged cove a forty-minute walk away. It boasted three small period houses, one abandoned, one where a ninety-year-old woman and her son lived, and Brett's house – the simple structure where D'Arcy was born. It was still owned by her mother though she had not returned to it or Crete for many years. Karinios was quiet, the water deep and clear off a stony beach. D'Arcy often went there to open the house and air it out. She kept it in repair but nothing else; it was just as Brett had left it.

Fishing with Max meant deep diving with a spear, and no one was better at it. D'Arcy liked to swim with him because he explored as well as fished, but she was better with a hook and a line than a spear.

'Come up for a drink. Laurence and Arnold are here – maybe they would like to go.'

Max waved and turned back towards her gate. She slid off the wall and went down to let him in. He was already there framed in the doorway when she pulled the wooden door back.

'You were quick,' she told him with a smile. He always made her smile; it was his virility and handsomeness, the aura of pulsating life emanating from him. She had never seen him down or depressed, not even during winter when it was cold and grey and some of the foreign residents became nervy with a need for a trip to Paris, London or New York. He just held more poker games in his house, went hunting in the mountains with his Cretan friends, kept the woman of the moment that little bit longer, or flew off in the four-seater sea plane he kept in a sheltered cove.

He would take parties of people in his old wooden sailing boat, weather permitting, for a day that might run into three or four. They might go to Sfakia where there was more action and he had friends, or else to Chania where he would stay and party with some of the foreigners living there. Or he might just vanish for a couple of months to play on some other island in the sun. His casual hold on life was stronger than that of men who held on to theirs with both fists clenched tight. D'Arcy understood that part of him so well because she too enjoyed life with a light touch. That similarity created an unspoken bond between them.

He bent forward, kissed her on the lips and told her, 'I'd like to fuck you out of your brains, D'Arcy Montesque.'

Her smile broadened and then she laughed. 'And what about Laurence?'

'Cards on the table?'

She nodded her head. 'A poker player plays his hand. Go on then,' she told him.

'He's my friend, but he's not strong enough to hold you. And he's an English gent, takes the measure of things. Deep down he doesn't understand where people like you and I are coming from. He's a man who still believes in approval and disapproval. I can wait. You're worth waiting for, D'Arcy. But do I really have to? Laurence and I have shared women before and never had a problem with it.'

'But this is love, Max, a little more than sex.'

He laughed, an uproarious sound, and grabbed her hand to run with her up several stairs to the terrace.

Chapter 3

Manoussos Stavrolakis was standing at the window of his office looking down. The heat of the day was just lifting and a light warm breeze was coming off the water. The port looked quiet and lazy and was cast in hues of pink-gold from the sun slipping slowly out of the sky.

Arnold was sitting alone at a small table drinking white wine and reading his *New Yorker* magazine, a familiar scene for this time of day. D'Arcy would be having her last swim. A luscious-looking girl with long blonde hair and legs that seemed to go on forever appeared. He had not seen her before. She would be staying with Max. He smiled. How did Max do it? He watched Rachel al Hacq – such tiny mincing steps. A wiggle to fuck by, they seemed to say with every click of her heels on the cobblestones. She sat at a table in a different cafe from Arnold and opened her notebook. She was a better poser than she was a poet. It was always good to be home. Manoussos had just returned from a tour of some of the more remote villages in his district. There was nothing unusual about that. He had been away for four days, and there was nothing unusual about that either. He had left his jeep in the cave, next to D'Arcy's 2CV, the Second World

War American jeep he had won from Max in a poker game one Christmas. Now there were two on the island, his and Max's. He was usually off duty, bathed and out of his uniform by this time of day and ready to play a game of chess with Arnold, but now he was being held up waiting for a fax to come through from Athens.

Manoussos was in charge of several dozen men keeping the peace in underpopulated places who checked in by telephone with him every day. He knew his job well, was diligent, and made frequent tours to show his presence and keep the men sharp. Other rookie policemen posted in similar remote places all over the island grew bored and fat and stale in their jobs. Not Manoussos's men.

Unlike some of their associates who worked in larger groups in the built up villages and towns along the coast under the Chief's jurisdiction, they had a different kind of action, and were envied for it. They made the newspapers and were feared and respected.

Manoussos and his men had caught more art thieves in the act, and retrieved more works, prevented more antiquities from being smuggled out of Greece, than any other group of art detectives in the whole country. And they were no special force, just policemen doing another part of the job of keeping the law enforced. But their successes in that field had given Manoussos his swift rise in Crete's police department at a young age. In his own quiet way he was a force to be reckoned with.

He saw D'Arcy round the point and come into view. Manoussos always felt uplifted when he saw her. He had loved her all his life . . . well, since he was six years old. They had lived and played in each other's houses and had gone to school together and had been first loves, first lovers, and still, until Laurence and she had fallen in love, had sex together whenever the moment was right, the passion was there. He still loved her, still wanted her.

Melina came into the port with two of the local boys she hung around with and took a table some distance from Arnold. Then the Plums, Tom and Jane, he looking happy, she glum – they were always that way – came into Manoussos's view. He loved living and working in Crete; she suffered in silence though it was clear that she would have preferred a London or New York life. Manoussos liked Tom, who was one of the Thursday night poker club, but found Jane irritating. He actually thought she envied her husband's huge success in the art world, that she wanted to be the celebrated painter but had settled for being his hostess instead. They sat down on their own near Melina and her friends after having greeted Arnold.

Katzakis the grocer and his brother were standing with several of the fishermen near the boats talking politics. Katzakis was always talking politics. The national pastime not only of Crete but Greece was talking politics. Life was as it always was in Livakia and that suited Manoussos just fine. This was one of the most unspoilt and interesting villages, beautiful and cosmopolitan in its own small way, because of the foreigners who had chosen to live here. It had become a fascinating and unusual place for the quality of most of its visitors: the famous and creative people who would arrive for the Cretan experience and leave after letting a touch of paradise enter their lives. Manoussos never took the zest and passions, peace and tranquillity, of his town for granted. Just as he watched over it now from the window of his police station, he watched over it when he was out of uniform and down there with his relatives and friends. He was too good a policeman not to realise that life in Livakia was a fragile thing, just like life anywhere else.

He heard the fax machine click on and turned from the window. The information he was waiting for came rolling out of the machine. He tore it off, read it, and a smile crossed his face, one of satisfaction. Interpol was indeed looking for the two men he had in holding cells in Iraklion. Now he was off duty and could get out of the office and have his game with Arnold.

Manoussos's house was not far from his office. It was on a narrow path of steep steps, an older part of Livakia where the houses were small and close together. On his way he was stopped by several old ladies, friends of his grandmother, who were sitting in their doorways. Like wizened black crows they watched and waited in the shadows to pounce on their prey, anyone to pass a bit of gossip their way. They were a hard lot, having lived a hard life. He greeted each of them, and received for his good manners the usual petty complaints. To be polite and respectful but brief with them, not usually paying any attention to their disgruntled opinions which they were very free with, took no more than ten minutes of his time, and didn't matter to Manoussos. Time was irrelevant in Livakia. He enjoyed his walk home every evening.

Manoussos lived alone in a house that had been handed down through the family for three hundred years. He was all that was left of his immediate family, that was why the old crones felt they had to watch over him, albeit from a distance, him, and Arnold who lived in a small house across the way from him. Manoussos had a housekeeper, Athena, a distant cousin who cooked and cleaned and shopped for him. When he arrived home she was already gone, having left him a cooked meal, and clean well-pressed clothes. She lived several houses away, came in to do her work every day, and only saw him when asked to. It was an arrangement that suited them both: he because of his need for privacy; she because she was disapproving of the women who chased after him. It appeared that the foreign women who arrived on the island could not get enough of sex with Manoussos. He was spoiled for choice and Athena and her cronies wanted him to settle down with a Cretan girl, although they all agreed the next best thing would be D'Arcy Montesque.

It was only when he was relaxed, neck-deep in bath water and smoking a cigar that Laurence had given him, that something one of the cronies had said came to the forefront of his mind. A complaint about Melina. She was doing some work for Arnold in his house, painting a room, only she was spending more time sitting in his garden with her friends. They didn't like her, didn't like her friends, but they did like their neighbour Arnold, who was kind and respectful to them and brought them token gifts when he returned from a visit abroad in thanks for their keeping a watch on his house.

He didn't much like the idea of Arnold's leaving the girl alone in the house. That might be putting temptation in Melina's way. Manoussos, if the occasion arose, would drop a hint to Arnold. No, Mark – he would talk to

Mark about it. Melina was terrified of displeasing Mark, whereas having the similar disdain for Arnold that Mark had, the girl would hardly be affected by anything Arnold might tell her. Manoussos had seen signs of that any number of times. A pity because Arnold was a better man than Mark would ever be, and could have been a kinder, more gentle influence on Melina.

Manoussos was an extraordinarily handsome man. He was tall and slender, wide-shouldered, rugged-looking and dark. Black curly hair surmounted dark sultry eyes, ever so slightly hooded and with a definite lusty twinkle in them. His face was Greek of the Classical period, as depicted in painting and sculpture: the perfect nose, wide-set eyes, good bone structure, sexy, succulent lips. He wore a bushy moustache that was exceptionally macho, and by contrast had dimples in his cheeks, and a smile that was broad and laughing and showed his strong white teeth.

When not in uniform, his dark sunglasses and police-man's hat, he dressed with a certain élan: jeans or cream-coloured linen trousers, fine white linen shirts, at times a Panama straw hat. He had learned many things in his years at the Sorbonne in Paris. Homosexuals came on to him there; he was the Greek male love they dreamed of, all male with a female heart at his centre. Women wanted him for his strength and beauty, for sex, and for him to take over their bodies and souls – something he enjoyed enormously. And they liked his Greekness, that Cretan temperament.

He was always amazed (and delighted) at how foreign women, most especially the English ones, dropped their sexual inhibitions the moment they left the white cliffs of Dover behind them. For a Greek bachelor it was a dream come true because even now, in the enlightened present day, to obtain sex with a Cretan girl was still a long drawn out family affair and meant certain marriage.

Manoussos had his game with Arnold, who was already half out of his mind with drink and managed to win anyway. Manoussos gave him a good game and several times thought he was going to beat his friend, as did the half dozen people who had drawn up chairs to sit round the table and watch them play. But chess was definitely Arnold's game. Very few times, drunk or sober, had anyone ever seen him lose a game. Max was his fiercest opponent, Mark his most angry. He could never accept that such a weak character as Arnold could beat him at anything.

There was no question that alcohol had dulled Arnold's brain but that did not stop him from winning games of chess, being the best swimmer in Livakia, nor being capable of surprising them all occasionally with an observation or insight. The greatest attraction about Arnold was that he had nothing to prove. The least attractive thing about Mark was that he was always trying to dictate something, prove everything, mostly his own brilliance.

From the chess game to the Kavouria. It was one of those great nights that casually came together most every night in Livakia. In the restaurant one table kept joining another until they were a chain of tables and people all sitting together. The mood was buoyant and there was much laughter and clever and interesting conversation as they drifted from one subject to another. There were half a dozen new faces, guests of the Plums and Max. A very pretty American girl called Susan appeared looking for Mark – a friend of a friend, her father was a well-known publisher who thought Mark was something special. She was dazzled, flirted openly, and thought she had found *the* writer to have a great love affair with. He thought she was right. A potential husband? He and everyone else knew she was wrong about that.

Mark was out to impress, and when Mark was out to impress no one could do it better. He took everyone on with his clever mind, did magnificent twirls and pirouettes with his intelligence and wit. He had the entire table enjoying every minute of him. It wasn't just the foreigners, the Greeks loved Mark for his passion for them and their island, and there were half a dozen or more of them at the table, challenging his thoughts and statements. The wine flowed continuously and platter after platter of food kept arriving. When all the other customers, having called out farewells to their neighbours at the long table, had left, the owners sat down with bottles of brandy and plates of fresh fruit and sticky sweets while a middle-aged fisherman and his young son played Bazouki.

It was nearly two in the morning when Arnold began slowly to slip from his chair and had to be propped up. That caused a tirade of abuse from Mark: 'I am sick and tired of having to drag you home and put you to bed, Arnold. If you can't hold your liquor, for Christ's sake don't drink. And you're drooling and you're disgusting! You look like a mad degenerate, an

58

imbecile! You spoil everything. God, you really don't belong on this earth!'

Only when Manoussos stood up and glared at Mark did he quieten down. He turned to the fisherman and asked for a specific song and the ugly moment passed. After several minutes, when the party was back in full swing, Mark went round the table to Manoussos. 'It's all right, he can't hear me, he's catatonic with drink. I only said what we all know to be true.'

'Not necessarily, Mark. You sound like a Fascist. I would like to think it was your own drink talking. But it's over, let's make no more of it.'

The two men shook hands and Mark slapped Manoussos on the back, a friendly gesture. Manoussos was distracted. He could feel the girl Bridget's eyes on him, and D'Arcy watching her watching him. The Swedish blonde whispered in Max's ear that she fancied a night of sex with the police chief. That was no problem for Max who adored sexual promiscuity and intrigue. He merely told her, 'Then bring him home with you, the more the merrier.'

But she didn't bring Manoussos home to Max's house, Manoussos took her to his. Not that anyone would have known. For all the sex and erotic game playing that went on in Livakia, it was handled with great subtlety except on rare occasions. Everyone knew sex was as important as food and consumed just as readily but only after the fact did people ever learn who went with whom, what so and so had done to so and so. It was all part of the sex game, the secrecy and intrigue, the not wanting to be obvious or to offend anyone's sensibilities. Each one knew that they were in a small community where the balance of an idyllic life could be tipped by bad behaviour, offence caused unnecessarily.

There were things assumed but never questioned, known but never discussed: sexual secrets, disappointments, failures of love or money. What had these things to do with friendship, people seeking their pleasures in paradise?

Livakia was silent in the dead of the night and so very dark it seemed to compel those that were talking to do so in whispers. Everything seemed to be incredibly still, without a breeze, and as can often happen just before dawn, the temperature rose and it was, if not stiflingly hot, exceptionally warm. The only lights to be seen were those spilling forth from the Kavouria on to the port. There was only a slice of a moon, bright and white, and the sky was peppered with stars. The smell of the sea was in the air; the sound of the water slapping against the boats was like a lullaby. The night seemed still young to the dozen or so people kissing each other good night, shaking hands and giving hugs as they split up and set off in various directions to wend their way home.

They were a small group climbing up through the narrow stone streets bound in by high whitewashed walls, moonlight as their guide. Mark propping Arnold up as he and Susan, helped by Laurence, tried to coax him to walk, straggled behind Manoussos who was flanked by D'Arcy on one side and Bridget on the other. Max, Rachel, and Jane Plum were leading the way and had vanished into the night by the time Manoussos arrived at his turning. He kissed D'Arcy good night, and taking Bridget with him, walked back to claim Arnold and deliver him home. Mark was more reluctant than relieved to let him go, and not for the first time Manoussos was aware that their friendship, though complex and at times not very easy, was an important factor in both their lives. He let Mark and Susan take Arnold home. Laurence kissed D'Arcy and placed an arm around her shoulders and they waved goodbye as they walked away, then they too were swallowed up by the night.

Manoussos used the key and the gate swung back. He led Bridget by the hand from the courtyard to his front door, swung that open and her into his arms, carrying her into his house. She was out of her blouse and had wriggled out of her mini skirt, had torn the strings of her bikini underpants and was sliding the triangle of white silk from between her legs while still in his arms and before they had even reached the bedroom.

Big-breasted to the extreme with an incredibly tiny waist and voluptuous bottom, and sending out an aura of sexuality, hunger for sex and a man, she was a delight. She had the face of an angel with blonde hair. She had an openness of heart and brimmed with sensuality. She was a lover of the erotic, had a passion for sex and men – it was coming off her like an exquisite and rare perfume. Junoesque and lascivious, she was quite crazy with desire for sex with Manoussos. She draped one of her long legs over his shoulder and leaned forward to unzip his fly. Bridget held his throbbing penis in her hand, closed her eyes and sighed. How great it was for Manoussos to have a woman who revelled in sex as much as he did.

He walked her straight through his bedroom and down

the hall to a large bathroom where he placed her on her feet and shed his clothes. They wanted to say things to each other, it was there in their eyes, but passion, urgency and lust struck them dumb. What need of words anyway? It was all being said with their bodies. He took her by the hand and they stepped into the shower, a large space of tiled walls and floor with a marble bench in one corner. He raised her up and she wrapped her legs round his waist as soon as he had impaled her on himself. The scream that escaped her lips was not of pain but of the pure pleasure of being penetrated by a man. He turned on the shower and the cold water hit them in a powerful spray, pouring over them. Bridget threw back her head and let the water run over her face and hair. Manoussos stepped closer into the spray of water and their bodies were transformed: made to shine like flesh-coloured satin.

Manoussos felt as if he was taking possession of a goddess. She had beauty, extraordinary strength, and was supple, raunchy but graceful; cock mad but with love and passion, sheer adoration for penis. In the land of the erotic, she was a queen, mistress of her own desires, her very soul. And she was so free, so uncomplicated and full of adventure in her lust. For a second D'Arcy came to mind and then vanished.

She was like a magnificent succulent dish to be savoured – Manoussos wanted to eat her alive. He started with her mouth and deep, lusty kisses while his hands caressed her heavy and luscious breasts. He played with them and the cascades of water flowing over them, buried his face between them while his penis throbbed inside her. He was a man lost in her lust, not his own. She somehow understood that, placed her hands firmly on his waist and, still leaning back and away from him so that he might continue his kissing and caressing, her legs still wrapped around him, she used her grip on it as leverage and proceeded to ease herself on and off his phallus. She had what Max called an educated vagina and used it with imagination, had a knowledge of how to please with every grip, every release; using her pelvis, she created a rhythm with her thrustings, had control of their exquisite lustiness and drove him into a sexual frenzy.

They came. And again, this time on the floor of the shower, lying in a shallow pool of water with the shower still running over them. He took her again and again in every way he had ever taken a woman. They had sex on the marble bench, her on her knees and he behind her, and it was then that they both realised they were making love in their lust. The realisation was sweet and made their hearts beat a little faster. It stirred their emotions and they were grateful for this one night of sex that would never happen again. They were human and loving creatures enough, that to experience a taste of the dark and delirious side of sexual depravity would not affect who and what they really were.

The sun was well up in the sky when Bridget made scrambled eggs and bacon for Manoussos, and he explained that Max would have to come and get her. Not because he was ashamed to walk her home to Max's house where she was staying but because his neighbours, the old crones, would be out on their doorsteps or peering through the windows, and though they all knew he was a womaniser, he did not like flaunting it in their faces. He was the keeper of the peace, he had a position to maintain, and that had to rate above all the other things he might or might not be. Bridget understood that. He made the call to Max's house.

A platoon of shiny red ants was on a quick march around the rim of the worn white marble sink. Arnold closed his eyes in the hope that they would go away and it was not true that they were back again. He opened his eyes. It was true.

There they were in columns of twos and threes, marching one behind the other, making an assault on the draining board, then splitting their column around the edge of a turned over white coffee mug. They marched on towards the bread box.

Arnold leaned across the sink to look through the window but was immediately distracted by the sight of its white plaster ledge. There the main body of the army was milling about, waiting for a signal to form ranks and take over his kitchen. Would he never be rid of them? How many times had he committed mass murder on those red ants? He thought he was done with them, had won, that his last raid had wiped them out. That had been the day before yesterday.

With a trembling hand he opened the cupboard and reached for his latest final solution. An old-fashioned remedy: a bottle of citronella. He had given up on the latest weapons, they were useless. This was more like guerrilla warfare so he had resorted to age old methods. He grabbed a wad of commercial cotton, the kind that is more grey than white and still has the seeds in it, and tore off a piece. He uncorked the bottle. One whiff was enough to turn his stomach and make him miserable.

As the brown liquid spread over the cotton, he realised he simply could not do it, chase after the ants yet again as they scattered, mopping up the hundreds of dead little beasts with their bug eyes and twitching legs. What for? Only to have them come back again in their endless march to drive him mad . . .

He washed his hands and as he placed the bar of yellow Fortnum's soap down in its dish noticed several of the enemy had been trapped in it. He felt terribly depressed. He stared at the soap for some time before he dried his hands, having first shaken out the towel, then reached into his hip pocket from where he pulled out a red cotton handkerchief and mopped his brow and neck. He was wet with perspiration. Nine-thirty in the morning and it was 92 degrees.

Arnold picked a clean glass off the draining board and examined it for the enemy. No ants. From the fridge he removed a bottle and poured out a half glass of ice cold Smirnoff vodka, topped it up with tomato juice, cracked a raw egg into the glass, and not even bothering to stir it, sat down at the kitchen table and wearily drank his breakfast.

On the table was his old battered shopping basket, in it a *Time* magazine, the *International Herald Tribune* (five days old), a battered copy of *Finnegan's Wake* and his beach towel. He looked around the neat, clean kitchen. Soon Kiria Marika, his cleaning woman, would arrive. She would deal with the tiny red devils. By the time he returned to the house at five that evening they would be gone, and even though he knew they would be back and on the march by morning, he felt momentarily relieved. How could this endless infestation have happened to him? Late at night, alone in the house, there were times he thought they had infiltrated his mind.

Arnold was obsessed with his army of tiny red ants. On occasion, when he was walking from his house to the port, as he was about to do now, he imagined he smelled of insect repellent. Other times his mind wandered away from insects only to be pulled back again because he imagined they were nibbling at his brain.

Normally docile and easy-going, he could live with them without being obsessive about them, as he had for years: part of life in a hot climate. But things were getting to Arnold of late. He was fed up with tolerating what he did not like about his life.

He sighed, thinking how foolishly he was behaving, and while lifting his glass and draining it to the very bottom, looked over the rim and was horrified to see the red devils, six abreast in some places, marching in a long column from under the back door across the floor towards the sink. He slammed the glass down on the table. It smashed. He grabbed his basket and fled from the house.

Arnold was on time, he was always on time. He never ceased to amaze people with his recuperative powers; how he could, no matter the hour or the condition he was in, rise, seemingly none the worse for wear, and carry on with one of his many schedules for living. Everyone knew that Arnold's schedules gave him a purpose in life, a reason to complete each day.

D'Arcy was early. She was halfway up the street and waving at him. He cheered up immediately. Arnold enormously enjoyed these morning swims with D'Arcy when he would wash the ants from his brain. They happened often, but D'Arcy and he usually met in the port at her favourite coffee shop. Arnold like most everyone else was just a little bit in love with D'Arcy, thinking her one of the loveliest creatures on earth.

They greeted each other with kisses, one on each cheek three times, the way Parisians kiss, and then she slipped her arm through his and they proceeded down his street. They stopped to have a word with two of his black-clad neighbours who were always cordial to Arnold and treated him with great respect. They liked him, liked the way he kept his house at the end of the cul-de-sac. It pleased them to have a stranger in their midst to cluck over, though they felt sorry for him because he was a foreigner in a foreign land. They talked to him endlessly about his lonely life, his need for a wife, and remained silent about his drunken walks home. They turned their backs to the occasional women he brought to his house. Mercifully they knew nothing about the rough Greek boys who sneaked in and out of the street in the dead of night, dragging, from some deserted place they had lured him to, an Arnold nearly catatonic with drink.

For years he had had enough control over his drunkenness never to allow the poor, illiterate boys from the mountain villages, to whom he was nothing but cordial in the daytime under the sun, into his house. His way had always been to have sex on the beach in the dark, hidden behind a rock, with the odd Greek boy or intellectually aware foreign female in Livakia for a brief visit. It was all the same to Arnold, who always excused his sexual encounters to himself as having been the product of a mad drunken moment. The foreign colony and the Cretan residents of Livakia knew nothing about that side of his life; they believed that drink was his mistress, and gave him all the sex he ever wanted. If they had ever suspected differently, they put it firmly out of their minds.

Now someone new had come into his life; he knew it wasn't love but a bizarre sexual attachment he was too weak to resist, a complex relationship he had been seduced into. Outwardly he had it firmly under control, but, like the tiny red ants, it was eating away at his emotions. Yet, in spite of that, he felt strong enough to deal with it, keep it under control. He believed he was master of the situation, that goodness, intelligence and kind gestures will always win out over the dark and cruel. It was the philosophy he believed in and lived by. The positive aspects of Arnold Topper that all who knew him loved him for.

There were few people on the beach and none of them from the crowd of the night before. D'Arcy held up her hand to shade her eyes as she looked out over the water. Arnold was doing knee bends. D'Arcy turned her attention to him. He looked happy. Mercifully after a certain amount of drink he never remembered anything, or so he claimed. She often wondered just how true that was. Clearly the humiliating incident between him and Mark had vanished from his mind, if indeed it had ever been there at all.

They spread their towels out on the sand. D'Arcy

removed the straw hat from her head and the full-length sarong from round her body. Arnold pulled off his tattered straw hat and shoved it in his basket, stripped down to his black silk knit bikini, removed his round horn-rimmed eye-glasses and carefully put them in the basket as well. They slipped their feet from their sandals. The burning hot sand made them hop from one foot to the other several times before they joined hands and ran to the water, waded in a short distance and dived into the sea.

The water was instantly refreshing. Nine times out of ten when they dived into the water together and finally surfaced Arnold would tell D'Arcy, as he did now, 'I miss that wonderful shock and shiver one gets diving into the ice cold Atlantic at Truro on the Cape. Now *that* was something!'

D'Arcy laughed, and scooping up water with both her hands she splashed it at him. Then side by side they began their swim. They were both excellent swimmers and loved the sea, any sea, so long as it was relatively clean. They swam a good distance and then floated on their backs for some time, eyes closed under the grilling sun.

Suddenly Arnold was pulled under. The commotion shook D'Arcy from her reverie and she was immediately at his side. It was unnecessary. With arms flailing, he shook himself free. A head bobbed up from the depths. It was Melina. She made another attempt to grab Arnold. She was a silly young girl, frolicking in the water, no more than that. The three swam round and teased each other for several minutes before embarking on a race back to the beach.

Still some distance from the shore, Mark joined them.

There was a glint in his eyes, a knowing smirk on his lips. D'Arcy picked it up at once. Melina would never have thought to join them or attempt to pull Arnold under the water and snatch his bikini had it not been instigated by Mark. She never socialised with the foreigners; sat in on the fringes of their evenings in the port maybe, and that only if Mark was there, but never more than that. This was a bold act. Oh, yes, Mark had set the girl up to inflict a little humiliation on Arnold. Had he thought that if he had Arnold unnerved, Mark himself could win the race, beat them to the beach? Not this time, Mark Obermann, D'Arcy told herself, determined that either she or Arnold would leave Mark trailing in the water behind them. She reached down and found added strength, swimming harder and faster. Arnold, who was swimming next to her, must have picked up on her determination that one of them should win: he was going all out for the shore.

Arnold won, to the applause of Laurence and Max who were standing on the beach. He walked through the surf and collapsed at their feet. D'Arcy had no problem coming in second. She collapsed against Laurence and remained there, catching her breath, until Mark appeared, Melina still far behind. Mark had the good grace to slap Arnold on the back. 'That was some swim, Arnold. Drinks are on me.'

Mark was a charming loser, too charming; he was always nicest when he was beaten whether it was in a race, a debate at the dinner table, or he had received a rejection letter from a publisher. He was one of those people who could always make you believe he had won, that you were somehow the loser. D'Arcy sat listening, observing Mark. He and Arnold were discussing a friend of Arnold's who was a frequent visitor to Livakia, at least once a year. Mark was trying to convince Arnold that his friend, a famous screen writer, should stay with Mark when next he came for a visit. 'Your house is too small. You don't cook, and the whole place needs painting. He would be more comfortable with me.'

It was at this point that an exhausted Melina arrived. She dropped down on the sand next to Mark and interrupted their conversation with, 'Too bad, Arnold.'

'Arnold won the race, Melina,' Mark told her, and turning his back on her, resumed his conversation.

He was quite through with her, dismissed her without another thought. D'Arcy could see that the girl was upset that Mark had been beaten by Arnold. Some minutes passed and then in a moment of pique she jumped up, scattering sand everywhere, and asked, 'Why are you talking to him? He's nothing. You always tell me that he should be wiped from the earth like a piece of dung, so why do you waste your time being nice to him? What about our swim together, our walk? You are better than him.'

All this she said in not very educated Greek and spat out so quickly that Arnold could never have understood half of what she was saying. D'Arcy got every word. She saw the pain in the girl's face, and the disappointment.

Mark was cool, icy cool, when he answered her without an apology, 'We had our swim, now I'm with my friends. Why don't you go find yours, or do some work, or read a lesson? Aren't you supposed to be doing some work for Arnold? Is that finished?'

After she left D'Arcy could not help but remark, 'That girl worships the ground you walk on, Mark. She only wanted you to win.'

It was at that moment that Rachel arrived, and all conversation stopped as their eyes followed her every movement. Her arrival at the beach was always a mesmerising performance: the shedding of her clothes, making herself cancer-proof against the sun. Today she was bubbling over with enthusiasm. They were opening Jimmy's house. She had spoken to the maid and Jimmy Jardine was arriving on the island later that day, alone, leaving his rock star entourage behind, his girlfriends, the outside world. He was in retreat, here to meditate and write. 'I've made up my mind – this time I'm going to spend the night with him,' she announced.

Everyone looked at everyone else, trying to control smiles, laughter even. Over the years Rachel must have made that statement a dozen times, but she had never been able to accomplish a seduction of Jimmy Jardine.

The men began to tease Rachel about her inability to seduce Jimmy to her bed. It was Laurence who gave her the tip: something he thought, at the very least, would get her into his house: Jimmy's serious commitment to Buddhism, his knowledge of Sufism. She must show an interest in that side of his life, let him know that all she wanted was to sit at his feet and talk about those things and what they meant to him.

The heat and the beauty of Livakia, the pleasures of life, the constant fun, seemed always to outweigh any minor unpleasantnesses that flared up there. The Melina-Mark episode of just a few minutes before was forgotten by everyone before the girl had vanished off the beach.

Chapter 4

D'Arcy had a good knowledge of Crete. She had travelled extensively over most of the 160-mile, roughly oblong island and had criss-crossed it thousands of times from its narrowest stretch of 6 miles to its widest of 35 miles. She loved every inch of it. The other foreigners living in Livakia had that same passion for Crete. They knew it – maybe not as well, except for Max, but enough to want to know it as she and Max did. Except for D'Arcy, Manoussos and Max, few of the Livakians took the road over the Levka Ori range of mountains as D'Arcy had a few days before. There were easier, less dramatic routes from Livakia, by boat up or down the coast to villages and towns where one could catch a bus, or else keep a car and then drive anywhere on the island. Only Max had the advantage of a sea plane as well as his jeep and a boat.

Laurence had no car, the hassle was too much, he used public transport and lifts from people. Arnold kept his convertible Volkswagen in a cave above a village several miles down the coast. Mark was too poor to have a car and didn't know how to drive anyway. The Plums had a car; Jane did the driving but wasn't very good at it so they rarely used their own but hired a taxi. All in all the foreign community had enough transport to keep them far from isolated unless they wanted to be. There was even a bus that did make the road twice a week to Livakia. Mark had dubbed it the Kamikaze Express. Only strangers and the desperate took their chances on its arriving anywhere at all.

Laurence and D'Arcy had been invited to dinner by friends of his who lived in a marvellous house in Rethymnon. Dinner meant staying overnight because it was on the opposite side of the mountain range from Livakia. D'Arcy had no problem with that, Rethymnon was her favourite town on Crete. It was on the north coast between Chania and Iraklion, smaller than those towns and filled with charm, a sleepy little place, looking very Eastern with its many minarets and wooden houses. Its buildings, like the great mosque in the fortress with its three domes and slender minaret, added yet another flavour. They seemed almost African. The ancient port, once made famous by the Venetians, and the early-seventeenth-century Loggia were always, for some reason, instant visual reminders of the history of Crete to D'Arcy.

'Sure we'll go. I always like going to Rethymnon,' D'Arcy told Laurence, looking very happy.

'But I thought you disliked the Chumleys?'

'I do, but you don't.'

'So this is a sacrifice?'

'Hardly a sacrifice. You get to be with your stuffy insular friends, I get a great dinner in a lovely house and to wander around town, saying hello to a few old faces I know they would never bother to speak to.'

'I don't know why you dislike them so. I've known Jeremy Chumley my whole life and no one I know dislikes him, or Celine for that matter.'

'Have you ever listened to their conversation? I don't think you have. You just accept what they have to say as interesting. It's not, you know. It's stultifyingly boring. When the four of us are together, the three of you talk in the past tense. "Do you remember when we were in India together? Saw Benjy the other day, remember when . . . Boo is divorcing, Tiggy is marrying. Bunny still asks after you. Are you going to the Chenedges' party. Oh, do you know Phizzy, D'Arcy? What is D'Arcy a nickname for, D'Arcy? Ha, ha, ha." Oh, really, Laurence, you left those sort of people behind when you left Eton and Cambridge.'

'D'Arcy, one never leaves Eton and Cambridge behind.'

Peals of laughter from D'Arcy, and Laurence joining her. It was late-morning and they were still in D'Arcy's bed. Having given up dinner in favour of lust, they had had a dawn breakfast on the terrace in the sun: fried eggs and bacon, slabs of cheese, toast, and English rough cut marmalade. They drank Fortnum's Royal Blend tea laced with sugar and a splash of Scotch whisky, a restorative after-sex drink, or so Laurence claimed. Exhausted from their romp through a landscape of adventurous sex, they had fallen asleep only after they had made themselves replete with food.

D'Arcy rolled on to her side and looked at Laurence. She knew he was right. What you are, what you have been, you carry with you all your life. It's what you add to it, what you do with what you've got, that makes the difference, or no difference at all. She loved Laurence just as he was, would never want him to change, nor for him to change his friends, but that did not mean she had to make them hers. She had thought he understood that.

D'Arcy slid her body over Laurence. She watched him close his eyes and felt his tremor of pleasure. He caressed her bottom and sighed, then dropped his hands on to the bed. She sat up, straddled him, and adjusted the pillows behind his head. They gazed into each other's faces and Laurence ran his fingers through her hair. 'I do like Jeremy and Celine, you know. I like all my friends like them,' he told her.

'I know.'

'You just don't understand them, where they're coming from. You think them silly with their love of nicknames – hot-house flowers rather than the wild thing you are. And maybe they are. But they like you, in spite of your not having a nickname or a normal background, an upbringing they cannot understand or accept. Your having a mother and several fathers but not one you can call your own; a name after a romantic hero from *Pride and Prejudice* but spelled more dramatically because your mother was an incurable romantic. You should give them some credit for that.'

D'Arcy was not offended to be told she was not a conventional girl from a conventional background. She did not, however, find that a hindrance in her life, nor had she thought Laurence did. For her it was just her life. She, her brothers and her sister all adored their mother for her beauty and her courage to have lived life the way she wanted to, bringing them up in the manner she felt would give them the best beginning. But what did offend her was the tone in Laurence's voice, the look in his eyes. He was being condescending about who and what she was.

She remained silent for several moments just sitting astride him. She needed that silence to compose herself, rattled by the way he was patronising her. She took a deep breath and reached out most tenderly to remove a lock of hair that fell on his forehead. Then she ran her fingers through his hair several times, all the while studying his face. She understood for the first time that they had a passion for each other; they loved each other but didn't know each other. There was, she realised, the possibility that they didn't even like each other.

Laurence understood what he had done. He could see in her face how he had offended her. He hardly knew how it had happened. He reached out to her and took her hand in his, drawing it to his lips and kissing it. 'D'Arcy . . .'

'No, please don't say anything.'

'I feel I must.'

'I don't think we can have a discussion about this. It occurs to me that you and I have never asked each other about our backgrounds. What we know are bits and pieces of each other's lives learned third-hand from other parties. It never occurred to me that our life's histories needed defining so that we might come to terms with them.'

'You're upset.'

'Not upset. Not even disappointed. Surprised.'

D'Arcy bent forward and kissed him on the lips. He wrapped his arms around her and caressed her breasts. She slid smoothly from his arms and the bed and went into the dressing room. She was slipping into a white silk kimono heavily embroidered with butterflies when she returned to him. Taking him by the hand, she led him out into the midday sun where she settled him in a chaise and brought him a cigar and a lighter, then went to sit opposite him on the terrace wall overlooking the sea.

The bedroom terrace was sheltered from all eyes and they often lay there in the nude, sometimes in the sun, at times in the shade under the enormous old fig tree. She watched Laurence smoke his cigar. Often she had thought he would make a good nude for Lucien Freud to paint. There was great strength, raw sexuality, in his nakedness. Such a contrast to the handsome, rather erudite face with its veil of secrecy, its depth of character, that was so inscrutable. Brett had always told her the upper-class Englishman was the Chinese man of the West. A man with two faces. That was what made him so attractive. He seemed relaxed, his usual self. That was possibly why she asked him to tell her what he did know about her and her family.

'Do we have to do this, D'Arcy?' he asked, but there was no annoyance in his voice.

'No, we don't *have* to do anything.'

Laurence was brief and to the point when he told her what he knew. It was quite a good deal and most of it accurate, and in a strange way that made his patronising of her a few minutes before even worse. She listened, and then when he was quiet went and sat down next to him. 'Maybe one day you will get to meet some of my family,' was all she said.

There had been no scene, the subject was closed. He had asked no questions, she had volunteered nothing.

His admiration for her, already great, increased tenfold. She had so many ways of seducing him, of keeping him enthralled. He loved her passionately for that, but his love was an ambivalent one. He disliked her possession of him as much as he loved it. She held him not with a string, not a single female ploy, nor did she play the games women usually like to play with men. He moved over on the chaise and asked her to lie down next to him. After removing her kimono, she did as he asked.

'You're too good for me,' he told her.

'You just might be right about that. We'll have to see, won't we?' That was not the answer he'd expected.

'After the Chumleys, shall we take a few days and go down to Phaistos, maybe visit the dig where Hannah and Yorgos are working?' he asked.

'That would be nice.' .

There were good things and bad about leaving Livakia for a trip across the island. Time changes everything. Other places on Crete had not fought as hard as the residents of Livakia had to keep the village and the old port as they had always been. They had struggled to keep the concrete and the plastic out and their own little world locked in. To look around at other places was to realise Livakia had retained the heart of the real Crete and to understand that they were living in paradise.

The years had taken a heavy toll on some places on Crete, and Laurence and D'Arcy would make their trip over long difficult back roads to avoid as much of it as possible. D'Arcy knew every short cut that was passable, every village worth stopping at, and that was why once the news was out that they were going away for a few days, Mark asked for a lift. Manoussos suggested that he follow them out and take them to a village that only he and D'Arcy knew. There they would see marvellous things and could break the journey for a picnic which he would provide.

Two days later, at six in the morning, the convoy of three cars set out: Manoussos leading in his jeep with Arnold as passenger, packing two cases of wine and five litres of Katzakis's best extra virgin olive oil, D'Arcy driving her 2CV with Laurence next to her and Mark squashed in the back with a whole lamb butchered and ready for the fire, and twenty loaves of bread. The rear was brought up by Max driving the other American Second World War jeep with Bridget, Elefherakis Khalikadakis (it was his grandmother's village and he maintained the church there) and a visiting house guest of his from Athens, Maria Kokas, who was balancing on her knees trays of Greek sweets oozing with thin and sticky honey syrup. Two burlap sacks of potatoes were lashed across the jeep's flat bonnet.

Manoussos had called ahead to his officer for that area to announce they were descending on the village for lunch and everyone was invited as their guests. Everyone in that convoy knew what Cretan hospitality was. Here was a poor village, with not even a bakery in it, and the moment the cars arrived every household would be emptying their larders to offer them food and drink. The only way to avoid stripping them bare of food was to bring enough to the village to feed them all well with quantities to spare. Even then the villagers would trot out every bit of foodstuff they had in the house to the picnic that had turned into a banquet.

The church and icons were treasures and the view of the mountains and the sea spectacular. There were marvellous ruins of early civilisations, and magnificent caves. The men in that village had a reputation for courage and bravery, were heroes of the resistance when the Germans occupied Crete during the Second World War. They were fiercely proud men who had fought hard for their freedom and their country and now even their children and their grandchildren carried those same traits in their blood. No man was going to rob these people of what was rightfully theirs. They were some of the most helpful people Manoussos had as allies against art theft on Crete, the extra forces his department could not afford. They were his guerrilla army for art as their friends and relatives had been for freedom during a dark time of war.

Eight miles before the village, when the convoy was still on a climb up a narrow dirt road with a treacherous drop to one side, a mountain rising high above them on the other, they heard rifle shots echo above the sounds of grinding gears and noisy engines. Manoussos raised his arm, a signal for D'Arcy to keep going, then, one hand still on the wheel, he raised the rifle lying between him and Arnold and fired two shots into the air. They were navigating a blind bend in the road. Once past that the steep grade of the climb eased off, and five men could be seen walking towards them, firing more shots into the air and smiling. They wore jeans tucked into high white leather boots, and white shirts. Some had a red sash tied about their waist, and they wore narrow black bands fringed and tied across their forehead.

Big rugged-looking men, dark and handsome, contemporaries of Manoussos, they shouted for the drivers not to cut their motors as they swaggered forward to shake the hands of the party in welcome. They walked alongside the cars which were travelling at what seemed like a snail's pace, slapping backs and asking about the road and their journey. Two of the men knew Max and ogled Bridget, one recognised D'Arcy, and they all teased her about the 2CV.

Here the road was even narrower. Three of the men walked ahead, clearing stones and throwing them down into the ravine. The others draped themselves on the open vehicles, hopping off now and again to give a push when they thought it necessary, shouting an order to cling closer to the mountain when they saw the tyres riding the edge of the road. There was the sound of the occasional rock crashing down into the ravine, an unnerving occurrence, but there was the drama of the landscape to distract them, rough and arid, barren of trees, all shapes and forms, beige and white and grey against a sky bright blue and clear. A pair of huge birds with enormous wingspans kept swooping then gliding on the warm currents of air not far above the cavalcade.

It was barely eleven o'clock in the morning when they finally arrived in the village and five o'clock in the afternoon when the convoy split up and D'Arcy drove away with her passengers plus an escort of two. They would be very late arriving at the Chumleys' for dinner.

Manoussos had given them the most wonderful time.

The village had been a jewel, the works of art of museum quality and the villagers marvellous: a community of very old Cretans and younger men, several children, and the women, of course staying in the background of the festivities. Other men arrived on foot from neighbouring villages, some a good distance away. It was a great party with great food: the lamb, covered with rosemary and olive oil, was roasted over a pit dug in the earth and filled with charcoal and wood that had turned to hot white ash. There were dishes of yoghurt and cucumber salad strong with fresh dill, earthen pots of cooked beans, and potatoes fried in olive oil, rosemary and garlic, salted and sprinkled with coarse black pepper. The wine never stopped flowing, and then came the tiny cups of sweet black coffee and the cakes.

D'Arcy, Max and Manoussos had even managed a spectacular walk with the sea far, far below always in view. There had been something very special about that place where they walked. The mind kept making side trips. There she was a goddess and the two men gods and this was Olympus where they dwelt.

Never had D'Arcy felt so connected to two human beings as she did during that walk with Max and Manoussos. She had always known ever since she was a child that she loved Manoussos, would always love him, but she had never known that she loved Max. She had been running away from him for too many years even to contemplate such an idea. There had been no clap of thunder, no bolt of lightning had struck her, this was no *coup de foudre* where she was catapulted into love. It had been a much slower realisation, one to be savoured.

The three barely spoke to each other on the walk; it was as if no one wanted to shatter the mood of a moment that was so personal to each of them. They walked separately and at times together, three abreast, holding hands, Manoussos with an arm round D'Arcy's waist.

They had been standing together on a large slab of rock that protruded like a ledge over the edge of the mountain. There was barely a breeze, the sun was bright and the heat dry and intense. They looked at one another and knew without having to declare it that it was time to leave. There was fire and passion and love so very strong, a powerful spirit, emanating from them. Souls soaring. This was a moment in their lives that would never happen again, one that would be remembered forever. Manoussos had taken D'Arcy's face in his hands. He had only ever seen her look as she did at that moment while in the throes of orgasm, when the inner D'Arcy surfaced and she gave herself up wholly to sexual bliss. He placed his lips upon hers and moved his hands to the buttons on her dress. One, two buttons, and she took over and continued.

Max approached her. He removed her hands and continued, stopping only when the buttons of her white cotton dress were undone and it was open to below her waist. Manoussos had stepped behind D'Arcy. He slipped her dress from her shoulders and it fell to rest on her slender hips. He caressed her shoulders and her back, and slipping his arms under hers, found her breasts and caressed them, removing his hands only to stroke her long red hair and watch Max take over where he had left off.

Max was a big man with large, strong hands that

he used gently. There was tenderness in his touch. He fondled her breasts, felt the weight of them in those hands, caressed their swell, the nipples, and then ran his hands over her midriff, caressing the flat of her belly, the curve of her hips. He took her breasts in his hands and kissed them. His lips sucked the stunningly elegant and subtle nipples. He transferred those kisses, that passion for her, to a kiss on the lips, and gave her a smile filled with affection, respect, even a hint of adoration before he took her hand in his and kissed it then walked round behind her. Manoussos took his place.

D'Arcy and Max watched Manoussos drop to his knees and lick her flesh, resting his face on her mound beneath the white dress, covering it, while Max stroked her shoulders and back. These were some of the sexiest moments of D'Arcy's life, of all their lives, and yet it was not mere lust. It was lust and much more than that. It was sex and much more than sex. It ended as innocently and easily as it began with Manoussos rising from his knees and Max slipping D'Arcy's dress back on to her shoulders; both men, Max from behind and Manoussos from in front, doing up the buttons for her.

They had smiled at each other and Max broke the spell that had taken them over. He did it with nothing more than a shrug of his shoulders and a sigh that was one of pure pleasure and contentment. D'Arcy placed her arms around his neck, grabbed a handful of his hair and hung on to it as she placed a kiss on his lips, then his eyes and his cheeks. She did the same to Manoussos and they left that place that they knew they would never return to because it was there that something very special had reached into their lives and that could never be repeated. They were not people to chase after rainbows.

All the way over the mountain range and during the remainder of the drive to Rethymnon, these were the things that kept slipping to the forefront of D'Arcy's mind. And more, the realisation that she was one of the most fortunate of women, truly blessed.

For Mark also it had been a memorable day. She thought she had never seen him happier or in better form than he had been in the village. He did have a way with the Cretans. Mark had held them spellbound with his knowledge of the history of the island, his stories of the bravery of the Cretan people, and all told in the most perfect Greek.

As a story-teller and an orator he could compete with the best. He had been witty and intelligent, passionate and serious by turns. He had natural timing, the pauses always in the right place, and had spoken with authority, to everyone's relief leaving his Fascist thinking buried in the recesses of his mind or heart. D'Arcy never knew where that side of Mark truly lived.

He had charmed everyone and had been patient and considerate with Arnold, translating when he thought Arnold might have missed something, watching the amount he drank, and even being discreet about that. He played backgammon with several of the men and recited one of the epic Cretan poems, going on for nearly half an hour without faltering once. Mark had held everyone in the village entranced and when he finally fell silent there was a tear in every Cretan's eye.

Here had been the Mark they all wanted him to be,

the Mark that they'd thought he was, the Mark he had been when they had first met him on his arrival in Crete. But time, and changes that had come about in his life in the last few years, had made Mark not only rude and uncaring, but bitter and sadistic as well. He had written two books in the years that D'Arcy had known him and had received moderate critical success. But his writing kept him poor. Mark was always going to be a not quite first-rate literary talent, and always poor. And that was the problem, his hatred of being second-rate and poor. He wanted it all: to be a great writer, wealthy, and have critical success as well.

Those things and having the sound of his own voice for Fascism silenced by the voices of free-thinkers, liberal democrats such as Arnold, frustrated him. He had only one friend who listened and agreed with him. And when she was visiting, a conversation between them was like hearing goose-steps.

If only Mark could be persuaded that such thinking was not going to make his or anyone's life easier or more palatable – quite the opposite. It can infect, destroy, ravage and poison minds and hearts, his own a case in point. And how many others who admired him for his thinking? More days such as they had just experienced, more love and good friends was what was needed. Maybe then that aggressive behaviour he took with the weak and less driven than himself would taper off and he could enjoy life as much as he had during the marvellous day they had all just had together. D'Arcy had great hopes for Mark, for all of them.

* * *

After their picnic in the villages, Manoussos, Max and Arnold returned to Livakia while D'Arcy and Laurence spent several days on the move round the island, visiting the odd friend, but in general just enjoying themselves and each other enormously. They were having a lazy lunch straight from the sea to the fire in a small taverna in a village to the far west of Livakia, when D'Arcy suddenly said, 'Let's go home.'

'Sure. This has been a great trip, D'Arcy, but, yes, do let's go home,' he agreed, taking her hand in his.

There was nothing more to it than that. The aquamarine 2CV, top down and layered with dust, was parked out of the sun and under a thatched lean-to close to the beach. They had choices: they could try and find a bed in the village and leave the next morning or they could leave immediately, but it was a long hard ride from that village up the mountains and across the range to get home. They would have to drive the last hours at dusk and more likely in the dark. While that was not a problem for D'Arcy, she had been driving for days and the prospect of another long haul did not inspire much enthusiasm.

They had very nearly decided to stay the night in the village and asked the taverna's proprietor if there was a bed to be rented. D'Arcy and Laurence were no strangers to the village or the proprietor who had joined them over a bottle of wine and assured them there were several beds in several houses they could be comfortable in. Or, he had suggested, 'We can lift your little blue bug and put it and you on board Sotiri's boat and you can be home in a couple of hours,' pointing to a large and handsome wooden boat sailing in towards the beach and a dilapidated wooden dock a hundred yards from where they sat.

When he could stop laughing at the idea of tossing the 2CV on to a boat, he continued, 'He's delivering my meat and supplies, and his next stop is Livakia.'

While it was very tempting, it was an impossible idea. To get the Citroën on the boat was one thing; to get it from the port in Livakia to the cave where D'Arcy kept the car was another. There were no roads in Livakia that could accommodate anything more than a man and a donkey. They all had a laugh and then once the boat delivery had been made to the taverna Sotiri joined them for a drink. It was he who suggested that they leave the car under the lean-to and take the boat with him to Livakia. In a few days he would be making his return trip. He offered to pick up D'Arcy in Livakia and drop her off to collect the car then. It began to seem like a good idea and after several more glasses of wine, a brilliant one. They pulled up the roof of the 2CV and locked the car. The taverna keeper appeared with a huge tarpaulin which they draped over it and tied down, and with no more fuss than that they boarded Sotiri's boat and sailed for home.

It was one of those magical boat rides that can happen on that coast. They sailed not too far out to sea and parallel to the rugged coastline, always a glorious sight to see but especially with the afternoon sunlight playing on the cliffs and along the deserted coves and beaches or on the occasional village. The landscape changed colour from beige and stone to lavender and pink, even a quite bright yellow, and then back to its original colour and all its hues and variations: cliffs of toffee and hills of gold.

'God's palate,' said Sotiri as he handed them huge slices of warm watermelon. He smiled at them and D'Arcy thought she had yet to meet a Cretan who, when it came to his island, did not have a little poetry in his heart.

They were sitting in the prow of the boat on packing cases due for delivery in a port further on from Livakia, D'Arcy in a wide-brimmed straw hat that had seen better days, Laurence wearing his grandfather's Panama that had yellowed with age. With eyes trained on the coastline and apropos of nothing he said, 'It's so difficult for me to think of you as having been born and brought up in this magically beautiful but in many ways unreal place. I can't even imagine how it could have happened to you.'

'Well, you'd have to have known my mother, Brett, to understand it. She was a pleasure seeker, who loved men and life and freedom. That was why she lived in Crete, and bore four children, had lovers, and gave us several men for father figures. Men who loved us and her all the more for her having not trapped them into a conventional married life she knew she could never sustain. Everything I am and do is coloured by my unusual upbringing here on this island.'

'You've told me that before and still it amazes me.'

'What amazes you?'

'The way you turned out without the trappings of the establishment. I think I envy you.'

'I know you do, darling. You must try and get over that.'

'You envy no one?'

'I don't even understand envy.'

'You can honestly say that you have no desire to know who your biological father is, as I do?'

'It never crosses my mind. All my life I've known he's one of two of the best men any girl could ever want for a father. That's always been good enough for me – for all concerned as a matter of fact. They don't know which one is my dad any more than my mom does. She loved them both, they both loved her. I'm a love child and so are my brothers and sister. Brett always made sure we understood that and appreciated it. We did and it made us happy.

'Happy, and wildly free and romantic was the way she brought us up. As a very young child I had a lifestyle which was materially poor, at times even desperately so. Sometimes we lived on credit from Mr Katzakis for months and months and were fed by some of our Cretan friends.

'Mother had a small trust fund and when money came in the first thing she did was pay her bills and take us for a treat, an excursion somewhere. We were all right without electricity and central heating and money, but then nearly everyone else in Livakia was really poor except for Elefherakis. Brett had many friends who would arrive and stay, and the fathers would come for long periods of time. It was all part of our rich life of fun and looking for fun. It helped that everyone admired my mother – they were dazzled by her beauty and respected her independence and her love of Crete, and the way she was bringing us up. In a strange way we had the most privileged life any child could want. Being brought up by a beautiful, eccentric mother, an incurable romantic who named her children after heroes of literature, has been no hindrance in my life.

'Brett was a product of the sixties, a mature beautiful woman who had been a chic, sophisticated deb and model. Then she saw an alternative way to live and love and be happy. Men always fell in love with her. It was a millionaire Greek ship owner who brought her to Crete. She fell in love with it rather than him. Periodically he used to return and fill the house with food and wine and we would party on his yacht. Then one day, when I was fourteen years old, my mother gave birth to her fourth child. A week later one of my fathers arrived on a lovely black schooner. We watched it sail into Livakia as my mother, with the baby swathed in a white silk shawl in her arms, walked round the port to meet him trailed by her three other children. He kissed her and helped her aboard, then he kissed each of us and swung us on to the deck. He had inherited one of the finest vineyards in France, carrying one of the oldest and best labels. He wanted to show us the world.

'The harsh years of near penury and then the influence of that particular father of ours did not so much change all our family's life as expand it with his wealth and generosity. It was through him that I learned the advantages of being independently wealthy enough to be able to seek out and enjoy my pleasures and satisfy my heart's desires. So you must see why I can't understand how you can be amazed by me. I'm just living my life the best I can on my terms, in my time. It's nothing more than the way I was brought up to live, the way I've always lived.'

Laurence pulled D'Arcy off the packing case and on

to his lap. He removed her hat and her lovely auburn hair tumbled down round her shoulders. He tilted up her chin and kissed her full on the lips, then again. They smiled at each other, and she leaned her head against his chest. He rocked her in his arms while slipping a hand beneath her blouse to caress her breast. His caressing was sweet and sensual and it stirred her soul. She felt her flesh, her bones, melt away into sweet bliss and she reached out to him to caress his lips and slip her hands beneath his shirt. She liked the feel of his firm, warm flesh and, unbuttoning his shirt, she kissed his nipples and licked them and then his lips. D'Arcy sighed and smiled at Laurence, they kissed once more before she closed his shirt and reached for her hat, replacing it on her head. They remained like that, watching the coastline of Crete slip by and listened to the sounds: the chatter of Sotiri and his crew from somewhere in the stern of the boat rising above the chugging and spluttering noise of the working wooden boat as it headed towards home.

Laurence was too moved by this woman he loved to challenge her about several things she said. She was a sophisticated, well-educated and talented woman, a Yale arts graduate who in her chosen field of industrial design had been clever enough to win contracts for work and patent several innovative designs for the motor industry that had made her a millionarie by the age of twenty-eight, at which time she retired to Livakia to live for her pleasures.

She wore her successes as if they were not successes at all, but as she herself might have put it, 'just life'. Was this innocence? Naïveté? Or was it a grand case of inverted snobbery? Was what she told him, and the giving of herself to him so totally in sex and every other way, genuine? He demanded complete possession of her and she gave it to him and he was trapped by her gift. She *was* amazing. No other woman had managed to capture him in love and keep him as she had.

D'Arcy and Laurence were standing with Sotiri at the boat's rail when they rounded a cliff that plunged dramatically straight down to the bottom of the sea. The port of Livakia slowly unfolded before their eyes. It was dusk and the night was coming down fast. People would be sitting in the coffee shops, walking down from their houses for a stroll along the port and the corniche, lights would just be being switched on, and Livakia would soon be looking from the water as if a handful of stars had been thrown down by a benevolent god enchanted by all things rare and beautiful. It was the perfect time to sail into the small but deep natural harbour and a perfect way to end their excursion.

Livakia inched into view. The only twinkling lights to be seen were those in the houses on the hill. The port itself seemed deserted; the Kavouria, though open, had only a dim light showing from inside. The cafe tables were out but where were the people? Something was going on, but what? D'Arcy checked the time by her watch, and then scanned the port. Not a foreign resident was in sight. Was there a party somewhere? But the foreign colony didn't party much in each other's houses. The church . . . there was a function in the church. But there were no lights on in the church. She spotted a light in Manoussos's office and felt inexplicably relieved.

Chapter 5

At last two people appeared, Manoussos and his deputy. D'Arcy watched them walking along the crescent-shaped port to where the boat was coming in. She took off her hat and waved it at Manoussos. Normally she would have called out to him but somehow there was a hush about the evening and the port, and she was reluctant to do so. Instead, she raised her arms and turned her hands palms up, shrugged her shoulders, as if to ask, 'What's going on here?'

Laurence was less sensitive. He called out, 'I didn't expect a band or a welcome committee, but where is everybody?'

Manoussos helped D'Arcy off the boat and shook hands with Laurence and Sotiri. He placed an arm round D'Arcy's shoulders and smiled at her. 'Good trip?'

'Great,' she told him, feeling less concerned about the strange quiet that seemed to lie like a blanket over everything in Livakia.

But that was before she realised the usual warmth of his smile was somehow not there, that there was a stiffness in his walk. His deputy, Dimitrios, had not looked her in the eye when he had greeted her nor had he looked

Laurence or Sotiri in the face when he had shaken their hands. D'Arcy began to stride along with a spring in her step, talking about their boat trip. They were passing the barber's shop. There was no one waiting in a queue to use the telephone, no one sitting in the chairs being worked on, not a soul lolling around waiting for his turn in the chair or merely there for a gossip. Nothing but the glow from a small naked light bulb, the shop's night-light, and the barber-cum-mayor leaning against the door jamb. On seeing them, he turned his back on them and walked to the rear of his minute shop.

D'Arcy stopped walking and stepped in front of Manoussos. She could not help but notice the flush of colour that had come into his deputy Dimitrios's face. 'OK, our mayor can sometimes be Mr Grumpy, but he is never rude. Or let me put it this way, I've known him my whole life and he has never been rude to me. Now *that* was rude. What's going on here, Manoussos?'

They were only a few steps away from some small tables set out on the cobblestones. Manoussos took D'Arcy firmly by the hand and led her over to one. The others followed and pulled up chairs. The coffee house keeper vanished into his shop. Manoussos snapped his fingers and a little boy came running with glasses of water which he nervously plonked on the table, slopping water everywhere. D'Arcy just as nervously began mopping the water up with Kleenex from her basket while Laurence gave orders for the boy to bring coffee for them all.

D'Arcy watched Dimitrios remove his policeman's hat and mop his brow and the palms of his hands with a neatly folded white handkerchief. Once more she gazed along the port, and then looking directly into Manoussos's eyes told him, 'Well, whatever has happened here since we've been away it must be bad because not even Arnold is here, having his first drink of the evening while waiting for a game of chess with you. Or has he gone off on his trip to Skafidia Padromi? He did mention something about wanting to visit someone there, or was it Kastelli Kissamu? I can't remember.'

Dimitrios put his hat back on and actually rose and left the table. The boy returned with a copper swing tray of demi-tasse cups of Greek coffee, hot and sweet. Manoussos raised his hand to stop the boy from banging them down on the table and himself removed each from the tray. He placed a cup in front of Laurence, D'Arcy, and himself. Even one on the table in front of Dimitrios's empty chair. He instructed the boy to go and tell Dimitrios, who was standing by the water, to return to the table.

Silence settled on them. Their eyes were fixed on Dimitrios as he returned to the table to sit down and pick up his coffee cup. Like robots they followed suit, placed the rim of the chipped white cups to their lips and sipped the hot black liquid.

Manoussos stroked his moustache several times, as if it were ruffled and he had to smooth it down, then he spoke. 'There is no easy way to tell you this. Arnold's not missing, he's dead.'

Dimitrios lowered his eyes. D'Arcy couldn't somehow grasp what Manoussos was saying. Her eyes were fixed on Dimitrios, who was clearly upset. She remembered that he always watched out for Arnold, made sure no

harm came to him. They were friends, he often helped
Arnold on his days off, liked the American and his little
projects. She reached across the table and grasped the
sleeve of his jacket in her hand and began tugging at
it. A profound sadness was pulling her down, disbelief,
hysteria . . . she could feel those things taking her over.

'You were his friend, Dimitrios, took care of him. We
all did. Wasn't anyone watching him? Oh, don't tell me
no one was there to help him?'

Laurence removed her hand from Dimitrios's sleeve.
He had actually to prise her fingers open. He was
harsh with her when he demanded, 'Stop this, *now*.
Pull yourself together, D'Arcy. We're all upset. Handle
it better.'

Tears filled her eyes and she covered her face with
both her hands and took several deep breaths. It had
finally sunk in. Arnold was dead and gone from Livakia
forever. His death would leave a gap in all of their lives.
It was Manoussos who rose from his chair and went to
her. He handed her a handkerchief and stroked her hair
before he returned to his chair opposite.

When she lowered her hands she was more in control of
herself. The first thing she did was to address Dimitrios.
'I'm sorry, Dimitrios, but it was such a shock. Only days
ago he was alive and happy, happier than I had seen him
for a long, long time. Forgive me? That was grief talking,
pulling at your sleeve.'

'We are all grieving, Kiria D'Arcy. We are all very
upset that such a thing could have happened here.'

D'Arcy, a quick mind at the best of times, realised that there was more than grief going on. She

turned to Manoussos and asked, 'What happened? When, how, why?'

'Let me tell you everything we know to date. The evening after our return from the picnic everything here was as usual. The following day Mark returned by boat at lunchtime. It seems there was a message waiting for him when you dropped him off in Rethymnon, a publisher he wanted to see was arriving in Athens. He made his way back home as quickly as possible to pick up a manuscript and planned to leave by plane for Athens the following day. He was very excited and so was everyone else who had heard about it.

'The Kavouria was filled to capacity – everyone in Livakia seemed to want to have lunch on the port that day. Dimitrios and I were talking business a few tables from where Arnold and half a dozen others were dining. It began from nothing, as all those little tiffs that flared up between Arnold and Mark began. One overheard it but paid little attention. Arnold asked, "How is the new book coming on?"

'"Fine, just fine. If it wasn't, Arnold, would I be making this trip to Athens? How is your war against the ants coming along?" Mark answered testily – you know, with that certain tone he could take with Arnold, especially when he had been drinking heavily.

'Arnold replied, "Well, I'm not winning. I can't understand it because my house is immaculate. There is never a crumb anywhere and yet still they come. It's so upsetting. You don't have them, do you?"

'"Of course I don't have them. You make entirely too much fuss about them and behave worse than any old woman. It's because you have nothing more important to occupy your mind than how to pour yourself into an early grave, and drive Melina mad while she's trying to get on with the work you hired her to do."

'Arnold became unusually annoyed at being spoken to in that way by Mark. His annoyance turned to anger and he was pretty aggressive with Mark when he told him, "I'm not making too much fuss, and since you have brought Melina into this, I might just as well tell you that *your* Melina has been no help. I paid her good money to come and caulk the windows and she did not do a good job. She left gaps and that's where the ants come in. She never properly finishes any job that she begins."

'It was Arnold's voice that was drawing attention from everyone around. His stuttering was worse than usual and he was loud, and yes, had had a lot to drink, but was not by any means slipping off his chair in a catatonic state. This was more than the spats we were all used to. In a very calm voice Mark asked, "Arnold, why do you take her for odd jobs when you always complain that she's no help and does everything badly? She does things perfectly for me."

'Then he began to laugh at Arnold and told him, "You poor pathetic thing, stop fussing. If you don't like the way she works then, tell me, why do you keep asking her to go to your house? It's not too clever of you to badger Melina to work for you, and tell her how bad a job she does, and then overpay her for it. She goes off thinking she's done a great job for you and you come here and tell everyone what a rotten worker she is, how she overcharges you. She doesn't take kindly to that. You're such a fucking hypocrite, Arnold! You disgust me. You overpay so she'll keep quiet about how much you fancy her. All your slagging her off is to cover up those pathetic drunken sexual advances she has to fend off. She doesn't like working for you, Arnold, she does it for survival money, and I'm going to see that she doesn't have to do it again. She holds you in disdain. A poor, hardly literate Cretan girl, Arnold, despises you for your weakness and hypocrisy – *that's* what you've been reduced to."

'Of course by that time more than a dozen people had overheard the whole thing. Too much had been said. Things that would not be forgotten easily and certainly not by Arnold since he was sober enough to understand every word. The two men were silent for a few minutes. Arnold poured out what was left of the bottle of wine in front of him into two glasses. I am sure everyone felt as I did, that the two men should leave it at that. But, alas, they couldn't. You could see it in their faces, too much had been brought out in the open, too many secrets revealed. Arnold leaned both hands on the edge of the table for support and said, loud enough for the entire restaurant to hear, "Mark, I think it's time you and I settled a few things. I think we should have it out like gentlemen."

'"Whatever are you talking about?" asked Mark.

'"I'm talking about the way you speak to Melina about me. There was a time several months back when she was only too happy to come and spend time with me. As a matter of fact, to lead *me* on as to how much she wanted to be more, much more, than a skivvy to me. It was she who did the running, the seducing. It was not just for the money either, though she wanted that and other little gifts. She enjoyed being with me and listened to what I had to say, appreciated my suggestions as to how she could better herself and her life. She didn't mock me in public as well as in private then, or steal from me as she does now."

'Arnold's stammer became pitifully pronounced and there were longer hesitations in mid-sentence but he carried on. Nothing could have stopped him. He was more angry and aggressive than I had ever seen him. This was an Arnold none of us had ever seen. He emptied his glass and continued. "It has grown increasingly embarrassing for me since that night at your house several months ago when you stopped Melina from coming home with me. I have seen you consistently poison her against me, and it's not just Melina, Mark. You ridicule me in front of other people and I don't appreciate it in the least.

'"There is something else I want to address here. I have been watching you spoil Melina, making her believe that she is more intelligent than she is, giving her authority to do things that she should not be doing: control of your house when you're away, telling her that she is indispensable to you and your life, that she belongs in it. You have no idea how she behaves when she's in charge. You've inflated an already over-large ego and have actually convinced her that she is more clever than anyone in Livakia. How could you teach her to despise me, treat me with disdain in public in the manner that you do? I want you to stop it, and for you both to treat me with respect, if for no other reason than that I am a human being."

'Tears welled up in Arnold's eyes but he sat fast and

never took his gaze off Mark. It was then that Tom Plum tried to stop it. He suggested it had all been said and it was time to go home for siesta, that he would accompany Arnold home. But would Mark allow Arnold the last word? Not on your life.

'He talked past Tom, asked, "Are those tears of anger with me, Arnold? Tears of frustration? Or are they tears of unrequited love for Melina? Forget her. As long as you have brought up that embarrassing night at my house, let me tell you, you were so drunk and made such a scene over Melina, demanding that she should take you home and have sex with you, that it was easy to let you know at last what a fool you were making of yourself."

'"Why a fool, Mark? Because you like having her for yourself and pretending you don't pay for it, as I did, as others do?"

'No one quite remembers exactly what happened next, it all happened so fast. Mark jumped to his feet and shouted, "Stop it, Arnold, you never had her. And you are being extremely indiscreet and libellous."

'Melina appeared as if from nowhere, which stunned everyone and silenced the two men. She had been sitting in the shadows, making herself invisible – you know how she can do that – and had probably heard all that had been going on. After filling Arnold's and Mark's glasses, she placed a newly opened bottle of wine on the table. She was flirting outrageously with Arnold, picking up his glass and placing it in his hand, wrapping his fingers round it and covering them with her own, moving the glass to his lips, undressing him all the time with her mischievous, sexy eyes.

'Mark, in a very angry voice, demanded she leave him alone, asked her if she was stupid and didn't understand she was being insulted by Arnold, and in front of everyone, or hadn't she heard what had been going on? She said she had only been trying to help. After scanning the faces of everyone around, faces that turned away because they were embarrassed over the entire incident, she demanded the key to Mark's house, declaring she wanted to go home. He told her it was in its usual place. And after glaring at both men she shoved her way past the seated diners and ran from the Kavouria.

'Arnold struggled to his feet. He raised his glass. His hands were trembling so badly the wine spilled over his fingers. He paid no attention, composed himself and told Mark, "It's not just Melina. The things you say behind my back to her are only a part of it. The things you say in front of other people, my friends, humiliate me. We've known each other for more than ten years, have been friends who have helped each other, protected each other as foreigners living in this community. I find that I'm still doing it for you but you're attacking me, abandoning me as a friend, and when you do that you're not just attacking me, you're showing yourself up in a bad light. It's not only that you're rude to me, it's your attitude and manner. I am the abused one and still I'm speaking to you as a friend. Something is happening to you, you're doing evil things and covering them up with your excellent vocabulary and perfect diction. Some day it will reverberate and you'll pay heavily for what you do. There are times I don't know you, you've changed beyond recognition."

'The two men were still on their feet. Arnold was

tottering, but bravely tried to keep his balance, a proud but beaten man. Mark – well, it was frightening to look at Mark. He sipped his drink looking handsome and fit with his youthful face, those cold blue eyes, and then quite suddenly the face seemed to slip: the eyes went first from ice to venom – the nostrils seemed to grow narrower, the lips became thin and curled. Arnold, perspiring profusely, appeared to feel cold. He shivered visibly, and announced to the table that he wanted to go home. Unbelievably, it was Mark who offered to take him. That seemed to galvanise everyone at the table. Chairs were scraped back and several other people offered. It was Dimitrios who took him home, undressed him and put him to bed.

'Forty-eight hours later Max found Arnold lying on that deserted beach where he liked to swim. You know the place, that small cove that's so difficult to get to, where he kept his rowing boat in the little grotto. He was fully clothed, not a mark on his body, his basket by his side.'

'When was that?' asked Laurence.

'Two days ago.'

'Poor Arnold. Well, at least it was quick and he didn't suffer,' said D'Arcy.

'I didn't say that,' said Manoussos.

'What do you mean?'

'I mean that there are no clues as to what happened to him except the expression on his face, and that did not show that death came to him easily.'

'His liver, his heart, anything might have given out. He was bound to have some discomfort before he died,' said Laurence, taking D'Arcy's hand in his because he thought she was beginning to look distressed again.

'He had had his annual check-up in Paris four months ago. In spite of his drinking he was in very good health,' Manoussos told them.

'You suspect foul play? Not possible surely, not here in Livakia? He was too cautious to get involved with anything or anyone who could do him harm,' said D'Arcy.

'We'll know more when we get the autopsy report.'

'Autopsy report?' D'Arcy jumped up from her chair. 'Then you do think it was a suspicious death?'

'I'm not ruling that out, at least for the moment.'

'Then it's not just grief that has sent everyone behind closed doors? It's suspicion, shame. People are angry. Arnold's death could be part of some sort of a vendetta, and now everyone will be wary of everyone else until the mystery is solved and they know no one else in Livakia could be involved.'

D'Arcy sat down again. She had heard about these Cretan vendettas all her life: the way they could break up a family or a village for generations. The aftermath could be horrendous even for those who just got in the way. She had never seen it first hand, or experienced the tragedy of those vendettas. The closest she had come to anything like that had been when she was a child and a man had hidden out for years in Livakia. He went away one day, just vanished. Several weeks later an unidentified body was found on a road on the other side of the island. The newspapers were asking about missing persons. He was without family or close friends so no one bothered to claim the body as their missing neighbour. They didn't want to bring the vendetta home to Livakia. An identification might have, and with it more murders for merely harbouring the man in the village for so many years.

Laurence too knew about vendettas, everyone who lived in Crete did. He spoke up. 'This will all blow over, this notion of someone's having such a serious grudge against Arnold as to declare a vendetta. That's ridiculous.'

'It may not be, Laurence. Arnold could be very insensitive to Cretan pride – not deliberately but out of ignorance. And we don't know all of what his life was like. Arnold had his secrets, as we all do,' said Manoussos.

For only the second time, Dimitrios spoke up. 'No one saw Kirios Arnold from the time I brought him home until Kirios Max found him. Where was he? The night after I left him he wasn't in his house. I went to see if he was all right the following morning. At eight o'clock he was already gone. No one saw him in the port all that day or night. Where was he drinking? Where was he eating? I thought he'd taken that trip he said he was going to make, so I didn't even worry about him. I never even thought to look for him. I thought it was a good thing he wasn't around after such a terrible scene with Kirios Mark.'

There was guilt in his voice, guilt clearly imprinted on his face. D'Arcy could see that as policemen he and Manoussos must take the death seriously, consider every possibility. But why was everyone else? True, the scene that everyone had been privy to the last time they saw Arnold alive did sound dreadful, embarrassing, but what was so different about it from the other scenes the two men had had over the years, and that none of them ever did anything about? Then it came to her . . . Melina. D'Arcy's whole body went tense. She had to close her eyes and take several deep breaths, to quell the sickness she was feeling in the pit of her stomach. Finally she looked directly into Manoussos's eyes. Her first question to him was, 'Where is Mark?'

D'Arcy could see the relief in Manoussos's face that at last she had figured it out and was asking the right questions.

'Mark is in Athens. He left here just when he said he was going to, at six on the morning following the incident at the Kavouria.'

'Does he know about Arnold?'

'Melina called and told him, I know that from Max. He called Max to ask about the funeral arrangements and offer any help he could. Max said he sounded really upset. He arrives back here some time tomorrow.'

'And Melina?'

'She is here. She's about the only one who is carrying on as normal. Her only comment on Arnold's death was that he had at last drunk himself to death just as Mark had always predicted he would, *and* he did it owing her fifteen hundred drachma and his car which he'd promised her if and when he ever left the island for good.'

'She's a liar! Arnold would never have run up a debt with Melina, she wouldn't have let him and he never owed money. And as for the car! Arnold would never lend it to her, never mind leave it to her. She covets that car, seeing it as a symbol of wealth and class. She sees

110

her lie as a way to get it. Probably only wants it for Mark anyway. Oh, the stupid girl.'

'Don't make any accusations, D'Arcy, you don't know whether what she claims is true or not,' said Laurence, looking very annoyed with her.

D'Arcy sensed his irritation, his calm, almost icy indifference, and she resented the fact that he could take the mysterious death of a friend with so little emotion. She knew Arnold's death was affecting her on many levels, not least of which was having to face up to her own mortality. Was that not the way it must be affecting most everyone else in Livakia who had known Arnold and cared about him? Policemen or not, you could see the emotion in Manoussos's and Dimitrios's face. Why not Laurence's?

As if he were picking up her thoughts he took her hand in his and said, 'This has been a shock to us all. But we must not let it get on top of us.'

She knew he was right and nodded agreement, squeezing his hand and leaning forward to kiss him lightly on the lips, grateful for his being there and that he did at least understand her distress, not only for the death of a friend but for the circumstances of that death, whatever they might be.

'Laurence is right about not letting this get on top of us, D'Arcy, and apropos of that, I have a favour to ask,' said Manoussos. 'I have got to get the town back to normal as soon as possible before breaches in friendships start erupting, petty grievances we all live with get blown out of proportion, and the village starts to turn into two camps, the foreign colony and the locals

– something we have never suffered here. And if, as I suspect, there has been foul play then blame will start coming into it and things will get much worse. I want you to get the foreign residents to come out of their houses and behave normally. The same long lunches at the Kavouria, the routine swimming and boating parties, the sitting round on the port drinking coffee, reading the newspapers, buying bread and bits and pieces, and gossiping. You too, Laurence. Why don't we start by having some dinner at the Kavouria and you can tell me about your trip? Shall we say at nine?'

Laurence and D'Arcy walked in silence from the port to D'Arcy's house, past shops that were open but empty and houses where, unusually, all the lights were on and entire families were at home. Strangely, D'Arcy found the early evening darkness particularly beautiful. Livakia was in a hot haze of dark pearly blue; the sky, filled with stars, shone a lighter shade and the moon had risen above the village, casting its light on the white houses, showing soft yellow in the incandescent lamp light. She had seen hundreds of early evenings like this one, some of them had even been shared with Arnold.

They were climbing the narrow lane that led to her house when D'Arcy stopped and told Laurence, 'You know where the key to the gate is. Let yourself in and open the house. I'll be right back.' And before he could say anything she turned her back on him and ran down the lane.

D'Arcy's closest neighbours were Cretans. One was a boat builder and his wife and their two handsome grown-up sons. They were friends; the sons often sat and drank at the same table as D'Arcy, the mother on occasion had had her in for a meal, at the very least a snack at Easter. They had had good relations for as long as she could remember and yet when she and Laurence had just passed the house, the father and son had walked off the balcony where they had been sitting – a deliberate snub. Her other neighbour was the schoolmaster and his wife, and she had actually stepped behind a curtain to avoid a greeting. The boat builder's door was the first one D'Arcy knocked at.

Twenty minutes later she pushed open her own gate. She was hot, she was tired, and she was sad. It hadn't been easy but she had been determined and had won through. The schoolmaster and the entire family of boat builders had accepted her invitation to dinner at the Kavouria. D'Arcy's rationale, that they were doing a disservice to Arnold and his death, as well as to themselves, by behaving as if he had caused a crime to take place and disrupt their happy little world, had appealed to their sense of fairness. She pointed out, rather bluntly, that fear was dividing neighbour from neighbour – so much so that they had forgotten that a man, a neighbour, had lost his life. When she asked them how they could allow fear to take them over, and insisted that was what it had to be because only fear or ignorance would have made them turn their back on her, and she knew them to be not at all ignorant but intelligent and kind people, she broke them down. There were misty eyes and profound apologies.

Walking through the first courtyard of her house, she looked up at it, the place she loved, cherished actually. It was large with inner courtyards and terraces on several levels. Nearly every room had a different view of the sea. It was a house with good spirits in it, a happy house, and she never came home without appreciating it for what it was and the pleasure and peace and contentment that the place seemed to generate. It was a house that had not come easily to her, she had worked hard and long to earn the money to buy it, even harder to make it a perfect place of simplicity and beauty. It was as people said a work of art to live in, the same thing she had made of her life. It had actually been Max who had said that, Max who best understood and appreciated the house.

She could see a trail of lighted rooms that Laurence had walked through to her bedroom and her bath. She entered the hall: period white marble floors, a large double cube – the perfect room, so all artists and architects claimed. The ceiling twenty-five feet above her head was of open beams and the gallery surrounding it had doors off it leading to other rooms, giving the hall stature. It was incredibly cool here, a relief after the hot evening, and the tinkling sound of water was enchanting. She had brought the marble fountain set in the centre of the floor from Damascus along with period Damascene furniture: inlaid ivory and mother of pearl, huge mirrors and elegant chairs, chunky chests of drawers, some with Bombay fronts and rippling curves, others square and flat, a pair of slender settees and small charming tables, all of which she'd mixed with Greek Island period provincial pieces and rough white Haitian handwoven fabrics. There was also a collection of Bugatti furniture, Lalique glass, and ancient Greek sculpture. The paintings were spectral: Miro, Motherwell, Francis Bacon, nine Rothkos, all of which Laurence disliked. He also disliked having a house with no more than one or two things in a room, the dining room and the kitchen being the only exceptions to the 'less is more' code that D'Arcy lived by.

She walked through the hall and down several steps to her studio. It was there she kept her drawing board, there where her office equipment was kept. A long fax was hanging from the machine but she paid no attention to it. She went directly to the telephone and called Max and then the Plums and Elefherakis. She made the calls short and to the point, and they all agreed to dine with her at the Kavouria, albeit reluctantly. Switching off the lights, she went from there directly to her bedroom, stripping her clothes off en route, anxious to steep herself in a long and luxurious bath.

D'Arcy's bathroom was a large room, almost her favourite in the house. It was square and had a beige marble floor and three sets of windows, glass doors that went from the floor to the ceiling and led out on to a terrace overhanging the sea. The walls were a soft ivory colour, the bathtub many centuries old, deep, oval and long, of cream-coloured marble. It was a Greek artefact found in Turkey, and had already been drilled to let out water. Just below its elegant rim, a lovely deep curved lip, there were carved swags of acanthus leaves, obviously wrought by a master sculptor. It was fed from the mouth of a carved lion with a chipped nose and magnificent mane of black marble mounted on the wall above the tub. At the far side of the room, the entire wall was of beige marble and all ten feet of it was enclosed by a clear glass screen. That was the many recessed-headed shower stall where at one end stood a white marble massage table: a two-inch thick slab on a pair of marble bases curved and ending in huge lion's paws. It was more than a huge shower stall, it was D'Arcy's mini-Turkish bath. A retired master of the art of Turkish massage had returned to live out the remainder of his life in Livakia where he was born. Most every week D'Arcy took advantage of his talents, as did a dozen other people in Livakia.

She sat down on an ivory chair in front of the marble table she used as her dressing table and broke down and cried. The sight of Laurence lying on the table, the shower playing over his body, reminded her of the times Arnold had been there to use the shower room for his Turkish bath. He was convinced that Andreas the masseuse was prolonging his life. Except for the drink, Arnold clung on tightly to his life, his beliefs. He was a pleasure seeker who'd enjoyed the life that had been snuffed out. By whom? One thing was for certain, Arnold had expected to live out a long and contented life in Livakia. How had that been snatched away from him?

It was some minutes before D'Arcy had herself under control. When she did she drew her bath and stepped in. She washed her hair under the flow of water into the tub then lay back and listened to the sound of the sea crashing against the rocks far below her house.

Chapter 6

In the days that followed life slowly returned to normal,
but with slight differences. People seemed just a little
wary of each other, there was a strained atmosphere.
But on the plus side at least they were able to talk
openly about the tragic death. Everyone had a theory
as to what had really happened to Arnold, where he
had been in those lost hours between the time Dimitrios
put him to bed and Max found his body on the beach.
Arnold's death was the main topic of conversation but
there were other things happening in the community that
no one liked but seemed unable to do anything about: a
pall seemed to hover over the old port where everyone
gathered, the Cretan residents of Livakia seemed to be
retreating from the foreign residents out of some sense of
shame that the death of one of the foreigners should not
have taken place in his own bed. There was a split into
two factions, those who believed there had been some
sort of foul play concerning Arnold's death and those
who didn't. The one thing that no one wanted to think
or speculate about was the autopsy report, although all
waited anxiously to hear its verdict.

Mark returned to Livakia. He had little to say about

the death, except that he was sorry that his predictions had come true and Arnold had drunk himself to death. No one bothered to point out to Mark that this might not be the case. The long lunches in the port resumed but they were no longer the same. The innocent frivolity had gone out of them.

They got better when some friends of Manoussos's and D'Arcy's, three handsome men of about their own age whom they had known all their life, came down from their mountain village some twenty miles away. They made the visit about twice a year and always stayed in Brett's house. The whole of Livakia was always pleased to see them; they were intelligent and amusing, mischievous and generous, and they cheered everyone up. They were tough and realistic about Arnold's death, sorry because they had known and liked him, and because, as they pointed out continually, he would have been appalled to have caused them all so much unhappiness. That as it happened was quite true.

Things got even better when friends of Elefherakis arrived from Paris. The pleasure seekers were back. The outings resumed and the long lunches became more interesting but there was as usual talk about Arnold and more speculation while they waited for the facts to be revealed and his Boston family to arrive.

Elefherakis was playing host to a party of thirty in the restaurant in the garden when the subject was yet again brought round to Arnold and his death by Rachel, who announced that she had taken it upon herself to write a poem she hoped the family would use for an epitaph. That had silenced the entire table. Her flowery poetry had always irritated Arnold but he had been too polite to discourage her. Rather, he had kept buying her books: T S Eliot, Auden, and Jimmy Merril.

The silence was broken by Elefherakis's guest, a French doctor, who asked, 'What was your friend Arnold like? You speak about his death but I have no sense of this murdered man's personality. I would like to know what kind of a man could incite someone to take his life and leave him in the manner they did.'

Ever since Arnold's body was found that was the one question no one had uttered, hadn't dared to think, except possibly Manoussos or Dimitrios. And here it was out in the open, what they all feared the most. The silence continued. Someone poured wine, someone else passed the basket of bread, everyone looked uncomfortable. Several minutes went by and then it was Mark who spoke up.

'Arnold was a man who never changed. That was probably what killed him.'

'Men don't die from not changing, and certainly not from lying down fully dressed on a beautiful beach. It is more likely that change *did* kill him. The changes you didn't see. People deliberately blind themselves to the changes in other people because it's so much easier to deal with the known,' said the doctor.

'I tell you, you are wrong about this man. Most of us here knew him for more than ten years and he never changed. He did the same things day in and day out, year in and year out. He ate the same things – just enough to survive in order to drink – year in and year out. He read the same literature, lived on the same amount of money sent him by his family to stay away from Boston, year in and year out. He had the odd infatuation, sex in rare moments of need, year in and year out.

'No, he never changed. He was, till his death, the same Harvard man he was on his graduation day. He made the same trip every year for a week to the family in Boston to let them know that he was still able to stand on his own two feet and still relatively coherent. Then the Algonquin for one week where he would look up every old New York acquaintance who was a successful writer, painter, museum director, or art historian, whom he would invite for one drink. Arnold would listen to them tell him how lucky he was to have got out of the rat race he had never entered in the first place and to have made a life for himself here in Crete. He had his fix: he could think of himself as in control of his life, sober and superior, and that too was part of the sameness.

'Even his clothes – never a change there either. From the Algonquin to Brooks Brothers to buy two new button-down shirts, a pair of trousers, and discuss with the same salesman the pros and cons of turning the collars and cuffs of his old shirts. Walking away, he saw himself as complete, the perfect Harvard gentleman aesthete. Another year done in New York then on to Paris to do it all again.

'Everyone at this table knows what I tell you to be true, Pierre. They have heard it all year in and year out: the Deux Magots, the expatriate friends, the grand dinner parties in his honour – we were never spared the details or the name dropping of the famous who adored him. Nor were we spared anything in his accounts of Rome.

He probably suffocated on the sameness of his life, its changelessness.'

For the first time since Arnold's death all those at the table were hearing an analysis of his life and his death, granted, in an abstract way, but an analysis nevertheless. D'Arcy was acutely aware that Pierre's question and Mark's response had just revealed that no matter what, Arnold's death was no straightforward one, and if it was murder, no straightforward murder either.

It was after midnight when the party broke up and Laurence and D'Arcy walked home to his house. They had hardly said a word to each other all the way home, but there was a sexual tension building between them that D'Arcy was quite enjoying. Though Arnold's absence and the underlying strain on the community was a constant reminder that all in Livakia was not quite right and things would never quite be the same, the pleasure seekers and the Cretans had resumed their old lifestyles as if nothing had happened – and that included the sex between Laurence and D'Arcy.

This evening had planted a seed in D'Arcy's mind, a question. This death, this tragedy, that in some way was touching them all, had she been in her own way responsible for some part of it? Had any of them been?

Those thoughts were swept somewhere into the recesses of her mind when Laurence led her through the darkness of his small garden to an old-fashioned swing, a wooden settee covered with floral chintz cushions and hung from rusted chains on a chipped metal frame painted several different shades of green. Laurence's junk was not confined to the inside of the house.

D'Arcy was wearing a white halter top and a short cotton sarong skirt with large white roses printed on a black background, and antique ivory bracelets, one thick one on each wrist. Laurence was carrying the jacket of tiny black and white checks that completed the ensemble, and of which she had had no need because the night had remained hot and humid. All evening long he had kept stealing glances down the table at her. She had been seated between one of the French visitors, not the doctor, and one of the boys who had come down from the mountains and was staying at Brett's house. She had looked every inch the great beauty, a seductress with her long auburn hair and provocative violet eyes, flanked by the two handsome men who were clearly making advances to her. She had flirted, had laughed as only D'Arcy could laugh, with bells in the sound, a smile in her eyes, and a gleeful heart. At times a serene look would come over her and her beauty became even more perfect, with a depth to it Laurence had yet to fathom.

D'Arcy Montesque was an enchantress whom many people wanted in their lives, and the reason he had kept stealing those glances at her was because he was suddenly aware that she was free to be in theirs and would always want to be. No matter that he knew it was only for a few minutes, for fun, that it would not be for sex since she had committed herself to him alone in that.

How had it happened that they should have done that? It had never been his intention. He liked having many women. He thought about having sex with every attractive woman he saw. He used to, would still have been doing so, had D'Arcy and he not happened. And what was all this monogamy and love about when the heart was really not in it? It was all over so fast, this life, all one's dreams and loves. Arnold being the most recent case in point.

He dropped her jacket on a three-legged wooden table near the swing and took D'Arcy in his arms, holding her in a long and sensuous hug as he stroked her hair, her naked back, and undid the two buttons that held the halter top in place. Laurence had a way of caressing her breasts, as if he was taking the measure of them, the weight and firmness, rendering them sensitive to his every touch and caress. He could torment her with desire for sex with no more than his hands on her breasts, could tease her and hold back on her until she begged him for more of himself, a kiss, and then more, and then all things sexual, and after that, anything sexual, everything, no matter how adventurous, how depraved.

He loved the warmth of her lips on his, the sweetness of her tongue in his mouth. His kisses were taking her over and he felt her giving in to him as she unbuttoned his shirt, slipped her hands beneath it to caress him, pinch his nipples, dig her long oval-shaped nails into the flesh on his back. He opened the hook that held the sarong round her hips and it parted and fluttered to the ground. He became even more excited, wanted actually to beat her for her lewdness – she had worn nothing under her skirt except her sex. All evening she had been open, ready and waiting to be taken had the right moment arrived and the right man.

D'Arcy was a sexual opportunist. He had always known that, had had her enough times on the spur of the moment in the most unexpected places to prove it.

She was courageous in her sex, for sex's sake, for sexual fun. How many times had he had a quickie with her when people were only feet away and had never known? They had been wicked in their lust many times, instigated, as it was now, by her wearing no undergarments. To know that he had only to lift her skirt at any time, anywhere, and she was ready to receive him with no questions asked was for him complete sexual control of this independent and vibrant woman. It brought out certain lusts and fantasies that he, like most men, usually kept buried deep for fear of revealing who and what they really were.

D'Arcy was well advanced in lust, he could tell that by the way she kissed him, her hands moving over his body, the way she was undressing him. She gathered his erection and his scrotum into her cupped hands and, lowering her face, buried it in his genital flesh, breathing in the scent. She understood his hunger for her to take him into another world of erotic bliss. He could tell by the way she licked him, covered him with her saliva, and then so gently fed him slowly into her mouth; the way she made love to him with that mouth. She gave everything. That was her secret weapon: to be able to give herself wholly to another human being without fear of losing herself. It was what he sensed she was demanding of him, although she had never overtly done so. It was something he simply did not want to do.

They lay side by side, facing each other on the swing, each of them resting on a hip, jack-knifed, her leg draped over his hip, one of their best positions because penetration was exquisitely deep and he could use his pelvis with ease and finesse to create a beat, a rhythm for fucking them into an erotic world where they could feel each other to the marrow of their bones, where their comings were long and luscious, and for a few seconds they could experience the bliss of the 'little death', that place of no return that could only be found again in a new coupling, another orgasm.

D'Arcy's heart was racing. These were her best moments with Laurence, when all reserve was abandoned, and he was on the edge of giving himself up to her as she did every moment they were together, whether in sex or otherwise. She experienced infinite joy in that giving, in making her partner happy. Would he ever take the chance to do the same? she wondered. Did he love her enough, trust her enough, trust himself enough?

Ever since their return to Livakia, Laurence had been obsessive in their love making, wanting her and the experience of orgasm all the time. Arnold's death had something to do with it, they were both aware of that. To see a friend's life snuffed out was a reminder of how short a time a man has for his pleasures, his heart's desires, and that was affecting everyone, not only Laurence. But it was Laurence that D'Arcy was living with and it was difficult not to see that he was changing in his attitude towards her and had been for some time. Only since their return had she become so certain of that, and it had everything to do with sex and little to do with love. That, alas, was their problem. The more sexually tuned they became to each other, the more thrilling their sexual life, the further he was retreating from loving her.

They spent hours on the swing under the spell of thrilling sex and when it became too cold they retreated into the house where lust and depravity took them over anew. There is no possible way that a woman can explain to herself or anyone else what great sex can mean in her life, how it can liberate her, set her free, and for a woman like D'Arcy who was born and bred to live as a free spirit it was like breathing or taking an elixir. A woman can stand a great deal from a man for a sip of such a drink. D'Arcy had been sipping from such a cup offered by Laurence because as time had passed and they had grown closer together outside the confines of sex, she believed that a mutual love was binding them together. She believed that whatever of himself Laurence felt he must hold back from her would one day be hers and they would at last come together, all barriers down. Love would win out.

The theory was right but was the man wrong? Lying in bed close against her lover's body while he contentedly smoked a cigar, she eating melting chocolate ice cream from a carton and on occasion feeding him a spoonful, both replete with great sex, D'Arcy knew that for most women such a question would never even arise. But D'Arcy was no ordinary woman.

It was about half-past five in the morning, she could guess that by the quality of the light. The sky seen through the window was cloudless and blue, there was a light warm breeze, the sea looked serene, the village still, a crowing cock somewhere far off in the distance all there was to break the silence. The question did arise, and another: what was she doing here in this mess of a room when a rich, ripe, beautiful day was rising? She wanted to take deep breaths of it, feel raw unadulterated nature all around her, before man and living took a hold on it.

She fed Laurence yet another spoonful of the delicious ice cream. A little dripped on to his lip and he licked it into his mouth. He wore the same expression of delight for the taste of the ice cream as he had when she had watched him lick her come off his lips. She asked no silly questions as some women might have: Was that what she was to him, another kind of ice cream to savour? Had she been fooling herself that they were something special together? Why wasn't she getting back at least what she was putting into their love affair? She merely kept looking at him and thinking how handsome and sexy he was – but who was he?

She scooped out several more spoonfuls of the ice cream for herself, then stuck the slightly bent out of shape and tarnished silver soup spoon into what was left and handed it to Laurence, announcing, 'I'm going home.'

'At this hour?'

'Yes,' she said cheerily, and was surprised by the lilt of happiness in her voice.

'Why?'

'Great love affair, wrong man.'

With that she unwound herself from him, but not before she had caressed his cheek and kissed him on it. He plunged his cigar out in the glass ashtray sitting on the bed next to him and put the carton of ice cream down. The weight of the spoon toppled it over and a brown stain spread in a small pool on the sheet. '*Merde!*' he said and moved away from it, picking up the carton and bending over the side of the bed to place it squarely on the floor. His attention went directly back to D'Arcy who was by now out of the bed and standing opposite him separating the clothes they had so hurriedly gathered up from the garden before leaving it to carry on their sexcapade in bed.

'What are you talking about?'

'You know very well what I'm talking about, and we are not going to hash it over. "You want more of me than I'm prepared to give," and all that crap, coming from you. And me making demands: "I want you to be free enough, to love me enough, to submit totally to me." I find having to make such a demand as that on a man a loathsome and denigrating thing for a woman. Ours is an uneven relationship. I don't know how to give less than I do and I don't want to anyway, while you don't know how to give more than you do and clearly don't want to. You demanded everything from me, total submission in sex and love, and got it. Let's just say I've waited patiently for the returns and they didn't come. So what? So nothing. We leave it like that, set ourselves free. Be grateful I've made it easy for us. I didn't say this is the end of us, I didn't say I no longer love you, all I said was, I'm going home and you're free to go on a sexual spree with other women.'

'Oh, I see what this is all about. You want to be free to have sex with other men. I saw you with that Frenchman, he clearly wanted you. And that rugged, sexy-looking Cretan who sat the other side of you at dinner, how would you have liked to have had him?'

D'Arcy was just closing the sarong round her hips and adjusting the skirt while slipping into her sandals. She looked up and smiled at Laurence. 'I have had him, many times, and long before I ever became interested in you.'

She placed the halter top round her and fastened it in place, then taking her jacket in her hand she walked to the bed and sat down on it next to Laurence. 'This is not worthy of you. Just once be honest with yourself. It's you who feel you are somehow being cheated of something in this love affair of ours. It's you who wants other women, not me who wants other men. I may be in love but I'm not blind. I see the way you covet the women Max has, every beautiful woman who crosses our path. You are a selfish, greedy pig of a man, Laurence, and for a long time I didn't mind that. I was always happy for you to be the man you are. I still am.'

She rose from his side and was slipping into her jacket when he asked her, 'Why suddenly now, this moment of truth?'

'Because of Arnold's death, because that French doctor last night made me realise that we are all fooling ourselves. Arnold met his death unwillingly. For a moment that doctor made me examine my own role in Arnold's life, all our roles, and that led me to take a look at us and what I really want from a lover.'

'I'll dress and take you home.'

'I'd rather you didn't, but thanks for offering.'

'Let me take you to lunch?'

'The Kavouria? Maybe. If I decide to go down to the port for lunch I'll see you there. I didn't say we weren't friends, just no longer lovers. I didn't even say we would never have sex again.' D'Arcy smiled at him and walked from the room.

* * *

She did not go down to the port for lunch that day. Instead she stayed at home and lolled around, not doing much of anything, merely enjoying the day and her own space. It was not a matter of trying to come to terms with what she had done. D'Arcy was as much a realist as a romantic, and more than those things she was a woman who liked to live, not stagnate. She had always been quick to see the first signs of decay in anything to do with her life or work, and to put things right before they took hold. She was a woman who knew how to keep her life trouble free, a woman who always did what she had to do and was quick to know when to cut her losses. She could not pretend that she was any the less in love with Laurence than she had been, simply more realistic about loving him.

What she hadn't bargained for was how much a part of her life he had become, how very much she would miss him and what they'd had together. What made her feelings for him, her sense of loss, easier was her certainty she had done the right thing at the right time for them both. She felt strongly that to be blameless was a superior way to live and afforded the greatest of pleasures. It was the road she took in life though not always the easiest passage. She thrived on progress, not stagnation. She was the most positive of beings, but found the very thought of imposing her own beliefs or codes on anyone else an abhorrent thing to do. D'Arcy Montesque was no missionary, just a woman who wanted to live the way she wanted to live.

There had been things to do round the house and in the studio. The fax she had found in the machine on her return from their trip to Rethymnon contained a fascinating and financially interesting offer for work: a design problem for the German automobile firm that had made her a millionaire. A desk was piled high with projects she was considering, letters to be answered, tax returns, the general mess of red tape it takes to keep a life afloat whether you are living in paradise or some major city in the world. There was E-mail on the computer she hadn't yet done anything about. The concentration was simply not there: Arnold's death, the unanswered questions and unease in the community, self-examination, the strained atmosphere that seemed to permeate everything, and now Laurence. These were her priorities in the days since her return. She needed nothing more now than to relax, lie around her house and gather her energies.

D'Arcy did not even go down from the house to the port to shop for food, but sent Poppy, the housekeeper. Poppy made a huge moussaka, and the housekeeper and the gardener and D'Arcy had it in the dining garden with a bottle of red wine. They talked, but not about the house and the garden. Instead it was village gossip, maids' gossip: the butcher, the baker, the candlestick maker sort of gossip. The three of them had known each other almost all their lives and were soon enjoying themselves thoroughly. They laughed a great deal, and then the inevitable topic, Arnold's death, seeped into their conversation.

Both Poppy and the gardener knew him well, had been very fond of him. To listen to them tell not at all disrespectful but bizarrely funny stories about Arnold was to remember him with laughter and understand why his death had affected them all in the way it had. These simple island people, like most of the Livakian locals, saw him as their pet eccentric, a little mad, a harmless foreigner for whom they had to care. One of God's unfortunates, a sort of upmarket village idiot whom the community loved and was bound to care for out of a sense of compassion. They thought of him as even more intelligent and special than Mark or any of the other foreigners because he was weak and could be taken advantage of, a price exacted upon him by someone who had, long before he arrived in Livakia, placed the evil eye on him for having such super intelligence. He had been a figure of fun to them. It was the gardener who said, 'And that's why Kirios Mark had so much trouble with him.'

It didn't shock D'Arcy that neither the gardener nor Poppy was surprised by Arnold's death nor the mystery surrounding it. But she was taken aback when Poppy said, 'No one in Livakia will be pleased if the killer was a Cretan,' before rising from her chair and starting to clear away the dishes.

D'Arcy spent that evening alone at home. It was a strange sensation being without Laurence, not unpleasant just strange. In the two years they had been together there had been times when they had been separated from each other for long periods: he at Oxford lecturing, she visiting Brett or away for meetings on some project or other, but that was different, there had seemed to be nothing strange about those separations. This would take some getting used to.

Early the following morning D'Arcy went down to the port. It was quiet. The fishermen had already taken the

boats out and the shopkeepers were just opening, setting
tables out in the sun in front of their establishments,
sweeping the cobblestones, taking time to have coffee
with one another or the odd early-bird customer waiting
for the bread to come out of the baker's oven. It was what
D'Arcy called the port's lazy hour and the time she liked
being there best of all.

She was sitting with the baker who was covered with a
dust of white flour, his ham-like hands, fingers and nails
encrusted with it, and the butcher who was waiting for a
boat to bring his order of beef and lamb, the latter still
on the hoof. Edgar and Bill, who were always the first of
the foreign residents in the port, there for the bread and
the post, joined them. They seemed particularly at odds
with each other but were obviously trying hard not to be.
Conversation round the table had got to the latest political
scandal in Athens when the boat the butcher was waiting
for rounded the cliffs and came into view. He was the first
to leave the table, then the baker to take his bread out of
the oven.

'I didn't want to say anything in front of them but
something's amiss. Our police chief was flown out by
Max just after dusk last evening. Rumour has it they
went to the coroner's office in Iraklion. Do you know
anything?' asked Edgar.

'About what?'

'The verdict.'

D'Arcy had heard nothing. The news gave her a terrible
sense of unease. Are our troubles just about to begin? she
asked herself. She had no need to hear the verdict. In the
many days of waiting she had vacillated as to what had

really happened to Arnold but all that had ended over dinner on the night she had walked out on Laurence. She knew in her heart someone or several people had been responsible for Arnold's death.

The two men sat staring at her, their own anxieties showing in their faces, waited for her to answer. Fortunately she didn't have to. The three of them were distracted by the sound of an aeroplane's motors. That in itself was disconcerting because Max rarely flew over the bay or the village and almost never taxied through the water to tie up in the port. He used his own bay, where he kept his plane, a twenty-minute walk from the village and his house.

The plane, like a great lovely white moth, appeared in the bright blue sky. It banked and then slowly swooped down and skimmed the water for some distance before it made a relatively soft landing, cut its motors and edged its way in. Dimitrios, who had heard the plane, was walking round the port to the place where the butcher stood ready to catch the line and pull the white moth in close to the quay. Edgar and Bill went to help. D'Arcy simply sat there unable to move. She was fighting back tears. She felt so deeply sad, as if her heart would break from the weight of her melancholy. She watched the men at their work securing the plane with hollow eyes, an empty mind. She was transfixed.

The door opened and the first one to step down on to the pontoon was Manoussos. He extended a hand and the butcher grabbed it and pulled him safely on to the quay. The next man was a stranger, a policeman. He very nearly missed the quay and fell into the water. Max appeared to grab the lines as the men threw them back. He gathered them up and vanished into the plane with them only to return and give his passengers a salute before closing the door. The men pushed on the plane's wing and it drifted far enough away from the quay for Max safely to start its engines and taxi out, make a full turn and take off again.

By this time a great many more people had arrived in the port, curiosity more than anything else bringing them out. They were standing round in small groups, clinging together, thought D'Arcy. The whispers and chatter ceased and a frightening quiet settled over them as Manoussos and his group passed by them. Hands were stuck out to be shaken, welcomes offered for his return. The question was asked and answered, and some faces grew very pale, others looked terribly pained. The groups dispersed, seemed just to melt away, some to sit at tables, others to return home.

Manoussos saw D'Arcy when he was a good distance from her. He shook his head from side to side as if to say, 'All is lost.' She understood. He went into the cafe she was sitting outside, then returned and placed another table next to hers. The other men drew up chairs.

'We're hungry. I've ordered eggs and ham and cheese, some coffee, and the boy's gone to get the bread. Breakfast for all of us.' Those were Manoussos's first words to her.

'Did you remember the honey? You always forget the honey.' Those were D'Arcy's first words to him.

'I forgot the honey.' He dutifully went back into the cafe to ask for honey to be sent to the table as well.

D'Arcy wondered what they were talking about. Honey, at a time like this? She was trying to get her head and her emotions together, that was the only thing that could explain such extraordinary behaviour. D'Arcy heard the young policeman before she actually took any notice of him. 'I've never been here before, have always wanted to come. It's even more beautiful and unusual than people say it is. I never thought I would come here on a case.'

Manoussos was approaching the table when he heard the young man. 'I think I had better introduce you to everyone, Stavros.'

The young man jumped to his feet and very nearly stood at attention. 'Oh, do sit down. We run a relaxed police station here in Livakia. That's not to say we are not respected, so that's the balance you will have to try and keep while you're here working with us. Now this is Dimitrios whom you will be assisting.'

The two men shook hands and then Manoussos carried on round the table with more introductions. There seemed to be an endless stream of boys running back and forth from the cafe slamming plates and cutlery, cups and saucers, on the tables. Platters of fried eggs arrived and thick slabs of ham. The men ate with gusto and the talk at the table was excruciatingly mundane. D'Arcy could not bring herself to ask a single question. Finally every morsel of food was gone, and empty plates littered the table. It was then that Manoussos sat back and spoke to them. The moment he began people left their tables to stand round and listen: the boys waiting on table, any passer-by. Proprietors came out of their shops and a small boy ran and brought the two Mount Athos monks who were getting into a boat to the table. A crowd of fifteen or so people had gathered and were listening.

'Arnold Topper did not die of natural causes. Although he was inebriated at the time of his death, he did not die of drink. He was suffocated, most likely by a person or persons who placed a plastic bag over his head during or just after a sexual encounter. There is no doubt that a crime has been committed and we are making a full investigation. It's to everyone's advantage that we have full co-operation and this case is solved in as short a time as is possible, preferably before the press gets hold of the story. The family has been notified. Any questions, come to my office. They'll be answered there if possible. Any information that anyone can contribute, even the smallest thing, could be a clue and help us.'

With that Manoussos rose from his chair and left the table to push through the crowd, followed by his investigative team. No one looked surprised. No one looked upset. Everyone looked frightened. Someone living in Livakia, or a visitor, had moved among them, dined in their restaurants, drunk at their cafes, bought provisions from their shops, had spoken to them, brushed past them, laughed with them, had shared in their lives – and then had gone out and taken a man's life. What evil, what betrayal! And how were they to say it would not happen again to any one of them?

Chapter 7

People were strangely relieved, though there was still fear in their hearts and it showed in their faces. The verdict had been bad, it could not have been worse, but it was at least declared and out in the open. That evening the port was swarming with people. Old and young, entire families, people who rarely came to the port at night, those who did only on holidays or when there was an event. The shops, restaurants and cafes were doing a booming trade. Three more policemen had arrived by boat and now Manoussos's investigative team's presence could be felt everywhere. They were interviewing everyone casually as they wandered about and not so casually in the police station. The place was alive with talk about Arnold and his undoing. And speculation as to who had done it? Well, there wasn't any. That was what kept everyone intrigued, the mystery of Arnold's death. And that was all they could talk about – how it was possible for a man, a friend, a neighbour, whom they had all known so well, to have met such a mysterious end.

Manoussos and his team were asking for information: anything that anyone could tell them about Arnold that might lead them to someone with a motive for murder. But equally important, possibly even more so, he had explained to his team, were the movements and behaviour, after Arnold's body had been discovered, of everyone who knew or had any dealings with him. A priority that must be checked out immediately.

There were about twenty people at the table at the Kavouria where D'Arcy was dining that evening. Among them Mark and Laurence, Rachel, most every one of the foreign residents, several Livakians, and sitting in a chair several feet from the table but near Mark, Melina. Max was sitting on one side of D'Arcy, Laurence on the other. Of course everyone knew that they had split up, that D'Arcy had walked out on him. It only took one person to be told about what had happened between them, that had been Max, and everyone knew. The usual form: no one asked any questions, no one interfered, it was accepted, as all things were accepted, friends' own affair.

Manoussos joined the table and was offered food. While he waited for it to be cooked, a plate was produced and passed down the table by the other diners. They filled it from the platters already there. Someone filled his glass with red wine. 'Just what was needed,' he told everyone and smiled. It was his smile that broke the lull in conversation that had occurred when he appeared at the table.

He broke off a piece of bread and someone refilled his glass, then he asked, 'Look, since you're all assembled here, would anyone mind if we talk about what's happened and I ask a few questions while I have my dinner? The more information I have the better, whether it's usable or not. If it's upsetting anyone, say so. We can talk about the weather, how romantic it is to look across the anchored fishing caiques and out across the water shimmering silver under that fat white moon.'

This was Manoussos at his best, the way they knew him, loved and admired him: direct, to the point, but considerate, witty even about a disaster to lighten the burden of sorrow he knew they were all carrying. And clever, oh, so clever as a policeman. They had to smile, they dropped their guard, and Rachel left her chair to go to him with a near empty platter. She batted her eyelashes and Manoussos removed the last remaining stuffed pepper and placed it on his plate.

He forked some food into his mouth and took stock of the people round the table. Mark seemed particularly subdued, but then he had been since Arnold's death. He had been drinking more, been in the port more: sitting round most afternoons and evenings, but more or less behaving as usual, Melina like a shadow sitting close by. She too seemed somehow more subdued, more polite, ready to do anyone's bidding. Mark seemed more anxious than ever that people be nice to her, offer her work. He was more solicitous to her. Manoussos saw the change in the way Mark looked at her. Guilt for how they had behaved to Arnold on the last night he was alive? Possibly. But Mark couldn't have slipped that plastic bag over Arnold's head, he had been in Rethymnon at the same time as Laurence and D'Arcy and then in Athens. And Melina? Arnold could have fought her off easily, he was incredibly strong. Laurence and D'Arcy's absence from Livakia eliminated them, not that they would have been suspects. No motive. Manoussos needed a motive if he had any hope of finding the murderer, and he needed information to find that motive. And no one liked to talk or hold the floor more than Mark did. He would start with Mark. 'Any theories, Mark?' asked Manoussos.

'About what?' He seemed somehow enlivened by the question.

'Why anyone would want to kill Arnold? What kind of a person that might be? What Arnold might have said or done to provoke someone to do such a thing? In spite of your differences, your irritation with him, you were good friends. You were closer to him than anyone. Did you have any inkling of anything different happening in Arnold's life in the days, weeks, or even months before his death?'

'The only change was that he fell off his chair more because time and drink had affected his brain and his nervous system more and that meant that I or someone else had to drag him home more often. He was increasingly more mean about money. But he was working just as hard as ever at surviving on a minimal level with as little effort as he could possibly make. You can imagine what torture that was for me, still the ambitious writer I have always been and always will be, fighting every day to survive and make my mark in this world. I'm living off no one, not even Arnold. I always paid back to the penny any money he lent me. We were both part of this community and so stayed civil to each other but that does not mean I had to respect him or his weaknesses or his life. I am desperately sorry he came to such a terrible end but he was a bore and a burden in this old port, and I am certain that, as disloyal as I may sound, I am not the only one who thought so. But you know the code here, a man has the right to live as he wants to live, in the privacy of his own soul.'

'Was he in love with someone?'

'Never!' answered Mark.

'I'm not so sure as you are about that, Mark,' said Jane Plum.

All eyes were directed on her. 'I know no more than that. I just had a feeling he was in love with someone, a very young someone.'

'What makes you say that, Jane?' asked Manoussos.

'Just a feeling. He once asked me if I thought huge age differences mattered where love was involved. I thought at the time it was an odd question for Arnold to ask.'

'Poppycock! Arnold knew the difference between love and infatuation and he preferred infatuation,' said Laurence.

'And Laurence would know about that,' said D'Arcy.

The remark passed over most everyone's head. Laurence glared at her; Max patted D'Arcy on the thigh under the table and smiled. She was annoyed with herself; it was a facetious, bitchy thing to say and had not been at all necessary. She'd thought she had risen above wanting to make digs at a man who'd promised so much in love and delivered so little. He'd deserved that little slap but she had not enjoyed delivering it. It would not happen again. She removed Max's lingering hand from her thigh, gave it a short, sharp little slap and placed it on his own, then smiled at him. The incorrigible Max threw back his handsome head and laughed, drawing everyone's attention.

'Sorry about that. I was thinking about infatuations – my own. We've all been there.'

The distraction over, Mark continued: 'One thing is for certain – if it was one of his infatuations who killed him, it had to be a Cretan. He hadn't had a foreign infatuation for several years, and I think we can all agree that none of us in residence here held him enthralled.'

No one at the table said a word. The Cretans sitting there looked uncomfortable. One of them scraped back a chair and, standing up, said, 'You should have more proof than theory before you make an accusation like that, Mark.' A second Cretan rose from his chair, his face like thunder. They were friends, very good friends, of Mark's.

'Oh, do sit down,' he said to the two men and rose from his own chair. Taking a bottle of wine, he walked slowly around the table to fill their glasses. He patted them on the back but none of the anger went out of their eyes.

'That was not an accusation. This is an open discussion of an event we would all like to get to the bottom of as quickly as possible. It was just a thought, as unpleasant as it may be. I think you have to agree there is a strong possibility I might be right and we have to face that, not get at odds with each other if that should be the case,' said Mark, not at all defensively. The men, reasonable types, had to nod their heads in agreement. Each of them hugged Mark, manly bear-like hugs, and sat down. Tom Plum shook hands with one of the men, D'Arcy smiled across the table at them and nodded, a silent expression of admiration for their calming their temper and facing the reality of the situation.

Manoussos's grilled lamb chops arrived, a heap of them, mostly long slender bone with a small eye of flesh in each. They were sizzling and smelled of roasting meat and rosemary. The aroma invaded everyone's senses, set off their taste buds. Yet another Cretan at the table shouted to the departing waiter to bring lamb chops for everyone, post haste. Some raised their glasses in appreciation. Manoussos picked one up with his fingers and ate the eye of meat off the bone while feeling quite satisfied that choosing Mark to do his work for him had been the right move. Long before the verdict on cause of death had come in Manoussos had worked out who had killed Arnold, but he had not one shred of proof as yet that he was right. He liked the way things were going at the dinner table. Mark had the bit between his teeth, he wouldn't let go now, but would he prove Manoussos right? He gave Mark more rope to work with.

Manoussos put down the long, slender bone, now stripped of its meagre flesh. 'A Cretan with whom Arnold was infatuated? Do we know of such a Cretan? Would that person be a man or a woman? What kind of a person would that be? We know that Arnold had many Cretan friends and acquaintances whom he liked and who liked him, but what sort of Cretan would he become infatuated with? And are we using the term infatuation instead of sex? He had had sex shortly before he died, remember. All interesting questions which need answering. It's possible Jane is right, maybe he had a secret love or infatuation, one he kept from everyone because of the person involved. What kind of a person or people would he keep from his friends? And if there was such a person or persons, then why would they turn on him, want to destroy him? Had he made promises he could not keep? Was this a crime of passion? A crime of lust?' Manoussos had everyone at the table hanging on his every word.

'Revenge. A crime of revenge. You've forgotten that possibility,' said Mark.

'Revenge for what, Mark?' asked Max.

'Arnold was not the angel he liked us all to think he was. He involved himself with boys and young men, not particularly for sex, though there was, on the odd occasion, that too. Poor people, simple in mind and less educated than himself, rough and ready types who did odd jobs for him as they do for us all. I can think of a few who were a bit simple he liked having around him and was not particularly clever with, in fact downright insulting to, and in public. Arnold should have known better than to shame them in front of people, but would he learn? Had I been any one of them I might have sought revenge. How could he expect to humiliate a proud Cretan in public and get away with it? He always knew what Cretan pride demanded.'

Mark was on his bandwagon, just where Manoussos wanted him to be. He gave him a little more rope. 'I wish we had been party to such an incident. It would have been useful to see how Arnold might have provoked someone, made himself their enemy.'

Mark looked anxiously down the table at Melina. He asked her if she would kindly do him a favour, go home and return with his diary. She left immediately, almost at a run, slavish as always to Mark's commands.

'I sent Melina on a fool's errand because I didn't want to embarrass her, poor kid. But she is a case in point. You all heard Arnold, that last night we were together. Melina is a simple girl. She was offended by his accusations, all exaggeration and distortion of the facts. Yet she turned a blind eye to the hurtful things he would say about her out of a sense of pity for him. Others in her position might not have, they would have sought revenge, but she did not. Instead she feels our loss and is sad for his death rather than being angry that he owed her money and didn't give her the few trinkets he promised. Promises were how he kept her working for him.'

D'Arcy was horrified. Mark had just delivered Melina to Manoussos: a suspect, on a silver platter. More than a few others at the table realised what Mark's megalomania had cost the girl, you could see it in their faces. Unbelievably Mark was not one of them.

'It's true, Melina was very forgiving, that was not the first time Arnold had humiliated her. I remember sitting with him on the beach one day when she arrived with those little boyfriends of hers and he called across to her for all to hear, "You, little thief, unless you return my watch by the time I go home this evening I'll report you to the police." They had a confrontation on the beach and I had to beg him to stop calling her a thief, he must have repeated it a dozen times,' offered Jane Plum.

'Didn't she ask him to stop, didn't she even defend herself?' asked Manoussos.

'Oh, yes, she denied taking the wristwatch and begged him to stop. I felt so sorry for her, there were tears of rage in her eyes.'

147

'How did it end?' asked Manoussos, ever so casually.

'Oh, the usual thing when people are having fights. She saying one day he would be sorry for what he'd said and running off with her friends. It all ended well enough, though. That evening at dinner I noticed that he had his watch on and Melina, when she passed by the table, waved to him. Months went by after that and he did his usual carping about her inefficiency with the ants and the painting of his kitchen, but nothing more than that. I think she was very forgiving indeed, and had a soft spot for Arnold as we all did. Yes, maybe it's true that someone else might not have been.'

D'Arcy had always thought Jane Plum a very stupid woman and spoilt. She never could quite see how she managed to hang on to Tom who was anything but stupid and a very great painter. What D'Arcy hadn't realised was that Jane was incredibly insensitive, she never thought before she spoke. Between them she and Mark were setting Melina up for an in-depth interview at the very least, even possible arrest on suspicion. D'Arcy could see that a motive could be attributed to the girl. And they sat there, both of them thinking they were doing her a service by explaining how Arnold might have offended some unknown Cretan's pride!

The very idea that Melina might have killed Arnold distressed D'Arcy. And if it were shown to be true, it would be the worst possible thing to have happened. How had they all not seen it coming? Or even the possibility of it? Had they seen it and just turned a blind eye, let it slide by them? Had they played a part, although unwittingly, in this tragedy that had landed in their midst? It didn't bear thinking about. D'Arcy put it out of her mind. She would not take on that scenario unless the girl was arrested.

Fortunately three platters arrived heaped high with lamb chops, and two bottles of wine, and the table burst into life again as eating and drinking resumed. Manoussos rose from his chair and went round filling glasses. When he came to D'Arcy he placed a hand on her shoulder and smiled at her. He perceived that she was aware of what he suspected and what he was doing, she could see it in his eyes, sense it in the manner in which he squeezed her shoulder.

She was the first to leave the table to go home. D'Arcy did not miss the look on some of the faces round that table: her friends sensitive to the fact that she was no longer with Laurence. They tried to act casually about it, as if it were the norm, and she was grateful for that, although it felt far from being the norm.

It was early, too early for her to go to bed, and so she sat in her garden, one of the lower level gardens that hung very nearly over the sea. A black, black night except for the white moon casting a wide beam of light on the water and a sky full of stars, the sound of the sea, and in the distance the lights of the old port. She'd always had those things in her life, and such nights as this one, for as long as she could remember. They were for her another kind of friend, another kind of love, a reason never really to be lonely in the deep sense of that word.

She remained in the garden for some time watching the lights slowly go out all over Livakia until it was very nearly in total darkness. She heard the men, her friends from the mountain village, walking on the path below the garden making their way back to Brett's house, and then silence again, nothing but the sea. It wasn't long after that that she heard the distant sound of creaking hinges: the opening of her garden gate. She made no move, her mind and heart were empty and still, nothing could break the peace and contentment, the spirit of place; she was one with it and herself. The footsteps on the stones were travelling in her direction. D'Arcy sighed. A smile appeared at the corners of her lips. It came from the heart. He stepped up behind her and placed his hands on her shoulders. She reached up and covered them with her own, and he kissed the top of her head and stroked her hair.

'It's been a long time, and still you knew where to find me.'

'Love is like that.'

He walked round the stone bench where she was sitting and, taking her hands in his, pulled her up and into his arms. He held her there for a long time doing nothing more than enjoying the feel of her again in his arms. They clung to each other in silence, passion building between them. Finally he tilted up her chin and kissed her full on the lips, at the same time sweeping her off her feet and into his arms. He carried her for some distance through the gardens before he placed her on her feet again and took her in his arms to hold her tight against him and kiss her again. Sex had now come into it, their erotic souls' craving for each other. She took him by the hand, he placed an arm round her waist, and together they walked through the remainder of the garden and into the house, directly to her bedroom.

They took their time undressing each other, savouring the excitement of once again seeing each other's naked flesh as it was exposed. And then began the celebration of that flesh. His kisses were long and lingering. He knew so well how to excite her with his tongue, lips and mouth. He loved her nipples, used to make them shine with honey and then lick them clean, eating away at them and then beginning again until she begged for him to stop and take her in long, hard strokes. He needed no honey now, he had been starved too long for the enjoyment of her and her luscious breasts. He caressed her arms. The feel of her skin on his fingertips set him aflame. He wanted to weep with joy for having her to himself again. He covered her with roving kisses until she stopped him. She held his hands behind his back and returned those kisses, to his face, his neck, his chest, where she sucked and bit hard into his nipples.

She led him to the bed and there lay down and placed her arms back over her head, raising her legs until they were bent at the knee, her feet flat on the mattress. He joined her there, on his knees facing her, and placing his hands on her knees ever so gently pushed them apart until they rested on the sheets. There she lay in complete passivity, open and vulnerable. Neither of them could wait any longer. He caressed her baby smooth shaven mound and whispered, 'My lovely mound of Venus,' stroking the long, so very sexy cleft beneath with his ample and rampant penis until it parted and he could feel her soft, pink, velvet-like inner lips. Her several orgasms like some sweet morning dew eased the way for him and slowly, with exquisite taunting and teasing, he took possession of her. She was soft and smooth as silk, tight and perfect. She was his velvet heaven.

She whimpered, tiny cries of ecstasy. She grabbed her hair with her fingers and dug her nails into her scalp. She followed his every thrust with squeezes of cunt and a rocking of her pelvis. Passion took them over, lust was their everything. He quickened his pace and she was right there with him. When she came this time she called in a strained and breathless voice, 'Manoussos, don't ever stop!'

They had been there before, they would be there again, in sex and love and passion. Theirs was a transient sex life, a transient love, they had come to terms with that many years ago, agreeing that there were such loves: one's that go on until death but are no more and no less than what they are. Manoussos and D'Arcy would always at certain times of their life have their erotic sprees, come together and let each other go. They had free love.

In the morning D'Arcy felt a special kind of happiness. Sex and men had come back into her life and she was willing and ready for them. She was delighted it had been Manoussos who had ended her two-year monogamous relationship with Laurence. Manoussos himself had that special feeling he always had when he sailed into erotic waters with D'Arcy. Life and sex were that little bit richer.

They had breakfast in the garden and talked about themselves, his life and loves, her life and love for Laurence, on the intimate level they had missed having with each other for the last few years. Inevitably the talk came round to the night before and the erotic road they had travelled together, its intensity, how much it had meant to each of them. Where it would go and where it would not, the other men and women who would once again separate them. How it had always been, would always be for them a matter of the right time, the right place. He took her again in the sunshine, standing behind her, bending her over the garden wall, her silk robe raised around her waist.

He adored looking at her like that: full and rounded tight flesh; the orbs of her bottom, the provocative long crack between those cheeks. He fondled them and ran his fingers up and down the crack; he parted them, and viewed her, and told her how beautiful she was, how wondrous the sex had been the night before. 'Do you remember last night when I . . .' He teased and taunted her with memories of their out of control lust, the things she said to him during her many orgasms, sex talk, lewd and exciting that she knew drove them further and further down that erotic road the end of which was for them both sexual ecstasy, a momentary oblivion.

She reacted as he knew she would, she was helpless to do otherwise, they wanted each other again, there and then, and there was no reason not to have each other there and then. From the waist down she moved under his hands, ever so slight rotations of her bottom, and she squeezed and sucked in and slowly released her vaginal muscles. The sensations she achieved were to make her feel alive again with sex, ready for him, wanting him. He knew how to set her aflame, how to hold back to increase the pleasure for both of them. By the time he thrust swiftly, in one powerful movement, she had to place her hands over her mouth to stifle her scream: ecstasy, abandonment to all else in the world, as she rode out her orgasm.

He stayed with her, never eased off on his stroke, and continued until she came again, stopping only when they came together. For D'Arcy to be taken in that position was always to feel a man more; such penetration was a deeper penetration, a more thrilling sensation, it was being filled by a man to bursting point and always left her exhausted, drained of all energy. When he finally withdrew, his hands still on her slender hips, she slipped from under them into a heap on the ground, drenched with their come. He lay down next to her and held her in his arms. Neither of them moved, he too needed time to restore himself.

Some time passed before he rose from the ground and went into the house to return with a pillow which he placed under her head. He made her a fresh cup of tea and spooned large dollops of honey into it. Bringing it to her, he lay down next to D'Arcy, and taking her in his arms, placed the cup to her lips. She smiled at him and drank the tea. He stroked her hair but they didn't speak. Much revived she sat up and placed the cup and saucer on the ground. She kissed him, a long and lingering kiss. Then she stroked his hair, his moustache, and smiled.

'You were my first true love and you will always be my first true love,' she told him.

'And you were mine, and nothing and no one can change that.'

He was dressed. She knew that it was over, time for

him to go home and change, become the police chief again. And that was the first time she thought about the dinner table at the Kavouria the night before, how clever he had been, and what the repercussions of his cleverness might be. Why did it have to happen? Why couldn't it all just go away? But it wasn't going to go away. She held out her hands and Manoussos took them in his and together they rose from the ground. She placed an arm round his waist and he an arm round hers and together they walked through the gardens to a gate less conspicuous than the other entrances to her house.

'Let me take you to dinner.'

'That would be nice.'

He kissed her lightly on the lips and was gone. She watched him walk away, the sureness of his step, that Cretan male swagger. He turned once to wave at her and call out, 'Nine o'clock, at the Kavouria.' She knew what that meant – they would dine together but he would be back on duty, talking, asking leading questions, observing. Would he have interviewed Melina before then? What more would he learn today that would lead him to Arnold's murderer? How she wished it could be a stranger to Livakia.

Later that morning the men staying at Brett's house called by and invited D'Arcy to go underwater treasure hunting with them and Max. All she really wanted to do was have a long sleep but they refused to take no for an answer. Rachel joined them; the Cretan men were too delicious, too perfect, for her to miss a chance of flirtation with them. They took Max's caique, an hour's sail to one of his most favourite coves. Once there they anchored a few yards off the beach and swam in to shore with their equipment.

Life in Livakia was never hurried, whether it be in sex, flirtation, dining, drinking, doping, swimming, work or play. Even the pressures and responsibilities of life were slower to be felt here. There was no rush to dive. D'Arcy stretched out in the sun to doze, Max checked his equipment, Rachel played oopsy-poopsy with the Cretan men and primped herself. D'Arcy gazed around her. What had murder and death to do with such pleasure seekers who harmed no one and in fact contributed to the community in none but positive ways? But then, on reflection, was that really true, that they harmed no one? Why else was Arnold dead? Why had someone taken his life? She sighed and looked around her. Her friends had left all thought of the dark side of life behind them, blanked it off, and were living for the moment. Not a bad way to live, she decided, and joined them.

In a half-sleep D'Arcy listened to Rachel and two of the men. She knew the three well and what was going to happen. The men would have her, discreetly apart from the party, in a cave where they would enjoy her in turn. They were not men for great sexual finesse but were fantastically well endowed and loved fucking foreign women. (Cretan women and especially young girls were impossible to enjoy before marriage. The virgin was all important to Cretan society and sense of honour; to defy the conventions was to write your own death warrant.) These two men especially liked the game of seduction and sex with women who pretended, as Rachel did, that they weren't interested. They had had her before and she had denied having sex with them; they would have her now and she would deny this intercourse as well. It amused the men and suited them all. Everyone knew what was bound to happen and everyone pretended they didn't, part of the Rachel game. D'Arcy fell asleep.

When she awakened they were gone and only the third man was there, talking to Max. The three of them climbed into their diving equipment and, holding hands, waded into the water. It felt cold and refreshing. D'Arcy, like Max, never tired of the sea and especially those first minutes when one submerges oneself and becomes one with the water and the sea world.

They swam together for some time then broke up and followed each other down to the sea bed. It was Max who spotted something. There was great excitement but it turned out to be nothing of great interest, only a shard. He gave it to Spiro. They explored for nearly an hour and then began their ascent. Max felt playful. He circled D'Arcy on their vertical rise, taunted and teased her in an underwater sexual dance. He took her hands in his and they rose through the water together. When they surfaced they pulled off their masks and Max shook the water from his hair and squeezed it from his beard.

'That was great,' he told her, and a smile broke across his face. He reached out and played with her long auburn hair, spreading fanlike on the surface of the water, undulating with the waves. He looked to D'Arcy like Neptune risen from the deep and come to capture her for his pleasure – all that was missing was his trident, the three-pronged fish-spear Neptune carried like a sceptre. Neptune, god of the sea. In many ways

Max was like some mythical god, not quite of this earth, too powerful, a man for himself and all seasons. But there was something different in the way he was looking at her today. His gaze had in it no more than a nuance of something more intimate for her than she had seen before. She put an immediate check on the closeness she felt towards him at that moment. Never, ever would she allow herself to fall into the Max trap.

She had seen too many women fall under the erotic spell he cast. He was famed for his sexual prowess and antics. Depravity and debauchery were his favourite pastimes; he seduced women and corrupted them for his and their sexual pleasure. As he had often pointed out to D'Arcy when he was making his yearly attempt at seducing her to his bed: 'I never take a woman who isn't willing and ready to come with me. I'm no rapist, I'm a libertine. One day I'll prove it to you.' It was a rare place you could go where his reputation hadn't preceded him. And it wasn't just the sex that made him so attractive. He was an adventurer, who did daring, thrilling things, a hard and ruthless competitor when he had to be, clever and witty and charming. And he had that thing most women adore: with Max to win was everything.

He told her, 'One day you and I, we'll no longer be able to dance around each other. We'll go for it, the fuck of a lifetime.'

Before D'Arcy could reply, he placed his hands on her face and pulled her to him to kiss her. It was a long and lingering kiss where he licked and sucked on her lips, ran his tongue over them and between them. She tried to wriggle away from him but he was too strong for her, and held her there with his kiss. She felt herself giving in to his sexy embrace and fought against it, resisted the sensations that kiss was engendering. Finally he released her but not before giving her a sharp but friendly slap on her cheek. She was still catching her breath, trying to compose herself, when he swam away.

Good company, laughter, intelligent conversation, men at their very best. There was an air of the erotic, sailing the sea in a restored hundred-year-old Greek wooden boat with Max at the helm. The hot sun and a clear blue sky . . . D'Arcy understood well that to seek your pleasures and gather them to you while you can was one of the essentials of life. This was something Brett had taught all her children and there was not a day that went by that D'Arcy was not grateful for a mother who had instilled the joys of life into her children. She threw back her head, and running her fingers through her wet hair and shaking it out she began to laugh: low laughter that gradually gained in volume. She was thinking of Laurence and his not being by her side. Max came to stand next to her in the bow. Her laughter had pulled him to her like a magnet and brought a great broad smile to his face. He asked her nothing, merely leaned against the rail and watched her.

Finally her laughter petered out and still with a smile on her face, she told him, 'I was thinking about Laurence – well, more about Laurence and me, our love affair. I do so hate a mean man and especially one who is so mean he cheats himself.'

'Women in love can never be told,' was all Max said before he walked away from her to bring the boat into harbour.

It was close to three o'clock when the diving party arrived at the Kavouria for lunch bearing three magnificent large fish to be cooked for them. Max and two of the other men had speared them on their second and third dive of the day. Succulent fish, fresh from the sea little more than an hour before, lacquered with olive oil, encrusted with sea salt and grilled over charcoal. They were served with a salad of ripe red tomatoes with fresh basil and spring onions and chunks of feta cheese dressed with the purest and richest extra virgin olive oil. How rich, how sweet, how good life could be.

Laurence, Mark and Tom were at a table drinking wine, several other people were still eating, and Melina was at a table nearby with two of her boyfriends. D'Arcy and the others greeted her in passing. It registered in D'Arcy's mind that since Arnold's death Melina seemed happier, better dressed, more sure of herself, still acting in her usual cocky manner but seeming less diffident, more assertive. She seemed somehow to be around more, sitting in the cafes and at the Kavouria. Where was she getting the money? Where was she working now that Arnold was dead? Was she working? Why did she suddenly seem to be always on the fringes of their lives? D'Arcy disliked herself for asking these questions. The girl was probably just being there, the way so many others were just being there, so why did D'Arcy feel there was somehow an ulterior motive to her constant presence? In the light of day and without Manoussos's leading questions, Melina hardly seemed a convincing candidate for murderer.

D'Arcy felt so relieved she turned round and smiled at the girl.

Three days later Melina Philopopolos was arrested for the murder of Arnold Topper.

Chapter 8

There was nothing clever about Melina; in fact she was simple. She was other things too: basically dishonest, very nearly illiterate, sly, and prepared to use whatever resources she had – sex, a certain hatred for her fellow man and the society he lived in, and a pathological belief that she had the right to do anything – in order to ensure her own survival. She was mean and corrupt and she was only fourteen years old.

The police chief and most all of the Cretans recognised her for what she was the very first day she arrived in Livakia and that was why they resisted her, waited for the time she would understand there was nothing for her in their village and go away. Their tacit resistance to her would have been their way of running her out of town had not Mark Obermann taken her up as his cause and dragged both the Cretan and the foreign community of Livakia into it: save a corrupt child, make an acceptable woman. Melina thought it was love. It was what she needed, what she wanted, and had never experienced before. She would do what she had to to keep it and so made tremendous efforts to please Mark. It was through those efforts that she was able to worm her way into the community, one that was never really happy to have her there in the first place, one that had always remained wary of her even though it had been reluctantly won over.

Manoussos was reviewing all that in his mind while sitting in his office, champing on a cigar. He rose from his chair and went to sit on the ledge of the open window. He was going to arrest Melina for Arnold's murder, not on suspicion of murder, but murder. He intended for her to make a full confession before he took her away to Iraklion and prison where she would be held until her trial. She might try a few lies, or maybe none at all. She was simple. Ignorance, Cretan pride, her own ego would demand that she tell him the truth about what really happened between the night Dimitrios put Arnold to bed and the morning two days later when he was found dead on the beach. He guessed she would have no remorse but instead be proud of what she had done.

Manoussos and his superiors in Iraklion had managed to keep news of the murder relatively quiet outside Livakia and would do so until someone was charged. Manoussos did not relish the thought of the media and outside world turning his village into a three-ring circus, but it was bound to happen. He would stave it off for as long as possible and do what he could to keep Livakia out of it. He made the decision that it would be better for the village and everyone concerned if he arrested Melina outside its limits and had her away and in Iraklion when the media got hold of the story. So far all that had appeared in the press was a small one-inch piece announcing that the body of a foreigner had been found on the beach. Would that they could have left it at that.

Manoussos called his team in to discuss the situation. When they were all seated in the one-room police station and the coffee boy had been and gone, Dimitrios passing round a paper bag of small sweet cakes, Manoussos went round his desk to sit on the end and tell them, 'You men have done a first-class job. Interviewing as many people as you have done in this short period of time, keeping your eyes and your ears open, and the concise reports you have produced, have all contributed to my belief that Arnold Topper was murdered not by an outsider but by someone he knew.'

There was a tinkling of cups and saucers and mumbling between the men as Manoussos went to the cork bulletin board and pulled out several drawing pins to rearrange the names of people written on various coloured papers. These were people who were close to Arnold or with whom he had had dealings in one form or another. When he was finished there was one name, Melina Philopopolos, printed on a green piece of paper on the right-hand side of the board and a myriad of rejected coloured papers and names on the left.

Two of the men shook hands, all smiles; Dimitrios looked knowing but there was no smile on his face. Manoussos returned to sit on the end of his desk again. 'I see we have some accord here. Let's talk about this. I'm open to anything that might persuade me that I'm not right about this.'

For forty minutes they hashed over several points in the case and discussed Melina Philopopolos as the probable murderer. Finally Manoussos took over once more. 'I would like to keep her arrest secret at least until I have her safely away from here. And I want no one, and especially not her, to know I am going after her. If she knew, I'm quite sure she would run away. There is also the possibility that those sympathetic to her might tip her off. There is the possibility too that she was not working alone.

'Here's the plan, and it's up to us all to see that it works and we get it right. I intend to ask Max de Bonn to hire Melina for the day to do some work for him on his boat. She'll accept, Max will see to that. Then he'll sail the caique to the scene of the crime, only at that point she won't know where they're going. That gets her out of Livakia without anyone the wiser. Dimitrios, you and I will already have started out on foot towards their destination, being conspicuous, greeting people. If asked, we're just doing our normal coastal check. For the rest of you men, it's business as usual, watching, listening, asking questions.'

Here Manoussos paused, waiting for questions. There were none. He picked up the telephone and called Max, asking if they could meet as soon as possible in the cafe. Manoussos began to laugh. 'Well, Max, finish her off as soon as possible and *then* meet me. This is important, I need some favours.'

The men began to laugh, made several remarks of admiration for Max and his sexual appetites, and then it was back to business. Manoussos continued, 'Max will pick us up as if by chance, offer to take us along the coast and back. Melina will still be unaware of what's going on. I plan to return her to the scene of the crime and hope to get a confession from her there. Max will then fly us directly from the beach to Iraklion, and I'll call in when she's been booked.'

'It sounds good, if it goes according to plan,' said one of the men.

'Why bring in Kirios de Bonn?' asked another.

'Easier, he's reliable, it'll be clean and fast. I don't much fancy a helicopter coming in and upsetting the whole village, and the huge operation Iraklion will throw at us for support when we don't need it. Overland is too long and hard a drive, and by boat and overland involves too many people when there is an alternative like Max and his plane.'

'You'll get a commendation if you can pull this off,' said one of the officers.

'The team will get the commendation,' said Manoussos to his men. Everyone looked pleased.

The telephone rang, Dimitrios answered. It was Max with a message. 'Kirios de Bonn says he'll be there in twenty minutes, and to tell you outside intervention too can be a turn on.' Even Dimitrios had to laugh.

Max did agree to help. He was extremely possessive about Livakia. He, like Manoussos, wanted his home and his privacy kept intact, shielded from the ugliness of the outside world. He had fought hard and gone through some seriously lean years and difficult times in order to find his place in the sun and was willing to go very far indeed to keep it. Right from the first, when he saw Arnold lying on the sand, he'd sensed something unnatural, mystery, deception, more than an accidental death, more than the loss of a friend of long standing. His first instinct had been that it was essential that everything must be done to learn what had happened to Arnold and then to get rid of this dark intrusion into their lives as soon as possible.

He listened to Manoussos's plan. Afterwards the two men remained silent for some time. Manoussos imagined that Max was thinking about Arnold. His first words to the police chief when he reported finding the body on the beach were in effect that, no matter how it looked, Arnold had not died a natural death. When the autopsy report came in, it was Max who said it was a crime of passion done by a woman with something to hide. He was therefore not at all surprised when Manoussos told him he was arresting Melina.

Max had always been indifferent to her. Some instinct had always told him to be pleasant but distant with her. He had heard the rumours about her sexual antics but had never wanted any involvement with her on that score. That was something, because Max – with the exception of D'Arcy and a couple of spinsters – had had, at one time or another, every willing female in Livakia. But she was not attractive or clever enough for him, certainly not pretty enough, although there was something raunchy about Melina. That, under normal circumstances, would have been enough for Max but somehow she had spelled danger to him, the kind of danger that was more sinister than fun.

He was thinking about those things while listening to Manoussos's plan. It was what prompted him to say, 'We have all been exceedingly stupid letting ourselves get sucked in by Mark's rhetoric. Only he found something attractive enough in Melina to save and somehow poor Arnold got suckered into a bizarre triangle.' Max was angry and slammed his fist down hard on the table. The coffee cups did a gig, and the table turned over, taking them with it. That was the first time Manoussos had seen the tougher side of Max in all the years he had known him.

An hour and a half later Max was rounding the cliffs leaving the port of Livakia behind him. Melina was on board with her blue plastic bucket and a mop. It had taken some doing to get her there. The many questions, the money transaction, assurances that she would be back in time for lunch. Then her persistence in wanting to know why he had never hired her before. She really didn't want to go, made excuses, but Max laid on the charm and upped the money. He actually found it fascinating to watch her grow more brazen, more crude, more rude to him the more he insisted he needed her and was depending on her to help him out. He had never truly realised what a nasty piece of work she could be, and yet he felt somehow sorry for her, for the way she was, the way she lived, possibly the way she killed. It was the only way she could find to live. He didn't like having her on board, didn't much like what he was doing.

She had not so much as touched the bucket or the mop from the time she brought them on board and placed them on the deck. Max found that irritating. He saw it as a kind of laziness and fraudulence once she had got what she wanted: the job, an agreement about money, even some already in her pocket. These were the same things Arnold kept going on about when she was working for him. She was a cleaner with a cocky attitude, behaving as if she had no intention of ever swabbing the deck, as if she was

169

just there for the ride. Well, as it happens that was exactly what she was there for, but she didn't know that.

The girl had a serious attitude problem. Having seen it once Max would never have had her work for him again. Why had Arnold tolerated her? Mark's nagging him to help her? No, it had to have been more than that. Once he realised that Melina had some kind of a sexual hold on Arnold, that she played on his weaknesses instead of his strengths, and Arnold had had those too, Max wanted to slap her hard across the face.

On board she was showing a side of herself she had hidden from Mark, from them all, had only dared to show Arnold whom she knew could never cope with it. Max controlled himself and led her along, allowing her to inflate her already swollen ego with thinking she had control of the present situation. Of course – control. That had been what it was all about, her controlling Arnold. He had got out of hand and so Melina had taken her revenge.

Everything went according to Manoussos's plan. Max picked up him and Dimitrios about twenty minutes further down the coast and Melina suspected nothing. In fact, once they were on board and were having cold drinks together she remarked how envious her friends would be of her having these three particular men all to herself, and began to use her body flirtatiously. It was crude but somehow pathetic.

They were no more than five minutes from the cove and the grotto, the very beach where the crime had been committed. The men watched her for any sign that she recognised the place but saw nothing to that effect in her expression. It was all so relaxed – the mundane conversation, the hot sun and a light breeze, the rugged and exciting coastline basking under them.

They were barely minutes from the cove and their destination when she asked, 'How far along the coast will we be travelling? Do we have a destination?'

Such a question, at that very moment? A slight inflection in her voice? Possibly imagined, or just a policeman's instinct. She knew exactly where she was, where they were going. For the first time, she suspected something.

'Does it matter?' asked Manoussos.

Brazenly, defiantly, she turned away from the rail to face Manoussos, Max and Dimitrios, and gazing directly into Manoussos's eyes she told him, 'I don't want to be too late returning to Livakia, I have things to shop for for Kirios Mark before lunch.'

Max spun the wheel and the caique swung round the cliffs and entered the cove. The beach and the grotto were clearly in view and Max headed his boat towards the makeshift and now collapsing weather-beaten wooden jetty that Arnold had had built there many years before. Quite suddenly there was an unpleasant tension in the air. It settled on the seafarers.

Manoussos answered Melina. 'You won't be going back to Livakia, Melina. Not before lunch, not ever.'

Her eyes turned mean and hard, filled with anger. She looked at each of the men in turn then leaned on the rail, her eyes fixed on the beach. She was silent for several minutes watching Max drop anchor, Dimitrios throw the line on to the jetty. Then, when all their attention was back on her, she asked, 'And why, you fine gentlemen, tell me why I won't be going back to Livakia?'

'Because you killed Kirios Topper, Melina.'

'How do you know that?'

'I don't know that, but you're going to tell me what happened here, and then I will know for certain that you killed him.'

She placed her hands on her hips and threw back her head, laughing uproariously. 'You are a pathetic policeman, you know nothing! All guesses. If you know so much, why don't you arrest me? I'll tell you why – because I am more clever than you. You are a very pompous man, and devious too to get me out here away from Livakia and Kirios Mark to make such a claim against me. You didn't dare to do it and make a fool of yourself in Livakia. No matter now, you make a fool of yourself here. Why me? Why do you pick on me for that stupid man's death?'

'Because you're the only one who had a motive.'

'Explain!'

'Motive is what induces a person to act. And you had it. A public humiliation that went too far at a dinner at the Kavouria two nights before Arnold was found dead.'

'He had been insulting about me before and I never killed him.'

'Not in front of Mark, or let me say, not in front of Mark when he had to stand up and defend you, openly declare an interest in you that sounded more than just a campaign to save a delinquent child.'

'You leave Kirios Mark out of this, you're not fit to utter his name!' she ground out. Then spinning round she shot looks more like daggers at Dimitrios and Max and spat on the deck. 'None of you is!'

Max was about to go for her but was held back by a look from Manoussos that said, 'Cool it'. So here was the key to a confession: Mark. Manoussos had it in his hand and he would use it.

'I'm afraid that I can't leave Mark out of this, for the moment anyway. You see, he's the only other person with a motive. Arnold had been a thorn in his side for a very long time. He might have decided to kill him off in return for the public humiliation Arnold inflicted on you that last night we all saw him alive.'

She laughed again but this time there was obvious hysteria in the sound. 'You're trying to frighten me because you know nothing for sure. Anyone, a stranger, could have slipped into Livakia in the night and killed Kirios Topper.'

'And why would a stranger do that?'

'For money, for sex, for fun . . . how do I know? I know one thing for sure, you leave Kirios Mark out of it.'

'Only you can leave Mark out of this killing, Melina, because I swear to you by all that is holy that unless you tell me exactly what I want to know, I will arrest him on suspicion, leak it to the press, and ruin his life whether he is guilty of the crime or not.'

'You pig, you whore! And everyone thinks you're such a good man, you deserve to be dead like Arnold. Worse, not like Arnold. You, I would have cut off your . . .'

It took Max and Dimitrios and all their strength to pull her off Manoussos, and they were both very strong men. Her rage gave her unimaginable strength. Manoussos received a small gash on his face, near his chin. She was so fast no one realised that she had a switchblade in her hand until the blood was flowing from the wound. She was screaming obscenities and completely out of control, her eyes glazed with hysteria. The two men could not wrestle her still until Manoussos slapped her hard across the face several times. That seemed to bring her back to her senses. They sat her down.

'You have to believe I didn't want to do that, Melina. I'm sorry but it was the only way to calm you down. Now you tell me the truth, the whole truth, and I promise to keep Mark out of it. You think about that while I tend to my face.'

That took some time because Manoussos could not stop the bleeding. Max produced disinfectant and finally the bleeding eased. A bandage and plaster were placed over the small but deep wound. Manoussos returned to sit next to Melina. Her face showed nothing now. He closed the switchblade and threw it overboard.

'Chief, that was the assault weapon, evidence.'

'What assault? I'm not charging her with assault, I'm charging her with murder. We'll all just forget about this little incident. It's going to go hard enough for her without a charge of assaulting an officer. I mean it, this incident stays right here between the four of us.' He was emphatic and the other two men knew that it was pointless to disagree with him, so they said nothing.

They could not read Melina's face. A strange silence settled over everyone. The longer they sat there the more uncomfortable they became. Yet no one moved, no one said anything, until Manoussos broke the spell by going to the cool box and returning with a tall drink for Melina. Her hand was trembling when she took it from him. She drank the entire cold lemon drink in one long swallow and then drew her arm across her mouth to dry her lips.

Max had to look away. He hated her, despised her, but for a moment she looked like a wounded animal he would have put a clean shot through to end its life, granting it mercy. Dimitrios removed his cap and wiped the perspiration from his forehead. He stood up and turned his back on her to look to the beach. For the rest of his life he would never forget the fear in Arnold's dead eyes. He wanted to see that same fear in Melina's eyes. He wanted her to suffer as Arnold had suffered but he knew that would never happen. She was a hard case, and she would weather this just as she had weathered everything else that had happened to her in her life. He knew his people and he knew his criminals. Only Manoussos remained emotionally untouched by her and the events that had taken place so far; he reserved judgement and would until he had heard the entire truth from Melina.

She handed the empty glass back to him. 'Have any of you ever been in Kirios Arnold's grotto? Ah, you have, of course you have, you were his friends, he would have taken you there. I've been there, many times. The water's so deep and clear and the colour, like a jewel, and the light off the water, the way it reflects off the walls and the roof of the grotto. I used to swim there with Arnold. He didn't like taking me there but I made him. I could make him do anything when he was drunk and wanted sex with me. But then when he was sober he would make believe that I was no more to him than a cleaner, a handyman to do odd jobs for him. Those were the times that he would not take me there. I would like to go into the grotto to see it one more time before you take me away to wherever they take killers. Not to swim, I know you won't let me do that, but in his rowing boat. You can tie my hands and my feet if you think I'll run away. We can all go. I won't ask you for anything else except that you keep your promise not to involve Kirios Mark in any of this. He doesn't even now know what I did.'

There was no pleading in her voice, no sense of shame or fear in her eyes. If anything there was a kind of stubborn simple pride. Max and Dimitrios would have whisked her away right then and there but they were not Manoussos and they were aware that he would not leave that place until he heard every last word about what had happened. They never even looked at him but made ready to secure the boat and tie up to the jetty.

'I gave you my word before, Melina, I give it to you again. Mark will not be involved.'

All Max kept thinking as he rowed them round the grotto was that his friend Manoussos was a giant among men and one with an enormous amount of humanity in him. How many men in his position would have granted Melina her wish? He certainly would not have. Max was prepared for the girl to take advantage of the situation, jump overboard, topple the boat, something. She did nothing. She behaved impeccably and surprised him further when, after having a good look round and imprinting the place forever on her mind, she told them, 'This place, it's magic. It wipes out the world. If I could have been born here, and lived here in this grotto, like a princess of the sea, maybe I would not have had to kill Kirios Arnold. I would have been a different person. Whatever happens to me, I will always have this to remember and dream about. I'm ready to go now.'

Back on the beach Manoussos asked, 'And now will you tell me what happened, how it happened, why it happened, Melina?'

'Yes, but I want to tell it to you alone, without them.' Hatred had slipped back into her voice.

'I'm afraid that's not possible. I want them here as witnesses. That's the way it has to be.'

She walked very nearly to the exact spot where Max had found Arnold's body and looked defiantly at Manoussos. 'I'm not sorry I killed him. Honour demanded it and I would do it all over again. You two Cretan men, would you have done less had you been humiliated as I had been that night? I don't think so. You would have demanded satisfaction as I did.

'Who was he? Nothing! A drunk who had everything, and was taking up space in this world, nothing more. And he called me a thief! He was mean and I was hungry. I worked for everything he gave me, promised and didn't give me, and the things I took from him he should have given me. He was the kind of man that should have been weeded out and destroyed because he was a cripple. A cripple pitied me! I think that's a joke on him, because look who's dead. I never would have killed him had he not publicly branded me a thief and a whore and refused to take it back, tell everyone it was a mistake, that he was sorry.

'I never liked him, never respected him. He was a

burden on Kirios Mark, he took up his time. Everyone's time. Yet you all liked him and respected him, I could never understand that. I despised his kindness, the secure little world he made for himself, and he was always trying to destroy the one I was making for myself. That last night, he stole my life away for the last time.

'I planned to kill him while he was still insulting me and telling Kirios Mark how he spoilt me, that I was not as intelligent as Kirios Mark pretended I was, that he should not give me the authority he does to take care of his house and make me important in his life. When Kirios Arnold made Kirios Mark accuse me of being stupid and send me home in front of everyone, Kirios Arnold was already a dead man. All the way home I was planning how to kill him, wipe him off the face of the earth. I knew Kirios Mark would approve, he always said the cripples, the deformed, the weak and the greedy should be weeded out and thrown away. That wealthy men like Kirios Arnold and his money ran the world against people like me. Well, no more would I have to carry that cripple home.

'I waited up for Kirios Mark to come home that night and when he did he didn't want to talk to me. He seemed angry with me. All he said was he would be gone in the morning, I was to take care of things while he was away, he would talk to me on his return. Maybe he was going to get rid of me because of Kirios Arnold, who was to know? He was very drunk and then he had one more drink and went to sleep.

'I saw you drag Kirios Arnold home.' And she pointed to Dimitrios. 'I saw you leave the house. I waited for a couple of hours, until all of Livakia was asleep. Then I stole into Kirios Arnold's house. I took his straw bag and found another and filled that with food and vodka, a bottle of wine. I took all the money in the house, his passport, and placed the baskets at the door. Then I undressed and slipped into bed with him.

'The truth is that he liked the power I had over him, though he pretended that it was he who had sexual power over me. I let him think that because it suited me. He felt guilty and generous because of the sex. Because a young, underage girl could excite him with sex, could satisfy him as no other man or woman had been able to before. I could get anything I wanted out of him once I had seduced him. You see, the things I did with him, in sex he would rather have died than have people find out about. I could drive him crazy with sexual desire, but it had to be at the right point of drunkenness, when he was still functioning but all inhibitions were gone.

'That was how he was when I woke him. We did it once in bed, just the way I knew would drive him crazy for more. He always wanted more. He had a lot of strength, a lot of stamina in that department. I usually tortured him by not letting him have sex with me except once. It was so easy to make him crawl for what he wanted, but not this time. This time I promised that if he took me to the grotto, we would do it there, all the rest of the night and for the next two days. I was free, no one would miss me because Kirios Mark was in Athens. I seduced him by telling him I had arranged sexual surprises and they would be waiting for us there. I knew how to tease him. He was lost, would have gone anywhere with me. It was easy, so easy. You see, he never remembered anything about the incident that had taken place only hours before.

'It was still dark but dawn was coming up by the time we had walked here and placed our things in the cave, that cave over there.' At that she pointed to a not very deep cave with a wide opening not three hundred yards from where they were standing. 'Come on, I'll show you.'

The three men followed her. They each of them had known that place, had been there with Arnold, it had been his shelter from the sun. To be there without him was to see it differently. He had made the place so much his own that without him it reverted to the rugged landscape of Crete, nature, powerful and pure. There was not a trace of his presence anywhere, it had died with his body on the beach.

She was so matter-of-fact about what had happened there, so detached from it, it was chilling to listen to her, to watch the cool satisfaction on her face. She might have been giving a tour of coastal Crete to three tourists. And the more she spoke about what had happened, the more sinister and dark a picture of events was etched in their minds. Could there have been a more sad, more tragic end to a life? It became increasingly clear that they had both been victims of one sort or another who had used each other, one to the death.

Max had had enough, heard enough, but he knew there was no turning back now. True he was with two friends, but he was with two policemen and a murderer and they were on a case. Ordinarily he had a fascination about other people's sex lives. He rarely found anything too bizarre, too decadent or depraved. A man's preferences were a man's right so long as they harmed no one. But these had, and he was revolted by what this teenage girl was telling him about her sexual games with his friend. She had never done one thing with Arnold for erotic pleasure, it had all been for power, to victimise, and for money. He would never forgive her or forget her for her evil. Nor forget Arnold for being a most civilised human being, kind of heart, if weak of flesh. He had been no more, no less than that.

They investigated the cave. Manoussos and his team had done that before and had not found a clue as to what might have happened there. They found none now.

They walked from the cave and Melina continued without even having to be prompted by the police chief or his assistant. She went into great detail as to how she had kept Arnold sodden with vodka to the point where his body still functioned but his mind was clouded with drink. 'You know, to just before the point when his legs turned to rubber and he would awkwardly, clumsily, slip off his chair into a heap on the floor – still babbling. You know the way that Kirios Mark could talk him forcibly to his feet? I could do that. I did do that, hour after hour, and then I would let him fall asleep, and then I would wake him and begin again. He never really recovered from one alcoholic haze to the next. He simply regained enough control to function on a minimal level for sex. Close to the end he had no mind left at all. All he was capable of was following my orders, and doing anything I demanded that would give him a greater sexual thrill. He was a pig for sex like all the men I've ever known.

'When I was quite finished with him, I helped him to

dress and lay down on the beach. He was passing out from drink, the days of sex, exhaustion. His mind was gone, his body slipping away into a deep sleep. He never even moved when I placed the plastic bag over his head. I sat astride him and I held it tight round his neck with my own hands and told him how much I hated him, despised him, that he wasn't fit to live. I had made the fool think I'd had sex with him for love, that I, Melina, loved him. And now the last thing that he would remember was that it had all been a lie. I had to shout it as loud as I could to make sure he heard me. He hardly moved for a long time but I know he heard me. He began to gasp for air, he opened his eyes and panic and fear shone in them. He was suffering but it was too late. He was over the edge and in what Kirios Mark would have called his catatonic state. It was over quite fast. It had been much easier than I thought it would be. I expected at least a little fight.'

No one said anything for a considerable time. It was a horror story, but just as horrifying was Melina. The way she had relived the telling of that story while staring down at the sand where he had lain, on the very place where she had performed Arnold's premeditated murder. The enjoyment in her face! When had anyone seen her look that fulfilled, that happy with herself? This was beyond sick.

There were several more questions that needed answering. Melina obliged with her answers. She never asked what was going to happen to her. She never asked where they would be taking her. She had had her satisfaction and that was all she wanted, nothing else seemed to matter to her except that Mark be left out of it. She had committed a crime of passion.

'Melina Philopopolos, as police chief of Livakia and the district of Livakia, I am officially charging you with the murder of Arnold Topper.'

Manoussos stated the time and the actual place of her arrest, the scene of the crime, that it was in the presence of his assisting police officer, naming Max de Bonn as the other witness. She showed no emotion at all.

'Handcuff her, Dimitrios.'

No one asked if that was necessary, no one really cared. The last remark that Melina ever made to her captors was, 'I bet you never thought I was going to make it so easy for you?' And then with a cocky smile she boarded the sea plane, its engines already revving up.

LIVAKIA and LONDON

Chapter 9

No one was surprised by Melina's arrest and confession to the killing of Arnold but everyone was disturbed by it. The tension between the foreign residents and the Cretans escalated as sides were taken. And sides were taken because on Manoussos's return to Livakia he asked the barber-cum-mayor to invite all residents to assemble in the port so that he, their police chief, could address them about the murder in order to quell all the speculation.

Manoussos had another reason for calling the meeting: he wanted to appeal to the Livakians not to discuss the case with any of the media that were bound to appear. He asked for a total blackout, no information to be given on either the victim or the murderer, and he got it. But at a price.

Demands for an explanation from the Livakians assembled in the port that evening as to why Melina had killed Arnold forced Manoussos to reveal at least part of her confession: her lack of respect for him had somehow poisoned her mind to a point where she no longer saw him as the man he was, but the man she imagined he was, and that was a man not worthy to live. She had killed Arnold because it was a matter of honour; she had sought satisfaction for the insults he publicly humiliated her with. Her claim was that Cretan pride had demanded it. The killing had been a crime of passion. *That* the Cretans could understand. Manoussos did not go into the seamier side of what she had claimed had gone on between her and Arnold. That they would not understand. It was too base, too unreal for them to handle, and in fact there was only Melina's word for it with no proof to back it up.

He stated his case: the less said the better. What they all wanted was justice to be done and the whole thing to go away as soon as possible. He did admit that he understood forgetting was going to be near impossible. The incident would probably taint the village with scandal forever.

Of course the fact that Melina had killed for Cretan honour was to strike a chord in all Cretan hearts even though they knew it was wrong, against the law, and that she must be punished. It was for that reason that she gained a certain amount of sympathy she had never had before. Arnold had lost some, much of this prompted by Mark Obermann.

He publicly came to Melina's defence. He wanted leniency for her and in order to get it he went on the attack against Arnold in every conversation he had with anyone who spoke to him about the tragedy. His favourite theme was Arnold's ignorance of Cretan pride and the respect it demanded. His inability to communicate in proper Greek which had caused a breach between him and Melina. With public humiliation of this simple-minded, uneducated, underaged girl, who was struggling without family and home to survive, he had brought his killing upon himself. It was the message Mark was spreading that alienated him from his friends in the foreign community and endeared him to the Cretans.

Mark knew very well that he was responsible for Arnold's death though Melina had been the one to carry out the killing, and that was something he had to live with. Up to the time of the murder it had been Mark who had continually planted seeds of poison in Melina's mind about the worthlessness of Arnold as a human being, until she did indeed see him as deserving death.

Mark's insistence that he would go on the stand as a character witness for her when her trial came up sat well with no one. That decision, once made, became an obsession with him and began to backfire on him. People were now openly holding him morally responsible, not so much for Arnold's death as for the girl's committing a crime, and thus putting a blight on the good name of their village. The blame was not set upon him publicly but in sly looks, dark whispers. After only a few weeks it drove him to flee from Livakia to Athens. That was the day before Arnold's family arrived in Livakia for a memorial service in the church. Duty bound to save face no matter how they might feel about where the blame lay for the tragedy that had befallen their village, most every person in Livakia who had known Arnold, and his friends from other parts of the island, attended the Greek Orthodox service where the black-clad priest officiated, assisted by the two monks.

It was all incense and chanting and candles among the icons and votives in the darkness of the church with the brightness of the hot white sunlight outside. The Bostonian Toppers looked more aghast than mournful, more ill at ease at what must have seemed to them some pagan rite in comparison to the memorial service they might have held in their small white clapboard church, as pristine and perfect on the inside as on the out, and with not an idol or a cross to distract them from God, only a bowl of flowers at the altar – white, of course.

They were accompanied by Manoussos. Max had flown them in from Iraklion, and he flew them out two hours almost to the minute after they had arrived. They had seemed more embarrassed than anything else. They had gone to Arnold's house and had left it with only one thing, the family bible. A request was made for Manoussos to find someone to send Arnold's personal effects, family pictures and private papers to Boston, and someone to take over the sale of the house and its contents. They had remained in it for ten minutes.

The memorial service had been a strange event in as much as people did mourn Arnold in the church, they did feel his loss, some quite deeply, and yet once they filed out into the sun, saw Max's plane skip over the water and angle up into the sky, taking the Toppers of Boston away, one could almost hear the sighs of relief. It was over.

It was inexplicable, but the shadow that had fallen over Livakia suddenly vanished. They had the sense that life could begin again, that it did go on, and that in some strange way Arnold would now be remembered for all the things he had been, and not the things he had not. That his life, whatever it was, had been valid, and his friends could live with that and his terrible death, as they would live with the memory of a twisted teenager who had brought the dark side of life into Livakia and destroyed something in each of them, changing them in some way, possibly even for the better. None of them would forget that she was languishing in a prison, locked up for her sins, and yet to face trial. That too they would live with. It would be a reminder of how fragile paradise can be, how delicate and vital was every minute of one's life.

D'Arcy was standing with Elefherakis, Rachel, Despina, a Greek neighbour, and her husband, the baker, and Jimmy Jardine – even he had come down from his house for the service. They were watching Max's plane turn into a small white dot in the sky. Laurence joined the group and placed an arm round D'Arcy's shoulders. In spite of herself she felt a rush of delight. Her feelings for him were still there. Still enjoying the sensation of his presence, she was distracted by Rachel tugging at her sleeve. D'Arcy gave her the attention she was seeking.

Rachel stood on the tips of her toes and looking up at D'Arcy discreetly whispered, 'Tonight's the night. At last he's interested! In the church he all but asked me to his house, and I intend to go and to sleep in Jimmy Jardine's spiritual bed.'

She beamed at D'Arcy and was already batting her eyelashes before she even left her friend's side. It brought back something deeply silly that seemed to have vanished when the mystery of Arnold's death had taken over their lives. D'Arcy couldn't have held back the laughter even if she had wanted to. It came from deep within, peals of it, until there were tears in her eyes. Her laughter released the tension that had become part of everyone's lives.

The group looked at her, smiles on their faces. Rachel slipped her arm through Jimmy Jardine's and twinkled up at him.

'That's beautiful, D'Arcy. You're washing away grief, like peeling off a heavy coat of the stuff. You're healing yourself, healing us all. The last time I heard laughter like that and saw happening what I see happening to you now was in a monastery in Tibet when a Buddhist monk, a master, was chanting to some children. Their laughter echoed through the cavernous halls of the monastery and I began to laugh with them. All the years and tragedies of my life fell away. I felt like a child. The master was a man of ninety-two and those years just seemed to slip away. He looked like a young man, he too was a child again. We were all happiness and freedom. Something I had probably never truly felt since I was four years old. He taught me that chant. It's used to release the true soul, get you in touch with your total being, the path to awareness.

'D'Arcy, I don't know how much you've studied, how many lives you've lived to get where you are, but that chant – you know it without knowing it, it's in your soul and you pull it out when you need it. You're blessed, one of the luckiest women in the world,' Jimmy Jardine told her.

'Make me one of the luckiest women in the world, teach me that chant, Jimmy,' pleaded Rachel, very nearly panting in her breathlessly sexy little voice.

Rachel was definitely on form, giving the best in her repertoire of seduction performances. Not one person in the group dared to look at another for fear of bursting into frivolous laughter and blowing Rachel's game as well as Jimmy's belief that D'Arcy was the aware human being, the spiritual soul incarnate he believed her to be, and which he had spent endless years trying to be.

Obviously inspired by D'Arcy and aware that life in Livakia was rapidly healing from a dark moment in its history, he dropped his guard and let Rachel into his life. 'I never thought of you as wanting to learn the Buddhist ways, Rachel?'

'Oh, I do. I do, Jimmy.' She saw her opening and was quick to jump in.

'Then why don't you come to my house tonight for supper and we'll talk?'

D'Arcy half expected to hear a burst of applause. Rachel had made it, she was in the door, but was she in his bed? The look of satisfaction on her face was one no one had ever seen before. Jimmy said goodbye to everyone and they watched him walk away, wondering whether he did or did not know what he was in for. D'Arcy imagined that he would be talking enlightenment, Rachel sex.

Looking smug she told them, 'I won't be joining you for lunch. I have to wash my hair, do my legs, give myself a facial – and don't worry if you don't see me for a few days. One of his ex-wives told me he's an animal in bed, a poetic animal but a very sexual one. Likes to go on long orgies of sex and poetry once he really gets going, and I intend for him to *really* get going.'

'Then you're not going to go into denial on *this* sexual romp?' quipped Laurence.

'Not on your life! I'm going to wear this encounter on my sleeve like a badge. You know, like something you win in the girl guides. I will have earned it.' Now everyone did burst into laughter. And Rachel walked away, eyes sparkling as if they had stars in them.

Walking to the Kavouria, Laurence and D'Arcy slipped back from the group. 'Now that this ghastly affair is over and we can put it behind us, I think we should talk. I miss you, and I know you still miss me. That's true, isn't it?' he asked her.

'Yes.'

'I knew it!'

'What should we talk about, Laurence?'

'Staying in each other's lives, both of us behaving in a civilised way when we have other lovers around, the possibility that one day we may get back to having more than the odd one-night stand together.'

'You assume a lot, Laurence.'

'Surely we still want each other that way, you can't deny it?'

D'Arcy ignored that. Yet again, she recognised something in Laurence she had never liked: his constantly trying to manipulate her. 'You have a lady arriving,' she told him in a matter-of-fact manner.

'Well, yes. From London. Caroline Finch.'

'That's what this is all about. This has nothing to do with *us*. Anything to avoid the direct route, always the devious but dressed up as diplomatic, whatever it takes to bypass a confrontation. Have your Caroline Finch, and a Mary and a Columbine. Have all the women in the world. You can parade them in front of me, I don't mind. Be assured I would never embarrass myself by making a scene over you and your inability to give yourself in love. Now, shall we join the others for lunch?'

D'Arcy rose early the following morning, dressed and went down to the port. Only Katzakis's grocery shop was open. The other traders were sitting around tables having their coffee and discussing politics. D'Arcy greeted them and after ordering eggs and a mound of bacon, bread, honey and coffee, took a table apart from theirs where she sat with her face turned up to the sun. The hum of voices and the sound of the sea lapping against the few boats still left in the port, the sound of a single bell being rung in the church high above the village resounding off the cliffs – the morning music of Livakia. The glory days were back. She let it seep into her soul and felt the power and the excitement of just being alive. It was enough for her, it would always be enough for her, life and love and living in Livakia.

D'Arcy was not concerned that love came and went in her life. For her it was just a cycle. She had no doubt that love would come to her again. Maybe it would be another love that was born, would develop and die. She was a woman who understood love can do that if it fulfils itself and has nowhere else to go, when the adventure goes out of a relationship, and eternal love is some far off dream. And then again maybe a new love would come along and be a greater love than she had ever had. Love eternal. If that were to happen it would come as all her other loves had: naturally, without artifice, both for her and the other person involved. Love, passion, sex, they had always come to her in the past, and she had no doubt that they would come again because she was receptive to those things if the chemistry was right. Time and chance were two things she believed in and never forced. She could wait. If it was to be, it would be.

The sun felt good on her face, it relaxed every nerve in her body. She gave herself up to it and sighed. She smiled when she felt his hands over her eyes and he kissed the top of her head. She knew it was Max by his scent. She had always found that light aroma of sandalwood and pine he wore very exotic and sexy. It went with the heat and the sun and the sea. She didn't move, said not a word. Not even when she felt his beard brush against her ear and he whispered, 'I'll have you yet, and I'll caress you better than the sun you're basking in now, and I'll eat into your flesh better than the sun's heat, and when that happens you'll never send me away again.'

Max bit her ear lobe, very hard, and D'Arcy squirmed in her chair. He removed his hands from her eyes, stepped in front of her and smiled. 'Good morning, D'Arcy.'

'Good morning, Max.' She found it difficult to hold back her smile.

'Dare I dream it might happen tonight?'

'You're incorrigible.'

'Well, at least you recognise that.' He touched the tip of her nose with his finger, and then her lips, and then he was gone. D'Arcy closed her eyes again, tilting her face back up to the sun.

It was just barely seven o'clock when D'Arcy was woken out of her reverie for the second time by the arrival of breakfast. She was ravenous and ate her meal with gusto. She left not a morsel of food on the plate and was having her third cup of coffee when she saw Rachel appear from a side street. D'Arcy had to check her watch for the time. Rachel never appeared in sunlight before ten or preferably eleven in the morning.

On seeing D'Arcy she rushed over to her and plopped into a chair. She looked quite worn out, dizzy with tiredness. 'I'm famished, I must have some food. God, you've left nothing on your plate. Don't go away, I'll be right back. The bastard never fed me!' With that she rushed into the coffee shop and came out seconds later pulling apart half a loaf of bread and stuffing the pieces in her mouth. Once more in the chair, she closed her eyes and sighed.

'You've just come from Jimmy Jardine's house. Well, was it everything you dreamed it was going to be?' asked D'Arcy, a smile on her lips and laughter in her voice.

'You can laugh! You haven't just spent the most boring night of your life and then not even been fucked.'

'I don't believe it!'

'This time you can believe it, it's God's truth. He did exactly what he said he was going to do: talked Zen and Zen and more Zen. He's been on a retreat so it was leftover macrobiotic food – disgusting! Eating that stuff can't be a way of getting to Nirvana, wherever that is. The poetry, his poetry, Zen poetry, we went through all that . . . interesting but too wise, when you could understand it, and far too worthy. Boring, boring. But still he was wooing me and he has that sexy look about him and, well, frankly, I remembered what his wife said so I tried every ploy to get him to crash out of Zen and slip between the sheets. Would he have it? Not on your life. He was a *pig*, not at all a gentleman. He accepted my sitting in his lap, my kisses and caresses, sat there like one of those precious stone Buddhas he reveres and let me make love to him. And all I got in return – not sex but more Zen. Oh, please!'

Rachel's food arrived and she ate while rolling her eyes in delight. In between mouthfuls she asked, 'D'Arcy, what do you think he does with all of those gorgeous, brainless beauties he brings here when he's not on a retreat?' Then, before D'Arcy could answer, she said with eyes flashing danger signals, 'Don't you dare tell me he beds them, fucks them silly and makes love to them. You do and I'll be very angry.' Then she paused and looked up from her plate. 'You'll tell me he wanted my mind not my body, and I'll tell you he was a schmuck – he could have had my mind *after* my body.' A smile slowly appeared at the corners of her mouth and then she broke into a grin and then both women had a good laugh over Rachel al Hacq's failed seduction of Jeremy Jardine. Her last words on the subject were, 'The man is too self-involved.'

The last days of September were still hot, the nights warm, but there was that end-of-summer feeling. With the end of the tourist season and the arrival of the more interesting travellers, the island was coming back into its own. Livakia was settling down again; it had weathered the tragedy, the divisions that had split the community, and then the media. The inhabitants had been so difficult with journalists and TV people that the media soon vanished, either because of the blackout on all information relating to the murder or just plain fear of stepping on too many Cretan toes.

Manoussos had called in some favours and a dozen big, strong, rugged-looking young men came down from the surrounding mountain villages to stay in Livakia and see off media intruders who might be disturbing the peace by re-hashing the sad story. A grateful Livakia took them into their homes, Rachel secretly into her bed, and all in all it worked. The unpleasant scandal that they could not wholly forget was at least fading from their minds, and life as they had known and enjoyed it slowly returned.

His name was Brandon Ketheridge and he was staying with Elefherakis, and had been there several days before D'Arcy met him. He was tall and broad-shouldered and slim, a man in his fifties with greying hair and dark sexy eyes. He was English, living in London, a writer of some renown, his name instantly familiar to anyone who read good literature. It was instant sexual rapport. There was about him that same erotic quality that most libertines have, a certain danger and excitement, mystery, the promise of sex unbounded, a habit of sensual indulgence – those same qualities that Max had and D'Arcy had always shied away from.

She had not the least intention of running away from Brandon Ketheridge. She could accept a short-lived, intensely sexual and satisfying liaison with him. He didn't live in Livakia, he wouldn't wear her as a notch on his belt the way Max would. There was no possibility of losing him as a long-standing close friend as there might be if she succumbed to Max's seductive sexual charms, and so when they met at the Kavouria a delicious sense of romance flared between them.

It began with a look across the table before they were even properly introduced. A sexual attraction so strong, so sure, that it left neither of them in any doubt that they would have each other, that this was the right time, the right place, for a romantic sexual adventure, the kind that flares up and burns bright before burning itself out. The kind that has nothing to do with love. The atmosphere their flirtation created left no one else in any doubt about that either. In fact, it made most everyone there hungry for an erotic experience in any form they could get it.

Once introductions were made across the table Brandon wasted little time. Not half an hour later he had managed to change seats with Elefherakis and was seated next to D'Arcy.

Half an hour after that, he said, lowering his voice, 'This meal is going to go on for eternity. Do we have to be deplorably discreet and remain?'

'I don't see why. I think we've already blown discretion.'

He smiled at her. 'I thought we might have.' With that he pushed back his chair and, very tall and very obvious, stood behind D'Arcy's and helped her up. He knew the form. In lunches and dinners at the Kavouria where there were gatherings of people who chose to sit together at one long table, people always paid an equal share of the bill unless specifically invited by someone. Brandon walked round the table to Elefherakis and, slipping money into his hand, said, 'For D'Arcy's and my share of the bill.'

There was a heated discussion going on around the

table and barely anyone paid any attention to their leaving. A table of nearly fifteen people often had someone popping up to go to the kitchen, the loo, to leave in a huff or change their seat. Laurence was one of the people who did pay attention to Brandon's and D'Arcy's leaving the table together so early on in the evening. He had Caroline next to him and was happy with her, in love actually. She gave him the things he had missed when living with D'Arcy, that certain Englishness that he loved but periodically ran away from. She was less free, more harnessed to life as written in the rule book of family, background, the acceptable face of any given social structure. She was bright, she was beautiful, she was sexy, and he was finding love on the rebound.

It was over for D'Arcy and him, and yet when she walked away with Brandon Ketheridge he wanted to stand up and pull her away from him. He missed her; didn't want her, but didn't want to lose her either. He was resenting the very same thing now that he had resented when he had been living with her: D'Arcy Montesque had more of him than he had wanted to give her. He turned away and kissed Caroline, caressing her hair.

Brandon was holding D'Arcy's hand as they walked across the port towards Elefherakis's house. 'You do know what this is all about?' he asked.

There was tremendous sexual energy vibrating between them; he could hardly keep the passion and the desire from his voice. D'Arcy liked his forthrightness, it added a shiver of excitement to the already thrilling prospect of an erotic tryst to remember. They had rounded the point and there was no light except from the stars and the moon, a soft low light cascading down the flight of stone steps that led up to Elefherakis's house. She slid her arms round his neck and placed her lips upon his and kissed them, licked them, slid the point of her tongue between them. His lips parted and there was a sense of their devouring each other in the kiss that followed. She wrapped a leg around him and he placed his hands under her skirt and caressed her bottom, helped to hoist her by it up on to him and there she remained, clinging to him with both legs wrapped tight as a vice around his waist.

D'Arcy's hands had already undone the buttons of his shirt and were roving over his chest. She liked his body, it was taut and virile. She stopped her kisses only long enough to tell him, 'Yes, I would say I do know what this is all about, what we're all about.' Then, gripping his hair tight in her hands, she placed her lips once more upon his.

He took over the kiss while tearing her silk bikini pants from between her legs. With one hand he was undoing his jeans; his other hand fondled the cheeks of her bottom. His fingers searched between those voluptuously round, firm, globes and under them until he found those most private of orifices. He so adored to master a woman, and knew so well how to excite. He teased them and fondled them, and took the first of the flight of steps to the house while doing so.

Their kisses were deep and searching. The warmth of their mouths, the taste of each other on their tongues – softness and warmth overwhelmed them, while his fingers were doing the work of exciting lust for them both. When she was moist and smooth as silk and he felt her giving into their kissing, and his playful and very sexy intrusions, he lifted her away from his body only enough, in one fell thrust, to impale her on him. She threw back her head, gasped, and the colour came rushing to her neck and face as she came. She couldn't speak. To open her mouth would have been to allow a scream of pure delight. The pain and pleasure, the agony and the ecstasy, of being taken over by such an exquisite sensation would have demanded nothing less of her. Instead she bit into the skin on the back of her hand.

'Kiss me!' he demanded.

She obeyed, and he continued going up the steep steps with her thus: clinging to him, kissing him, impaled upon his sex.

There was nothing tender or sweet about the sex they had together that night, but it was thrilling, erotic. A kind of sexual madness took them over. Both aware of that, they revelled in it, didn't want it to stop. They were on a sexual odyssey, an epic adventure, they were going on a series of wanderings in an erotic land. This was the beginning of a long and adventurous journey.

For his part Brandon had never met a woman so ready for such a journey. There seemed to be a fire in her that smouldered, was instantly ready to be fanned into a huge hot flame. She wanted it all, to taste, to experience every aspect of sex. She was a woman experienced in lust, and yet . . . it was as if she could go no further in her life until she had made this journey with him. He admired her, felt respect for her, even a little love for the courageous D'Arcy Montesque. He knew he could take her to the edge of depravity and she would enjoy it and come to no harm.

D'Arcy had thought almost from the very minute they gazed into each other's eyes that there would be no turning back from this liaison with Brandon Ketheridge. Now as the dawn light spilled into the room and across the four poster bed she knew it to be true. He was indeed a libertine in every sense of the word. He was licentious, a man who did as he pleased, a sexual free-thinker, hungering for every new sexual experience he could find. Never before had she felt the need as she did now to know that side of sex, to experience it and come out the other side of such an affair as she would have with Brandon.

As she lay in bed with this stranger, she found her desire to be with him in such extravagant sex as he promised inexplicable. She knew she was acting out of character, or was she? She had the most acute sense of wanting to live, of being free and wanting to soar to heights she had never been to before. She wanted never again to close her eyes to other worlds, new experiences, out of a sense of fear. It was just as easy to walk away with one's eyes open. If indeed she did want to walk away from something. Brandon, lust with a libertine . . . for the moment all she wanted to do was to stay by his side, enjoy his sexual life with him. She knew her strength, how solid a human being she was; she had nothing to fear. Before Arnold's unfortunate death she might have shied away from Brandon, but not now. There had been a basic change in D'Arcy. She felt a responsibility for all her actions which she had never quite felt before, and had no fear of that responsibility. She knew this odyssey she was embarking on with Brandon would somehow enrich her life, lead her one step further towards her place in the sun. Nothing could have stopped her from taking it.

Grey sky and a chilling rain – a perfect London afternoon. D'Arcy had always liked London, it was one of her favourite cities. She had only been with Brandon in Livakia for two days before he whisked her away. They had had breakfast and he had told her, 'I'm leaving in an hour and you're coming with me. Elefherakis has arranged for a boat and a car to get us to the airport.'

'Just like that?' she had said.

'Yes, just like that,' he had told her with a wicked smile.

And here she was riding in a taxi through Hyde Park, dressed in a smart linen suit, her passport in her handbag and no luggage, not even a toothbrush.

'I feel like I've been kidnapped,' she told him.

Brandon smiled and picked up her hand to kiss it. 'Of course you do. That's because you have been, for sex rather than ransom.'

It was true. She had known what he was doing before the boat had even left Livakia. It was a strange sensation for D'Arcy, this feeling of being a captive. D'Arcy, who valued her freedom above all else. D'Arcy, who had never enslaved herself to anything or anyone, and certainly not to a man for sex. Yet she didn't question it. It was merely something she was doing, something that was happening to her, and she did not resist.

'Some ground rules that you must obey. You're mine

and only mine for as long as you want to stay with me, we want to stay together. No outsiders or friends to distract us from each other.'

'That's why you whisked me away from Livakia?'

'Precisely why. Are you unhappy about that?'

'No. If I had been I wouldn't have come.'

He grazed her cheek with the back of his hand. Not once since they had first laid eyes on each other had that intense sexual feeling between them waned. It was there always, with every look, every touch of his hand upon her. Only hours after their first sexual encounter there was something else added to that feeling: affection for each other. Yet strangely even that affection was bound up in their erotic togetherness; that was the basis of it, that and what they were prepared to do with each other and for each other to satisfy the lust that was for the moment in command of their lives.

The taxi rounded Hyde Park Corner and sped through the park parallel to Park Lane. He pulled her closer to him and slipped his hand beneath her skirt. Already obeying him, she wore no undergarments. He had told her that was the way he wanted her as long as they were together and had proved to her several times why. Brandon wanted her open and ready for him, waiting to be taken instantly by him at any time and at any place. She stared at the back of the taxi driver's head in fear that he would look in his rear view mirror and catch them, but she could not help herself. She wanted the sensation of Brandon's teasing fingers deep inside her, his thumb working her clitoris as he drove her on with whispers, 'Come, I want you to come, here, now!'

The moment he felt her body tense and she put the back of her hand to her mouth to stop herself from calling out as she came over his fingers, he held her in a hug as tight as he could and closed his eyes, to hide his own excitement for her and her sexual hunger.

She went limp in his arms and leaned against him. She had been holding her breath and now she wasn't and her breathing was fast and nervy, her heart racing. He drew his fingers across her lips and she licked the trail of come off them then watched him lick his fingers, savour the taste of her.

'You're delicious,' he told her.

Not many seconds later the doorman of the Connaught Hotel opened the taxi door and, shielding them from the rain with an enormous black umbrella, escorted them to the entrance. D'Arcy's knees felt like jelly, she was unnerved and yet excited, unimaginably excited by the danger and the thrill of sex in the back of a London taxi. That and the fact that she knew that Brandon Ketheridge could make her do anything sexual and she would be willing, without thought or consequence.

She excused herself and went into the ladies' powder room where she had to sit down at the dressing table to compose herself. She looked in the mirror and touched her hand to her cheek. She felt a need to do that to prove to herself that the image in the mirror was real. D'Arcy, for all her looks, had never really got caught up in the fact that she was, like her mother, ravishingly good-looking. That hers was a sensual and vibrant kind of beauty to be admired and loved on a grand scale.

In the mirror of the Connaught ladies' powder room she

saw that for the first time and understood herself as never before. It took her somewhat aback that it should be a near stranger she was out on a sexual odyssey with who should awaken her to herself in a new and different way.

Chapter 10

In the dining room, D'Arcy sat across the table from Brandon and listened to him order their lunch. 'We'll have the terrine of *foie gras* served with a vintage Madeira wine jelly and baby leeks, followed by the roast duckling. I like it prepared with the maize, ginger and lemon syrup. The usual trimmings, the poached white peach, and for vegetables, the purée of celeriac, mange tout, a pancake of rosti potatoes. We'll choose our puddings later.'

D'Arcy was somewhat amused that when the maître d' had offered her a menu, Brandon had told him, 'That won't be necessary, I will order for us,' and the menu had been whisked away. She watched him as he ordered the wines. His choice was extravagant and perfect for the meal he had chosen. He had what she thought to be heroic, sensual good looks. Brandon looked every inch the depraved sensualist, and she was mesmerised by him. Sitting across from him she was aware of her lust for him – it was like a fever that had to burn itself out, and if the price was obeying him and his every whim, that he should have complete control over her to the extent that she had not even a choice as to what food she might want to eat, then so be it. As lost as she was in this erotic journey she was on with him, she was aware that she had not lost herself any more than he had. D'Arcy thought it time to tell Brandon she had a few ground rules of her own.

The waiter gone, champagne cocktails on the table in front of them, he raised his glass and said, 'You will be brave and will never shy away from the new, the never experienced, on this odyssey of ours.'

D'Arcy, without one second of hesitation, touched the rim of her glass to his and said nothing, just took a sip of the cocktail. 'Another one of your ground rules?' she asked.

'If you like,' he answered.

There was a smile in his eyes, on his face. Everything he said, everything he did, was sensual and exciting, constantly seductive, thrilling. It was like being on a rollercoaster, dicing with death: the death of her ego, and being born again as nothing more than a sex object who was being nurtured by another sex object. It was a bizarre and dangerous place to be in one's life, like jumping out of a plane, going into free-fall. Did he know how well matched they were, that he in turn was nothing more to her than a sex object? She thought this might be the right moment to tell him.

She slipped her foot free from her shoe and ran it up and down his leg several times. He felt her stockinged toes high up on his thigh and briefly a caress between his legs. The smile on his face was more broad now. 'I knew from the moment I set eyes on you that you were a woman who would speak to me with your body.'

'Would it surprise you to learn that this sexual slave of yours has a few ground rules of her own?'

'Ah, then you do understand that that is what you are to me?'

'And the only way you want me? Yes, I've known that from the start.'

Waiters arrived and hovered round the table covered in its crisp white damask cloth that safely hid the fondling of Brandon's genitals by D'Arcy's stocking-covered toes. After their first course was served, Brandon, who did not look at all surprised, asked, 'And if I don't accept them, or that you should even have them?'

'But you will. It's too late for either of us to turn back. This adventure is too great, it pulls us forward. Sexual oblivion on a grand scale? No, you won't reject that or my ground rules because they'll suit you as my erotic master, and me as your sexual slave.'

'I'm intrigued. State your rules.'

'You are never to ask me anything about my life, past or present, personal or business. Only anything that has to do with sex. You are never to take me into your life except sexually. I don't want to know anything about you, not the way you live or love or hate, only anything you want to tell me that's erotic and will add to our sex life. You are never to buy me flowers, or perfume, or a gift of any kind unless it is something sexual for us to play with. I don't want to go the theatre or the ballet or a concert or even out for another meal with you. If I am to be your sexual prisoner, then that's what I want to be. If you're to be my master then that's the way I want you and as nothing else in my life – not a suitor for my affections, not a romantic lover I might want something more from. We have to be everything to each other sexually, and nothing more. I guess that pretty much states my set of ground rules.'

Brandon placed the last forkful of *foie gras* in his mouth and drank his entire glass of Sauternes. The mingled tastes of the goose liver and the slightly sweet white wine lingered in his mouth. Sensual, erotic tastes that excited the palate nearly as much as D'Arcy's little declaration had excited his lust for her. He was certain that she'd known it would. His glass was refilled and he raised it and asked her to raise hers. 'You were quite right, I do like your terms. That's it then?'

D'Arcy placed the palm of her hand over his glass to stop him from drinking and told him, 'Not quite.'

He looked amused. 'And?'

'And when the time comes for us to part, when it's over, it's over for good. No return performances. No phone calls. Just memories of a time of sexual madness we shared.'

She removed her hand from his glass and he placed it to his lips and drank; only then did she finish her own wine.

They had no difficulty with the food, it was delicious; what they did have difficulty with was the erotic tension that kept building during their meal. When the dessert trolley was wheeled in front of them, Brandon chose the trifle, his favourite pudding at the Connaught. D'Arcy was hardly able to eat it. The food had been full of rich, erotic flavours and now this seemed the most sensual of puddings; every mouthful of cream and jelly and custard and sponge soggy with sherry was sex to the taste buds.

Brandon watched her spoon the pudding into her

mouth, licking her lips without realising it. He laughed. Caught out! He was delighted he had her so finely tuned and receptive to the erotic that even a pudding was playing its part. He knew what she wanted: him, the taste of him in her mouth, to lick him from her lips.

He made a move to rise from the banquette where he was sitting and the waiters arrived to pull the table away. He grabbed D'Arcy with one hand and pulled her from her chair. They were halfway across the sumptuous busy dining room when he signed for the meal. The maître d' most charmingly and with a knowing smile removed the dessert spoon she was still holding from her hand. Neither D'Arcy, Brandon, nor the maître d' missed the smiles of approval and envy on the faces of several of the men in the room.

The rain had never stopped. To travel the distance from the Connaught's entrance to the taxi was to feel that English chill that can come with autumn and a steady downpour.

'I never know how to dress for the English weather,' D'Arcy told Brandon. In the back of the taxi she snuggled up close to him for warmth.

The moment she told him that she realised how mundane all conversation was going to be with him. They were on another plane with each other, a place she had never been before, and she sensed that he was aware of that as well. As if to confirm her thoughts, he pulled her roughly to him with his hands on her face and tilted it up to look deep into it. The look he gave her before he kissed her, an erotic kiss that ravaged her with its passion and hunger, was telling her, 'You're beautiful and sexy and mine, and do shut up or you'll destroy something we will never be able to capture again.' That was the thing about them: they were so well matched in their lust, and their desire to be together in it, that they understood each other. These were two people who would never diminish what they were.

A kiss – how can a mere kiss send a woman out of control of her life? How can sex take one over and add so much to one's life that all else can be put in jeopardy? For the first time D'Arcy could understand that sex, as pure sex and nothing else, on the grand scale, was not so much the dark side of a man or woman's nature but a powerful experience of pleasure and pain and life, an enhancement as well as an adventure for those pleasure seekers of this world who want to know what life is all about.

Who was to know what drove Brandon and D'Arcy into each other's arms, what drove any man and woman together? But they were, in a house in Belgrave Square. A large and beautiful house of many rooms where they remained for eight days in an orgy of sex and where D'Arcy surrendered her life to lust. Never once did she feel that she would come to any harm in the arms of Brandon Ketheridge. Every minute of their time together was a sensual delight: the food they ate, the erotic films they watched, the pornographic literature he read to her. His collection of erotic art, from antiquity to the present day, was sexy beyond anything she had ever imagined: sexual acts, raunchy and thrilling, elegantly depicted in Persian drawings and Indian water colours. There were too Danish hardcore porn films that were less beautiful but powerfully exciting for Brandon if not for D'Arcy.

She watched them, and disliked them, and never did they watch that sort of sex film again. Nothing to do with prudery, merely that for D'Arcy they were distasteful and nothing she would want to be a part of.

As a sexual slave she obeyed her master but he was smart enough to know where to draw the line for his greater pleasure, and that was not having a sexual slave who merely obeyed, it was having one who obeyed and enjoyed and took off on every order he gave. What he did demand of his slave was that she fulfil every sexual fantasy she had ever had because he intended to satisfy every one of his. They did. Some things D'Arcy tried she would never try again but there were other things that she would definitely do again, with the right man, in the right place, at the right time.

It could have gone on for longer because the sex was great but it couldn't because, as splendid as it was, it simply was not enough without romance, love, friends, work, the outside world and its trials and tribulations. They had to come down from Elysium, that place of ideal happiness: and it had been a special kind of ideal happiness for D'Arcy and Brandon.

No words, no explanations were needed, they were drifting away from each other and they both knew it. He opened a bottle of vintage Krug, his favourite champagne, and a one-pound tin of the best Beluga caviare and they lay naked on cushions in front of the fire with their delectable repast. He dipped his finger into the mass of glistening black beads and scooped a large dollop of it out to feed it to D'Arcy. She sucked it off his finger and rolled her eyes with delight before feeding him some in the same way.

They drank and ate and fondled each other, and in spite of what they knew, they played lewd and very sexy games with the wine and the caviare. She had come several times before she placed cushions behind his head, the better for him to watch her, and cushions under his bottom, and mounted him, impaling herself upon his pulsating sex. They held hands, fingers interlocked, and she rode up and down on him, moved round and round in little circles. She could hardly catch her breath and her heart was racing, so acute was her pleasure. To be in control of his every movement, to have him where she wanted him, caressing every morsel of her most intimate self, to feel his hardness brimming, ready to come as he fed her more caviare from his fingers, was over-the-edge lust. They were both holding back, wanting it to go on for a little bit longer before a crescendo of orgasm sent them soaring higher, higher, closer to yet another few moments of sexual oblivion.

He squeezed so tight on her fingers D'Arcy felt pain, as if they were going to break. Never taking his gaze from her eyes he pressed a deep kiss on her lips and then on her breasts. His kisses turned to sucking and biting hard into her nipples. She knew what he wanted – to be ridden by her, harder, and faster. She obeyed and there were tears in his eyes when he raised his head from her breasts and gazed once more into her face. His voice was husky, filled with emotion when he told her, 'You're the best of times, a goddess in your own right, a lustful angel, a lady whore who should wear a crown of jewels more grand than the Byzantine Empress Theodora. Farewell, my lovely.' There were droplets of blood on one of the pale smooth cone-shaped nimbuses surrounding her nipples.

They came together, not quietly, and their orgasms were long and strong and frighteningly exciting. They were near to fainting, were certainly for several minutes off somewhere in a vast void of sexual bliss, gone, gone, gone . . .

D'Arcy awakened from a deep sleep. She was in Brandon's bedroom, in his bed, and alone for the first time since she had met him in Crete a week before. Crete, Livakia, her house, her life . . . she had left them all behind once she had come under the spell of Brandon Ketheridge. How had he done it, enchanted her into this most amazing sexual journey he had taken her on? How vulnerable, how ready she must have been to make it, to want to live to the very edge of life. Now she had been there and was back. It had been a fabulous voyage of discovery in many ways other than sexual, and it was so good to find herself again, and her life as she had known it before Brandon. It was like returning from a foreign land.

She went to his bathroom. Like his bedroom it was large and rich, elegant and with a certain masculine charm. She stepped down into the black and white marble tub recessed into the floor. It was large enough for four people and she turned on the several taps used to fill it swiftly. She bathed and thought about what she would do, where she would go when she left his house.

She was dressed and rang for Minnou, Brandon's Thai

217

servant, who had attended them punctiliously during her stay. He arrived with the Chinese girl Su Lee who lived in Brandon's house as a permanent sexual object, a plaything in his life. She carried a silver tray with a sumptuous tea for one on it into the bedroom and placed it on a round Biedermeier table in front of a window overlooking the garden. D'Arcy wanted to say something to Su Lee but she didn't know quite what. The young woman had been at times part of Brandon's and her sexual fantasies, and D'Arcy had shared with this girl some of the most intimate experiences she would ever have or not have again. Yet they had nothing to say to each other.

D'Arcy stood by the window powdering her nose, the last touch to her make-up. She looked at the girl eyeing the Fabergé compact D'Arcy was holding. It was very small and exquisite – oval, black enamel, trimmed and decorated in platinum and with a small diamond clasp. D'Arcy snapped it closed and held it in her hand as she told Minnou, 'I'm leaving now. I want to thank you for being so kind to me while I have been here. I've left you a little note.'

With that she went to the large Biedermeier desk and fetched an envelope into which she had slipped five twenty-pound notes and handed it to Minnou. He tried to resist, guessing there might be more than a message inside, but D'Arcy told him, 'Please, I insist. I don't imagine we will be seeing each other again. Where will I find Mr Ketheridge?'

'Mr Ketheridge will be here at any moment. He asks you please to wait in the downstairs sitting room when you have finished your tea. And so I'll say goodbye.'

He very politely bowed his head, they shook hands and he backed away. Su Lee went to D'Arcy and smiled. There was affection in the smile but she found no words any more than D'Arcy had. They were after all not friends, just two women who had played together in lust. D'Arcy had been an intruder into this beautiful young girl's life with Brandon, whatever that life was, and she had been a delight when she might have been a problem. In appreciation of that D'Arcy raised the girl's hand and placed the compact in it, closing her fingers over it.

When D'Arcy came down to the sitting room Brandon was there. He came to her and gave her a hug then asked, 'Is there somewhere I can take you? The airport?'

'No. If I might, I'd like to use the telephone. I think I'll stay a few days for some shopping.'

'In the hall.'

This mundane conversation, how it pained them. They could see it in each other's faces. She called several hotels, but with no luck. He went to her, took the telephone from her hand and called the Connaught, immediately managing to book a suite of rooms for her. 'Don't look so concerned, that's the least I can do for you. And I will keep to the terms we agreed. We both know when over is over and out.'

There was one more hug and he said, 'An affair to remember?'

She replied. 'Yes, an affair to remember.' Then she was gone from his house and into a waiting taxi.

D'Arcy turned round to take one last look at the house

in Belgrave Square where she had been a prisoner of lust, and then she sat back and relaxed. She sensed that that odyssey she had been on with Brandon had been much more than sex. It had to do with her life, her future. A new kind of excitement came over her as she thought about the unknown and what it might bring. She sensed it would be love and contentment and something more that she had never had before. She felt happy and secure. She could wait for it to come. Her emotions were aroused, principally gratitude at being who and what she was, and tears came to her eyes. She opened her handbag, the only thing she had brought with her from Livakia, and saw a small jeweller's box inside. There was no note. She was surprised. So that was where he had been when she had awakened. She looked at the closed box for several seconds and then she opened it. Inside was a pair of antique Byzantine earrings. She gasped. They were magnificent. Large and long, of twenty-two carat gold and blood red rubies. They belonged in a museum or on an ancient Queen of Byzantium. She knew she must keep them, she knew he had sent them as a memento of where they had been, how far they had gone together.

She arrived at the Connaught with no luggage but several smart Bond Street shopping bags. The luggage came later, empty, but was soon filled with goodies from Fortnum's and Harrod's Food Hall, Carlucci's and Camisa's. A little something for everyone. She did Jermyn Street for shirts from Turnbull and Asser for Manoussos and Elefherakis, and one for Max – she usually bought him a box of cigars. A blank notebook, its cover all flowers, for Rachel. Her housekeeper, gardener,

Katzakis, so many of her Livakian friends, got small mementos that she picked up from all over London, little nonsenses that were practical and which she knew they would like. She was on a happy shopping spree for herself and her friends until the day she returned for more tea and coffee from Fortnum's. She spotted a large tin of Royal Blend, Arnold's favourite tea, and plucked it off the shelf, annoyed with herself because she had almost forgotten to buy it for him. It was in her hand and she was handing it over to the tailcoated assistant when she realised why she had forgotten to buy it. Arnold was no more, Arnold was dead, and Melina was no more than a young life wasting away in a Greek prison.

How could she have forgotten that? She came over quite dizzy and could hardly catch her breath. The sales attendant came to her rescue and ushered her to a chair. A glass of water was produced, and she was, after several minutes, quite recovered, but feeling foolish and embarrassed over the incident that had caused such a flurry.

She went to have some lunch and sat alone, quiet and contemplative. This London life and such extravagance were too much for her. She had never been born to it, it had no meaning for her, it was hard work and not at all rewarding. Oh, yes, it was fun to have the things she had bought, and even more fun to know that she could afford to go on such sprees, but it was poor fodder compared to the way she lived and worked in Livakia. She had fought hard to climb out of poverty, and she had fought even harder to retain her understanding of the meaning of life and pleasure instilled in her by Brett. So extravagance was fun, but in the end all whipped cream with no real cake to bite into. She was ready to go home.

Nevertheless she remained in London several more days for the exhibitions she wanted to see, the theatre, a concert, some ballet, lunch and dinner with several old friends. She had dined at Wilton's and the River Cafe and Tante Claire and several more first-class London restaurants. The food had been delicious, a far cry from the simple Greek cuisine of the Kavouria, and yet there was a sameness about the dining and the socialising, the rushing about to enjoy the big city life. In Livakia she never sensed that sameness to every waking hour. She never missed her extravagant excursions such as the one she was presently on. But in London she did miss Crete.

On occasion she thought about her days and nights with Brandon, and was amused when she saw a full window display of his latest book in Hatchard's. She actually stood there for several minutes and said to herself, 'I've been there, done that,' and walked down the street with a broad smile on her lips.

For her last morning in London she walked the streets and window shopped and bought Brett a birthday present to keep for her next birthday celebrations. And then she took the plane for Athens, and made her connection for Crete. From London in the morning to Livakia and dining at the Kavouria at eleven that same night. Life was indeed rich and wondrous.

Nothing had changed. The pace was the same, and the faces, though some were missing. Max was on a trip to Africa, and all the talk was of that. Everyone knew that he had African connections. That had been where he had made all his money, selling commodities to poor African countries. He had gone into it broke, struggling for survival in Livakia, and after three years had returned with millions in Swiss bank accounts, vowing never to work like that again. The life of a playboy was all he was after, he claimed, and that was the way he lived now.

He kept the business side of his life, how and where he'd made such vast sums of money in so short a time, pretty much a secret. But what he had not been able to keep secret was his fascination with and the many things he loved about Africa and the African people. Max had the third fax machine in the village, and like D'Arcy was linked to the outside world by computer technology.

The Livakians were fascinated by the secret, mysterious side of Max's African life that had been, a glimpse of which they would get when, on rare occasions, he would have as house guests some important black Africans or else some stunningly beautiful, tall and slender black woman from Somalia or Ethiopia, as lover and companion for his usual brief period of time.

The talk about this latest trip he had suddenly taken off on was full of the usual speculations: gun running for some under-dog faction trying to take over a small country that could no longer bear its dictator bleeding it dry, or maybe organising mercenaries for the rebel faction of another. And when they weren't speculating on Max they were talking about Mark, a subject on which everyone had an opinion.

He was still in Athens but continually calling one friend or another, asking about the atmosphere in the village and for all the news. It was obvious he was under stress and drinking too much, missing his home and his friends. People were candid with him about their distress over his attacks on Arnold after his death. Mark was seeking forgiveness with every phone call, expressing how much he wanted to return but felt that he couldn't, the time was not yet right. And then, while talking one evening to Elefherakis, he said that he had taken legal advice and that as much as he wanted to he would not appear in court in Melina's defence. There had been a drunken confession to Elefherakis: he was infatuated with the girl and the dark side of her nature, and had been from the first time he saw her and picked her up and brought her into his house. He was in love with Melina though, before her arrest, he had not been able to accept that. Now he could and could do nothing about it.

D'Arcy was appalled at what she was hearing, thinking Mark's moral dilemma would haunt him forever. Aloud she said, 'He loves her but he's deserting her. I don't understand that.'

'I do,' Elefherakis told her. 'He's afraid of incriminating himself. He sees any further involvement on his part as putting himself under suspicion with the Greek authorities and his friends, both Greek and foreign, alienating himself even further from Livakia, his home and his work. He needs to clear his mind of this tragedy and the part he played in it so that he can come home and write.'

The table was quiet while listening to Elefherakis. It remained quiet until Manoussos spoke up. 'We Greeks are very generous. When he does return we'll receive him with open arms, even though we might never forget that he has been very foolish and destructive. Live and let live.'

D'Arcy was seated next to Manoussos. His humanity never ceased to amaze her. Now she reached up and pulled him towards her by his shirt collar, leaning closer and kissing him full on the mouth. Everyone began to clap and hoot and holler, and together, still in their kiss, they rose from their chairs and continued it in an embrace. Someone called for more wine, someone else for a platter of deep fried courgettes, and everyone teased them as they sat down.

Laurence watched D'Arcy and Manoussos from across the table. He tried to quell his yearning for her. He missed her kisses. But the yearning was short-lived as Caroline whispered, 'Why don't you kiss me the way that policeman kisses D'Arcy? Are they lovers?'

He lied to Caroline, only because he could not bear to think of Manoussos or any other man having her as he had had her, even though it was he who had really wanted his freedom. 'Maybe once, when they were children. They grew up together. Who knows about now?'

'I've brought you a new shirt from London,' D'Arcy told Manoussos.

He smiled at her and squeezed her hand. 'It's my day off tomorrow. Max has offered me his boat while he's away – we'll sail down the coast for lunch and visit Yannis, OK?'

Elefherakis, D'Arcy and Manoussos left the Kavouria together. They walked along the port and listened to D'Arcy talk about London, where she had been, what she had done. No one mentioned Brandon, though both men knew that she had been with him. Manoussos left Elefherakis to walk D'Arcy home; he had some reports to write, a fax to send, if they were going off in the morning. D'Arcy and he made arrangements to meet at seven on Max's boat, he kissed her and they parted.

In her house, D'Arcy offered Elefherakis a brandy. There was an autumnal chill in the air. D'Arcy lit the fire and then excused herself. When she returned she had in her hand the jewel box that Brandon had left in her handbag. She sat down next to Elefherakis and opened it. He clicked his tongue against the roof of his mouth in admiration of the earrings and said only one word: 'Magnificent!'

'It really is too much from a man who knows we will never have a repeat performance of what has been.'

'Obviously not.'

'What do you think I should do?'

'Wear them.'

Then they both looked away from the small treasure she had been presented with and D'Arcy gave Elefherakis a dazzling smile. 'That's what I thought,' she told him.

'At every opportunity,' he added as he plucked one from the box and carefully placed it on her ear lobe.

All the way home from her house to his, Elefherakis could not stop thinking about D'Arcy and how she had looked in her earrings. He imagined her naked with nothing on but those earrings and the Byzantine gold bracelets he had given her on her twenty-first birthday. With every year that went by she resembled her mother more and more. When she touched his arm, gave him a smile in a certain way, as she had tonight, there was so much of Brett in her he could hardly control himself for the desire he felt for her.

When she had kissed Manoussos in front of everyone he had recognised the sexual aura they created as a couple and it had made him dizzy with desire. He found her the most exotic, sensual woman he had ever known after Brett, and he wanted to make love to her, to fuck her until she screamed for him to stop. It had been like that in the past, a long time ago. He would have her now, maybe only once more, but yes, he would have her before the night was out. He was practically at his door when he turned round and walked, very nearly ran, back to her house.

When she answered his knock at the walled entrance to her house, he could see it in her eyes – she had expected him to return. 'It's been a very long time, my coming here like this,' he told her.

'Years,' was her answer.

She had changed into a diaphanous nightdress, her body could be seen through its seductively misty sheer silk. Like the finest spider's web, the silk rippled in the night breeze. She took him by the hand and together they walked along the paths and up the steps to her house.

Leading him through the rooms into her bedroom, she asked, 'Why now?'

'Why not now? You've come back from London and Brandon with a new sexual edge to you. Exciting, thrilling. I want a taste of this new you with nothing but your Byzantine earrings in your ears and your golden bracelets on your wrists.'

They smiled at each other. It was a knowing smile,

filled with affection and sexual memories of what had been. 'Wait here,' she told him, and walked from the bedroom into her bathroom, closing the door.

Elefherakis undressed and laid his things neatly over a chair. He went to her wardrobe and made a search for a dark blue silk damask robe of his that, years ago, when D'Arcy had admired it, he had given to her. He slipped it on but didn't bother to tie the belt. The bathroom door opened and she stood there with the light behind her. It made her hair, so long and luxuriant, look more tantalisingly red than ever. She wore her earrings and the bracelets on her wrists and had rouged her nipples so that they looked dark and sultry. Her mound, shaved of hair, had been decorated by Su Lee in henna, a pattern of squirls and curlicues. This was how she presented herself to Elefherakis.

He was dazzled by what he saw. She was standing very still, an erotic goddess. He walked up to her, opened his robe and placed a kiss upon her neck. He stepped closer to her, until he was hard against her, and held her with his strong hands cupping her breasts. The touch of his erect phallus against her body thrilled him.

'Don't say a word,' he commanded.

He touched the earrings and then the bracelets and then caressed her mound and told her, 'It suits you, you're ravishing.' Rubbing up against her, the feel of her skin, the scent of her, made him crazy with desire. She had always done that for him, from the very first time he had had her. D'Arcy had something about her sexually that made him take her roughly. She was like the calm before the storm and he wanted the storm, instantly. Wildly, ruthlessly to take sexual possession of her.

He had been one of her first lovers, seducing her after he had discovered that she had been having sex with Manoussos. She had been fifteen years old, his Lolita, and he had helped to create in her the erotic, very carnal lady that was now standing before him. He took her roughly, again and again, and the more she gave way to his lust, the more control he had over her sexuality. Elefherakis was powerfully strong and when he came he crushed her to him in an embrace which D'Arcy feared would break her bones. He had taken her standing up, pressed against the wall of her bedroom. Elefherakis had tremendous sexual stamina and control and he had been a long time in coming, long enough for D'Arcy herself to have come several times. Now, when he withdrew from her, he had to prop her against the wall with one hand or she would have slipped to the floor.

He was short of breath from his exertions but looking at her, still with her earrings in place, as ravishing as when she had stepped into the doorway, only now with the look of sexual bliss in her eyes and the expression on her face, he was able to calm himself. He was delighted to have had such a gift as D'Arcy had just given him. A woman who created herself as he had wanted her, a carnal goddess, wanting to be riven by him. Only a woman as generous and wise, as stable and secure, as D'Arcy could bestow such gifts as total submission to a man's lust and yet never lose her essential self; she merely lent it. He placed an arm round her and together they went to her bed.

*   *   *

The following morning D'Arcy was on her way to meet Manoussos when she saw Laurence sitting alone over coffee. This was particularly early for him, and where was Caroline? She would have liked to avoid him but that was impossible. He rose from his chair and she was yet again reminded of how good those two years had been with him. She put that out of her mind. There was still an attraction there but . . . They greeted each other and D'Arcy hurried past him just as a beautiful tiny Italian girl who had been at the Kavouria the night before went rushing into his arms. He looked round and seemed relieved that they had not been seen by anyone except D'Arcy.

She had heard that from the first day Lady Caroline had arrived in Livakia he was also sneaking round having erotic liaisons with every other attractive visitor to the village, and she was none the wiser for it.

It was only much later in the day, when they were sailing back to Livakia and D'Arcy had an overwhelming desire to make love to Manoussos, that she realised that since she had left Laurence she had been on a sexual spree with men other than him, to satisfy carnal desire, for pleasure and the sheer fun of sex, for the excitement and the adventure lust can afford, and for the bliss of orgasm . . . but more than all these things because she was trying to forget love.

Chapter 11

It was mid-October now and the skies were clear of cloud and as blue and bright as if it were mid-summer. These were days when the sun was hot and the weather warm enough for swimming, but the nights were drawing in. In the evening they still sat out at tables in the port but wore a shawl or a jumper. A breeze with the scent of the coming winter in it rustled the white paper tablecloths. Only house guests arrived, no tourists. They would stay away until spring of the new year.

In the weeks after D'Arcy's return from London, there were other returns: Max's to a hero's welcome. He had been found out. Much to his consternation, he made the cover of *Paris Match* as the guiding force behind a flight of thirty cargo planes of food aid: wheat, beans, milk, into Somalia, all privately sponsored by several African countries. No fuss, no bother from warlords, no hold ups on the airfield, no ransom for trucks or petrol to run them to the most needy in the remote areas of the country, no stealing, no looting. He was either piloting or on the ground, overseeing the army of workers unloading the cargo planes before the propellers had even been cut. In twenty-four hours he had done what no aid organisation had been able to achieve, no UN diplomats had been able to negotiate. He put a great many people and countries who had failed in their efforts to help the people of Somalia in the shade and there was little they could do about their own embarrassment. He went in unofficially, with no other intention than that of delivering his cargo, and had pulled a lot of strings to do it. The photograph that appeared showed him in a beat up fedora, dark sunglasses, an open white shirt and jeans. An Uzi machine-gun slung by a leather strap over his shoulder lay under his arm, a pistol in a holster on his hip. The only thing he would say about it was: 'That fucking *Paris Match*! It's an invasion of my privacy.'

Edgar Marion and Bill Withers returned after several weeks in New York. They had fled there in distress over the murder and how it was affecting Livakia. When they returned their habitual bickering was gone and they spoke happily about New York and were as amusing as ever.

And then there was a surprise return. Laurence was sitting with Max on the quay. Tonight was to be poker night at Max's house and the game was short handed. Lunch over, they were lingering with yet another bottle of wine and talking about who should replace the absentee poker player. Max's poker night was a serious social event among the men of Livakia.

She was still quite a distance away when she caught Laurence's eye. He was immediately distracted from his conversation with Max. She was tall and slender and dressed in a pair of wide white linen trousers, a long-sleeved fingertip-length shirt with a dropped shoulder worn over them. The light was behind her and you could see the faint outline of her slim figure. She wore flat sandals and her walk was a slow and elegant stride. She had very long thick wavy auburn hair with shades of gold in it worn swept back. No make-up on her face but a magnificent bone structure and a skin that had a luminescent quality, like smooth clear alabaster. She was probably the most beautiful woman he had ever seen. To see her was to fall in love with her, this vivacious and fascinating creature who enchanted Laurence even before he realised that he was, for the first time, seeing the woman he had only known before as a legendary figure: Brett Montesque, D'Arcy's mother.

She had appeared as if from nowhere, strolling along the corniche towards the port. When Max realised that he had lost Laurence's attention, he followed his gaze, turned and rose from his own chair to watch her. He smiled, feeling real pleasure to see Brett again. He saw Katzakis with a broom in hand about to do his afternoon sweep of the cobblestones in front of his shop. Without taking his gaze from Brett, Max called out to him, 'Katzakis, raise your eyes and see who's come home!'

Katzakis walked across the stones to stand next to him. 'Old friends, they stay with you all your life,' he said, handed Max the broom and started walking across the port to greet Brett. By the time he reached her several people were already by her side, shaking hands, kissing her first on one cheek then the other. There were hugs from Maria and her husband Manolis, the owners of the Kavouria. Max handed the broom to Laurence and went to join Brett's welcome committee. The poker game was immediately forgotten.

233

People were receiving Brett with love and admiration on a scale such as Laurence had never seen them show anyone before, with the possible exception of D'Arcy. Their hearts were genuinely in it, there was a bond between them and Brett. Later on, when he had left the broom behind and joined the group around Brett and was introduced to her, he listened to them all catching up with each other's news. That was how he realised they had that same bond with all of Brett's children and her two men. These were people who had shared hard times together, years of living from hand to mouth, and Brett, just as they had, had struggled to bring up her children and give them the best she could. This cool and elegant beauty with a quiet simplicity, a certain stillness, who had an enticingly mysterious quality about her, had shared her life with them, been part of their community. She had lived in Livakia when the village was very poor and only sparsely populated, the villagers struggling for survival and helping each other in the hard times, when a foreigner living among them was an oddity. Several of them remarked how sad they had all been when she had sailed away with her last-born infant in her arms, and the other children they had loved and cared for.

Brett took a white handkerchief from her pocket and wiped away the tears at the corners of Maria's eyes. 'I never thought I would ever see a tear in Maria's eye. What is it about Brett? Why do they love her so much?' Laurence asked Max in a near whisper.

'They share similar traits: Cretan courage and pride, toughness and resilience, a joy in life and love, and a passion for their island. And in all their years here, Brett and her children never abused their trust and friendship. To men and women alike she was the romantic they could never be, living a life they could never have. She lived openly but discreetly with two men, was a fabulous mother to four children, had many lovers and still managed to win the Cretan women over to her as friends. She seduced them by just being true to herself and they learned from her what a real liberated lady can be. And of course there was something else – she was then, as she is now, an incredibly beautiful, self-contained woman. To them she looked like a combination of one of those exquisite, seductive and charismatic goddesses of Classical Greek mythology who had come to live among them. Look at their faces, that's how they think of her even now.'

'Max.' Brett extended her hand and he took it and kissed it.

'Welcome home.'

Laurence watched them talking. Max seemed different with her, full of admiration. He made her laugh and it was soft and with a lilt to it, just like D'Arcy's. There was that same softness in her honeyed voice, and she spoke in short sentences and was sparing of words, also like D'Arcy. He suddenly realised that all these qualities he was so enamoured of in Brett were those same qualities that D'Arcy had had and he had thrown away. The fact that D'Arcy engendered from everyone who knew her the same sort of adoration as Brett was receiving now was something he had never taken notice of before. Laurence was appalled to discover he had been reticent to give D'Arcy those same things unconditionally from sheer inability to express the depth of his feeling for her.

He heard Brett tell Katzakis, 'They are fine. Look, here they come now, the fathers of my children.' And she stood up and waved. Several people including Katzakis left the group seated and now drinking ouzo to go and greet the two men walking into the port on either side of D'Arcy.

Seeing Brett and the two fathers was to throw into Laurence's face his own snobbishness, one of the sides of his character which had held him back from a real commitment to D'Arcy. Her illegitimacy, her unconventional upbringing and the life she was now living had in the end defeated him, and now he was realising his own small-mindedness, his meanness of spirit. He had been seduced by D'Arcy, loved her, been fascinated by her. How could he have let her go?

Brett and her longtime lovers, whom the Cretans always referred to as her 'husbands', were fêted night after night by their old friends. And they in turn entertained with picnics and excursions to places in Crete they wanted to visit, and people they wanted to see. One of her 'husbands' was beloved, a hero to the Cretans because he had fought in the resistance against the Germans who had invaded Crete during the Second World War. Even now, fifty years later, he was beloved by them, an adored figure. Elefherakis spent a great deal of time with Brett, and Manoussos was most always given a seat close to her at dinner parties; he had been in and out of her house as much as his own as a child. Edgar and Bill gave a grand dinner party for her and sat with her at every chance they could get. She had always been a heroine to them.

All this Laurence watched in wonder. It was one thing to hear about a legend; one could always have doubts about the validity of what one heard. Laurence had always assumed that exaggeration about Brett and her seductive charms was the real order of things. How he would have loved to have been proven right! He had his chance to speak at length with Brett several times while she was in Livakia: a day out in her company, being seated next to her at a lunch party, a walk with her through the gorge along with several others. He was only proven wrong.

He had used Brett and her lifestyle, how she had brought up her children, against D'Arcy. Had he expected D'Arcy to revert into someone who would one day be an embarrassment to him, thanks to her unconventional background? He had no idea what he'd expected but it certainly had not been that he would be overwhelmed by the stock she came from, that he found she was every inch her mother's daughter and more remarkable than he had dared to give her credit for. He knew days before Brett and her husbands left Livakia that he had to have D'Arcy back, that she must return to him. He would go to D'Arcy as soon as Brett left, tell her how much he loved her, what a fool he had been, how he had come to his senses and would break off with Caroline.

Brett and D'Arcy's fathers had arrived on a three-masted schooner. They had dropped anchor just off the bay where Brett's house stood and that was how she had managed to surprise everyone by merely appearing in the port. It was no grand entrance, and when she left a week later it was with no grand exit. Only D'Arcy waved goodbye to her parents in the dawn light as they set their sails for the coast of North Africa.

For days people did nothing but talk about how very good it had been to have Brett back, how she had hardly changed with the years, and how clever she was to have kept her two lovers by her side. It was revealed only after she had sailed away that she had given a rare Byzantine icon to the church in Livakia, a gift from her family for the years of kindness the village had shown her. People flocked to see it.

For several days after Brett sailed away D'Arcy was incredibly busy. She had finished the bit part she had been commissioned to design for the German automobile company, and it had been accepted. She seemed to be constantly tying up details with lawyers for the contract and the patent rights. Laurence bided his time. He knew very well how she worked, as did everyone else in Livakia: a stint of isolation, concentration till the work was done, and then when she had achieved her objective it was over, forgotten, and she was back to the life of pleasure seeking.

The day D'Arcy emerged triumphant was the same day that Melina's trial for murder began in Iraklion. Manoussos was there, Dimitrios and Max. They were all witnesses for the prosecution. Much to everyone's relief the story was very much played down by the press. The Livakians were taking it in their stride; they did, after all, know what the outcome was going to be. Melina would be convicted of murder and given a lenient sentence because it had been a crime of passion by a young girl with an unfortunate history.

That was discovered by her defence lawyers with the help of some very discreet sleuthing by Manoussos who secretly came to Melina's aid when not one character witness, Mark having withdrawn from his promise, could be found. Her history, combined with its being a crime of passion, was her only hope for leniency.

Now all the talk round the village was of who and what Melina really was. She had been born in a small village on the side of Mount Ida. Her mother, the poorest widow in the village, strange in many ways, some said retarded, died when she was born. In life she had been looked down upon by all the village for her poverty, her volatile nature, widowhood, and giving birth to an illegitimate child. Not one man went forth to claim the infant and give it a name. Someone left the baby, only hours old, at the priest's house in the next village. That was how Melina's life began. At six months she was in an orphanage in Iraklion and at five years old in a foster home where she was physically and sexually abused, barely fed and on rare occasions schooled until she ran away from the alcoholic fisherman who had kept her. That was four years before she arrived in Livakia. And for those four years the child had wandered round Crete, living from hand to mouth and dependent on the generosity of strangers, each of whom she had abused or stolen from in turn. Her whoring was played down in the courtroom as was her sexual relationship with Arnold, much to the relief of all concerned. The prosecution didn't need it, the defence didn't want it.

D'Arcy came down to the port and sat at a table near the water. She opened the cardigan she was wearing. There was still heat in the sun, more than she had realised when she had dressed that morning. Plates of ripe purple figs, slices of ham, and a bottle of Domestica white wine were set before her. She ignored them all. She could not seem to get Melina and her life story out of her mind. She might have had she not continually received calls from Mark, still in Athens, reminding her of the girl's isolation. He displayed a decidedly strange sense of guilt one minute, complete lack of remorse for his part in the disastrous farrago the next.

The call she had had from him this morning, just before she left her house, had been pathetic, and when she had tried to put Mark out of his misery by telling him that Melina had been born a damaged child, and briefly discussed her history, she was shocked to find that he knew nothing about it, nor did he want to. 'Once this damned trial is over, I'm through with this dreadful mess that Arnold has caused and I'll be able to put it behind me and get on with my writing,' he had exclaimed quite sharply before hanging up on her. Could he be so blind? Or was it a matter of, had he to be so blind?

A shadow crossed her table and the warmth of the sun disappeared. It brought her out of her thoughts and she looked up. Laurence loomed above her.

'May I sit down?'

She was actually relieved at the distraction. 'Sure, why not?'

He took a seat next to her and the sun came back to warm her face. She plucked a fig from the chipped white plate. 'Have one, they'll be the last before winter.'

She watched him split open the fig and suck out the

sensuous pink flesh of the fruit. How she liked his looks, how she had liked sex with him, his intelligence, wit and laughter. D'Arcy missed him. She took a slice of the pink ham and an already peeled fig and rolled them together, taking a bite.

'You seemed very far away.'

'Only as far as the courtroom and Melina.'

'They expect a quick verdict and then we can put her in the past tense.'

'Can we as easily as that? I wonder. What about Arnold? A quiet, unassuming, considerate human being in spite of his minor defects and overpowering weaknesses – will he be relegated to the past tense so easily? I somehow don't think that such a shocking end is easily forgotten, any more than his killer will be. Do you really think it can be, Laurence?'

'Life goes on, D'Arcy. We live, we make mistakes, we suffer for others' mistakes – but life does go on. That's what I want to talk to you about . . . us. My having made a grave mistake about us, and how I had to lose you to understand how much I love you, how much more of myself I want to give you, and without reservation. If you will give me another chance?'

D'Arcy was silent for several minutes. She looked away from him and out over the water. It was ten in the morning and the port was busy with people arriving to do their morning chores, or having a coffee while waiting for the boat to bring the morning post. She was acutely aware of her friends' and neighbours' lives going on all round her, so much so that she turned in her chair to look away from the sea and at them.

'Why don't you say something, D'Arcy?'

She turned her attention back to him, and gazing straight into his eyes answered, 'Because I don't know what to say.'

'You still love me, you still want me and for us to be together, that's what you could say. That's what would make me happy, put me out of my misery.'

'What if that's true, Laurence? It doesn't mean that either of us has changed, that we can give each other what was missing in our relationship before.'

'We can try, work at it.'

'We did try, we did work at it, for two years. A fundamental change will have had to have taken place in each of us if we're to be happy together. I don't know that that's happened. I don't want to live with a man who has to work at loving me, who is always trying to give of himself as much as I need from him. That's too much like hard work and only breeds resentment. I don't want a man who resents loving me. I didn't realise that when I left you, but I do now.'

'You left me too hastily. We should have talked this out.'

'That's true, we should have. So what? We're doing it now, and does it change anything? I don't think so. And how genuine are your feelings now? We have to ask that, not only you of yourself, but me of myself. Arnold's death has reminded us of our own mortality, not just you and me but everyone here in Livakia, and that's affected us all in one way or another. The details of his life and his weaknesses have been set out to be scrutinised, and along with looking over his we've all had a good look at our own. Maybe that's what's brought on this change of heart of yours and no more than that. And if that's the case it's not enough to build a life on.'

'But how will we know unless we give each other another chance?'

D'Arcy finished her ham and fig titbit, and had a drink from her glass of wine. Then she spoke. 'I don't suppose we will.'

'I love you, D'Arcy.'

'And Caroline?'

'I never loved her as I love you. I've never loved any woman as I love you.'

'Does she understand that?'

'No, but she will. I'll tell her that I loved her on the rebound and she'll understand that. She's sensible, and very English. Pride and good breeding will demand that she leave me with a stiff upper lip and no scenes.'

D'Arcy, as sorry as she felt for Caroline, could not keep herself from bursting into laughter. Laurence couldn't help but laugh himself.

'We're wicked to laugh,' D'Arcy told him.

'Yes, we are, but it's true. You know how we English hate to show our feelings.'

'And you do love her?'

'Yes, I do, but not as much as I love you. I love her for all the things you are not and never can be, things I know now I can live without.'

'I wonder.'

'You haven't said you love me.'

'I'm not sure that I do anymore. Maybe it's a love hangover and nothing more than that.'

'I've never known you to be so blunt, so questioning of your feelings.'

D'Arcy stood up and he followed. They gazed across the table at each other. 'Laurence, I want to believe you love me, that you've changed and are willing to share a life with me, not just looking for another game of love-lend-lease. You do what you have to about Caroline and I'll do what I have to about you.'

She began to walk away. He reached out and grabbed her by the arm. She gazed down at his hand and then at him and he released her. He made no apology, merely asked, 'That's it?'

'I think that's quite a lot, Laurence. The ball's in your court,' were her last words to him before she walked away.

D'Arcy did want to believe she had acted hastily in leaving Laurence but if that was true only his actions, his behaviour, could make her believe it. She was still attracted to him sexually, emotionally; even now his intelligence and dry English sense of humour were something she enjoyed enormously and liked having in her life. And there was also something essential and not to be forgotten – he did love her, she was certain that he did, as much as he could love anyone other than himself.

The following day she made a trip to Chania and when she returned three days later stopped briefly in the port and then went directly home. D'Arcy was quite exhausted. She had taken the mountain route home and it had been an arduous journey: two small landslides and one puncture which, thanks to two hunters to whom she had given a lift, she had got over without too much difficulty. The 2CV had as usual behaved admirably.

It was late afternoon and she was lying on the chaise on the terrace of her house. She heard someone below in one of the lower walled gardens. She knew it had to be Manoussos, he was the only one who visited her via the gardens. She rose to sit on the wall overlooking them and called down to him, 'You're home then.'

'Yesterday,' he called up to her, and took the steps two at a time.

Tired as she was, seeing him somehow gave her new energy. She remained seated on the wall and waited for him to arrive. When he did, he kissed her and stroked her hair and sat down on the wall next to her.

'I saw you from my office window, that's how I knew you were home. Max and I came over the same road you took to come home. He was with me in my office when one of my men called in his report and said he had seen you on the road heading for home. Max is worried about you and the 2CV. He says I'm to talk you into accepting a gift he wants to make to you, a four-wheel-drive jeep like the ones we have. It might be a good idea, D'Arcy, if you're going to continue taking the remote mountain roads.'

'Oh, never mind all that. Melina? She was convicted, of course?'

'Yes.'

'What was her sentence?'

D'Arcy could not understand it. She thought she had emotionally distanced herself from the tragedy of Melina's life and yet when she was waiting to hear the girl's fate, she felt her blood run cold. She knew that all colour had drained from her face and that Manoussos was seeing her as pale as a ghost. She placed her hand over her mouth as she felt the nausea rise. She held it there, hoping to hold back the sickness she was feeling in the pit of her stomach. Tears filled her eyes.

Manoussos placed an arm around her shoulders, took a handkerchief from his pocket and put it in her hand. Then he walked her to the chaise where she had been resting and from the table next to it took the jug and poured her a glass of sweet iced mint tea. He held it to her lips and she drank the glass nearly empty. A sigh that seemed to come from the depths of her soul and she was right again, very much in control of herself.

'I don't know what came over me. It was as if someone had walked over my grave.'

'Are you all right now?' There was serious concern in his voice. This was unlike D'Arcy, a side of her he had never seen before.

'Yes, quite all right. I promise you I am.' And she smiled at him. 'Was her sentence fair? Has justice been done?'

'Can justice ever be done for the crime of taking another man's life? That's real sin, real evil. That being said, she was given a fair trial, and I do believe, with certain reservations, her sentence was a just one. Fifteen years. Melina will still be a young woman when she is set free, but what kind of a woman?'

D'Arcy had no idea what she had expected. Life in prison? Thirty, forty years? Fifteen years didn't seem much for Arnold's life. Yet fifteen years in a Cretan prison with hardened criminals: never to wander under a blue sky and a hot sun, to swim in the sea, to smell the wild rosemary and basil in the hills, never to see the stars and the moon. Locked doors for fifteen years. For a gypsy like Melina, that was a life sentence. She didn't read or write, had no friends, no family, not even a bad lover like Mark to help her through the years. All these things raced through D'Arcy's mind even though she felt no distress about the sentence, felt nothing except the consequences of it.

Manoussos had said it all when he had asked if justice is ever done in cases like this. Even if Melina had been given a death sentence, a life for a life, would justice have been done? D'Arcy didn't know and probably never would.

'Manoussos, you said you have reservations about the sentence?'

'Melina needs more than punishment, she needs serious help. Fifteen years for a fourteen-year-old girl to make herself ready to step back into society, with no one to help change the direction of her life? She is a hardened criminal, but a very young one. Society helped to create this monster. Should it not at least take on the responsibility of teaching her a better way to live, give her twisted and abused mind some attention, a chance of healing in these years she's to be locked away? I don't want a killer with no remorse for her crime roaming free on Crete in fifteen years' time, or anywhere else for that matter. These are big reservations, and ones I intend to do something about. A psychiatrist, a social worker, whatever and whoever I can find who will be a constructive and healing element during her years in prison – that's all I can do for Melina Philopopolos and my law-enforcing job, maybe even for myself.

'Now enough about Melina. Let's talk about Max, and a new jeep. In fact, I think I want to break a confidence and tell you something that Max told me, only because I think it's something you should know. Something he blurted out one night in Iraklion, when we had had a little too much wine and were under some emotional pressure during the trial. You know Max, as soon as he realises he has placed himself in a corner, he cleverly wriggles his way out of it. But it was too late. I pretended I didn't take it all in but I did and . . .'

Manoussos was interrupted first by the opening of a door and then the sound of Laurence calling, 'D'Arcy, it's me.'

It would be unfair to say that she had not thought about Laurence and their conversation in the port during the days she had been away. She had. She had wanted to believe that he loved her and in those days away had come a long way towards believing that they might indeed have another chance for a good life together. She was therefore not surprised by his visit, more delighted. Presumably it meant he had sent Caroline away.

It was Laurence who was surprised. He had not expected to find D'Arcy with Manoussos, or anyone else for that matter. Manoussos was his friend, but more than once when he'd seen him with D'Arcy Laurence had wished his friend was a little less handsome, a little less attractive to women, that the long-standing friendship and erotic past he had had with D'Arcy did not exist, that they didn't love each other nor were as close as they were to each other. Everyone in Livakia knew that whatever they were or were not to each other that was the way it was always going to be for them. Laurence stood there, not knowing quite what he wanted to say.

Manoussos might have been surprised to see him there a week ago, but not now. He had seen Caroline and her luggage stowed on board the boat that would take her down the coast to catch the aeroplane for London. He had only to look at D'Arcy's face to see the happiness in her eyes, a certain lustful cheekiness in the way she moved, the way she held her head. She was interested once again in Laurence, and that was enough to send Manoussos away. He always wanted for D'Arcy what D'Arcy wanted.

He was in uniform and Manoussos always knew how to use that to best advantage. 'Well, I've got to get back to the station. See you.' He kissed D'Arcy on the cheek and patted Laurence on the shoulder as he passed by him. 'Maybe see you guys later at the Kavouria, or the garden restaurant. And then again, maybe not.'

'Yes, maybe,' answered Laurence, and shot a friendly punch at Manoussos's arm.

That was it. It was just as simple as that. They were back together, even Manoussos had seen that. Laurence felt joyous, he wanted to shout the news to the whole world. D'Arcy felt the same way, her every gesture told him that. And then she said, 'And so it begins, the second time around. They always say that it's better the second time around.' There was a softness in her voice, a lovingness, a sensuality. He felt no hesitation in going to her, giving himself up to her.

He had her in his arms before they even heard the door shut behind Manoussos. He licked her lips with his tongue. He kissed her eyes and the tip of her nose and chin, and then he kissed her full on the lips – a kiss that was deep and searching and full of lust. They were here, wanting each other in a celebration of reunion and love. 'Tell me you love me, you've missed me?' he begged her in between kisses.

'I love you, I did miss you, and, oh, does it feel good to be back in your arms,' she told him in a voice husky with desire.

He had her blouse off and his hands fondled her breasts. He wanted her as he always wanted her, giving herself up to him in uncontrolled carnal lust. The sun was going down and there was a cool breeze coming off the sea. They walked from the terrace into the house leaving a trail of clothes as they disrobed. He sensed in D'Arcy a new kind of eroticism, and that was before she slipped away from him into the bathroom and reappeared as she had before Elefherakis.

She did it again, that same thing she could always do for Laurence – break through any last vestige of sexual inhibition he might have. He had never seen her as she appeared to him now, the ultimate seductress, a magnificent sexual goddess in her golden earrings and rouged nipples, the henna-decorated mound, golden bracelets on her wrists. Walking towards him, even her long and shapely legs were another erotic image of sensual excitement. They were both aware that they had come together for a night of sex where they would, each of them, pare themselves down to the basics of sexual desire, where they could put aside their egos and the outside world, any moment but the very moment they were living in, and take each other over for the sake of erotic passion, sexual oblivion.

He was sitting on the end of the bed. She went up to him, straddled him and sat on his lap. In the hope of composing himself, he closed his eyes for a moment, but there was no hope of accomplishing that. She had already seduced him, and his mind was racing over all the many different ways he would have sex with her, how he would master this depraved woman he loved, how he would like to tame her, no matter how harsh the method, but tame her for being the sexual animal who had her sexual teeth into him and would never let him go.

D'Arcy placed her arms round his neck. She rubbed her breasts up against him, and kissed him full on the mouth. His lips parted and their kiss deepened: the warmth and smoothness inside their mouths, tongues licking, mouths sucking – they each of them felt themself drowning in sensuous kissing. She ran her fingers through his hair and pulled tight on it. She was brimming, on the very edge of orgasm. Not yet, not yet, she told herself, and so pulled back from the kiss, put her hands on his shoulders and leaned away from him.

Laurence no longer saw her as the woman he loved, but as a woman who wanted to go on an erotic journey with him as captain of their destiny. He knew what took her over the edge, every erogenous zone that could make her his sexual slave, how she lived to give herself up to sex. He took her raunchy rouged nipples one at a time in his mouth and sucked deeply on them until he heard her sighs of pleasure, felt the sexual tension in her become very nearly uncontainable, and it was then that he raised her up to sit her hard down on his fully erect and pulsating penis. So harsh was his thrust that she cried out, lost control of herself, and came in a long and thrilling orgasm. He pulled back her head by a handful of her hair and before he ravaged her with another kiss, told her, 'I love you, I have always loved you from that first time I saw you, and I want you as I have never wanted any other woman I've ever known. I give you my life.'

LIVAKIA
and IRAKLION

Chapter 12

For several days, sex and togetherness took over D'Arcy's and Laurence's lives. Happiness, and especially a new kind of happiness with someone you believe yourself to be in love with, can be like an aphrodisiac: you always want more of it and to fill your life with such a profound feeling. Well, at least D'Arcy did.

No one seemed to be surprised that Caroline had vanished from Livakia and Laurence and D'Arcy were together again. It hardly caused any comment at all, any more than Mark Obermann's return had. He arrived with yet another pretty young thing who was dazzled by the idea of being the life and love of a possibly great literary figure who lived a romantic life on a Greek island. He settled into the community as if the tragedy had never occurred and was once again accepted by everybody. Arnold's death was never mentioned, not even in passing. If Mark and Arnold's other friends, who had for so many years shared the life of the expatriate with them, were sad that Arnold was no longer among them, there was no hint of it.

The boyish good looks, the Mark Obermann charm, and a love light in his eyes for the new girlfriend, gave the Cretans a basis to think of Melina's relationship with Mark as one based on charitable, brotherly love – that is if they even thought of it at all. They felt now as they always did, close to him because of the unswerving love and loyalty he showed to Greece, the Greek people, and in particular Crete.

D'Arcy, when she could for a second step back from her own happiness and observe Mark's return and everyone's reaction to it, could see that Laurence was right: life does go on. Except for the absence of Arnold, the laughter and wit, the minute trials and tribulations of living in paradise were very much the same. Mark drank more, much more, but he spouted the same old rhetoric and was still the great orator and brilliant intelligent mind, still the enchanter, the seducer of women promising sex and love in every glance. She wanted to enjoy him as she once had but the memory of their last telephone conversation before his return kept putting her off.

He had told her, 'It's all right for you, you who have everything. Oh, how I would like it to be all right for me. Of course I'm in love with Melina, of course I hated Arnold, despised him actually. Yes, I did poison Melina's mind with my detestation of Arnold. I have never stopped wanting Melina, never for a day will I stop wanting her. I love everything about her – her body, her illiteracy, the fact that she was orphaned from birth, her poverty, her cunning, her dishonesty, her sexual depravity, all that's dark and evil in her nature. Yes, I have enjoyed and loved it all. She loves me, had often told me she would sacrifice anything for me, and she proved it. She killed Arnold, as much for me as she did for herself. I thrill to her adoration of me. The fact that I returned her love, embraced the dark side of her soul, was enough for her to get rid of the one thorn in my side. The living ugliness, weakness, failure, most especially failure. All that I despise was there in Arnold. Did she not do us all a favour by ridding us of such a drag on our society?

'I would not have chosen for her to murder Arnold but she did, and I have no intention of suffering his death as I suffered his life. If that means deserting Melina, believe me she will understand it. Her kind of love would.'

D'Arcy and Laurence were walking to his house after having lunch with half a dozen others in the garden restaurant. She was taken aback when he commented, 'You don't seem to find Mark as amusing as you used to, and he was very amusing at lunch today. Have you lost your sense of humour?'

They were in a narrow lane, climbing steps walled in by high white walls. D'Arcy stopped. She had been amused, very much so, but then she had remembered that last conversation and it was true, she had been distracted from her amusement for a few seconds. Had it been so obvious that Laurence should have picked it up? Well, obviously it had. She had never mentioned that conversation to anyone and somehow she couldn't bring herself to mention it now to Laurence. 'No, I don't think I've lost my sense of humour. I actually found him extremely amusing, except for a few moments when my mind wandered away.'

He slipped his arm through hers and they continued their climb in silence. When they arrived home they opened a bottle of wine and took it to the bedroom, undressed and slipped between the sheets. It was siesta time but neither of them felt much like sleep. Laurence slipped an arm round her shoulders and she leaned in to him and rested her head against his chest. He kissed her several times and removed the book she had planned to read from her hands. She didn't mind. She kissed him lightly on the lips, caressed him. She felt easy and comfortable with him.

He stroked her hair and commented, 'It never ceases to amaze me how you can be so lovely and sweet, and at the same time such a whore in bed.'

D'Arcy's first reaction was to pull away from him in disbelief at what she was hearing. They gazed at each other. There was a look in his eyes that told her she had not misheard him.

'Don't glare at me like that, it was meant as a compliment.' He smiled at her, even gave her a little laugh.

'A compliment! You can't tell the difference between a woman who is steeped in sexuality, enjoys every aspect of the erotic and wants to share it with the man of her choice, and a woman who is paid for sex, who derives no personal pleasure from it? Are you mad?'

'Let's put it down to a bad choice of word and leave it at that.' And he pulled her back into his arms.

'I should think so, unless you do think that all women are whores?'

'Well, they are to a certain degree, even you must admit that.'

'Laurence!'

He laughed again, clearly enjoying this conversation with D'Arcy. 'You all use sex to hold a man, your mother being a case in point. Like mother like daughter, you might say.'

'How did my mother come into this, Laurence?'

'Well, she's a good example, isn't she? She's managed to keep two men for decades.'

'And you think she kept my fathers for all these years by sex and sex alone? Not only are you insulting Brett, you're blind. You've spent time with her and you didn't see what an unusual and special person she is? She has many more qualities than sex appeal and they have kept two extra special men constant in her life for all these years. Unless, of course, as I suggested before, you see all women as whores, and if that's true it must include me.'

'Look, if we're going to talk about this, darling, let's be frank. Can you honestly say that you've not cultivated the sexual side of your nature to capture a man and keep him? You've been doing it your whole life only you're a hopeless romantic like Brett, and dress it up as something more than that.'

'Max was right about you, you don't deserve me, and let me tell you why. Though you appreciate me, I'm really more than you want to take on. This stupid conversation, why are we having it? Because these last days together we've come closer than we have ever been, you've let go of your emotions and you want that to stop. You have a pattern, have worked it out, the very same way you worked it out before. You figure you've given me enough to live and be happy on, and I'm dizzy in love and I'll accept that it's better to have you and what I've got than not to have you at all. Hence your pulling back, putting me in a position where you leave me little to do but retreat, and all because you can't bear showing emotion. How very English of you, but not very English gentlemanly.'

'You are only partially right. You forgot to take into account our conversation of last night. I don't think I want a woman and certainly not a wife of mine chasing after lost causes. I've never asked you for much, D'Arcy, probably the only thing I have ever asked you to do for me was to give up this notion of yours to go to Iraklion to visit Melina and befriend her. I detest this idea of taking on the responsibility of helping her to make her years in prison constructive. The girl doesn't even like you and you never liked her. Are you playing the lady bountiful or is it moral guilt for having never done anything for her before she became a murderess? I would guess it is neither, just a romantic idea that you can contribute something to a wasted life.'

'Is that why you're so angry with me, why you feel you have to call me a whore, because I insist on doing something you disapprove of, getting involved where you would not?'

'It's an indication.'

'Of what, Laurence? That you can't control me, my heart? In that you are damned right!'

'You're no social worker, D'Arcy.'

'Nor do I intend to be. I'm just a whore with a heart.'

'Now you're being facetious.'

'Now you'd better go and call Caroline, and never expect me to return to you again. I told you before I wasn't sure about us. Now I am. We may have

260

been good lovers, you and I, but we've missed out
on love.'

D'Arcy was far more upset at this break-up with
Laurence than she was the first time around. Upset
with herself for having given him the benefit of the
doubt, and by the downfall of love. If she had learned
nothing else in those first days when she and Laurence
had come together again it was how good it was to be
in love, to have a romantic feeling for another human
being. That was what she had been looking for and the
only real reason for her return to Laurence.

One day they were inseparable and with eyes for no one
else; the next they were estranged, civil but at a distance
from each other. In a matter of days everyone realised
that it was over for them and this time it was final. Several
days later, D'Arcy watched him board the boat that would
take him down the coast where he was going overland to
the airport and back to England to give a series of lectures
at Oxford. But not before he approached her and took her
aside from the people she had been talking with to tell
her, 'I'm sorry it didn't work out for us. You may not
believe this but I will always love you and want you.'

'But not enough,' had been her reply.

'I can't let it end like this. Please can we be friends?'

'I think that's about all we ever were, erotic friends.
Now I suppose we'll be platonic friends.' She offered
him her hand and he kissed it and then kissed her on the
cheek and turned away.

What she had wanted to do was hit him over the
head with her shopping basket but they lived in a
small community that had seen enough violence and

bad behaviour among the foreigners. She had no desire to add to it.

It had been clouding over for several days now and people were spending more time in their houses, inviting others home for a meal more in the evening. D'Arcy was enjoying some solitude, catching up on her reading, going out for the odd dinner at someone's house or eating alone. She didn't much feel like entertaining. The days passed and life was full, peaceful and contented.

Several times while she was working in her garden she saw Max walking below on the way to the cove where he kept his plane. Most of the time there was someone with him. He always called to her and waved and invited her to go along with them. D'Arcy realised that there was something constant in their friendship and that she would have been the poorer for not having Max in her life. A day passed and she didn't see him and suddenly she realised that she missed him. She had somehow never missed him before and D'Arcy understood that she had always taken Max very much for granted.

The next time he came by, she called down to him, 'Hi there, handsome.'

His smile warmed her, his laughing eyes teased her. 'Hi D'Arcy, want to come with me?'

There was always a sexual innuendo in his every greeting or look. His asking, her rejecting sex. It had been going on for years, this flirtation that was almost but not quite a joke between them. She answered him with a question of her own. 'Want to come to dinner this evening?'

'What are you cooking?'

'I'm not going to tell you, let me surprise you?'

'Dinner *à deux*?'

'Maybe, maybe not.'

'No sex?' he teased.

'No, no sex, Max. God, you never do give up.'

'Well, so long as there's no sex involved, I'll come.' And he laughed and waved, calling out, 'Nine o'clock. Thanks, see you then.'

D'Arcy felt really pleased at having asked him. She called Manoussos and invited him to dinner as well. She thought of asking Rachel to make up the numbers but then thought better of it. She decided to indulge herself with the company of these two very attractive men. It somehow seemed right that it should be just the three of them.

After she finished her work in the garden she went into the house and sat down with her housekeeper, Poppy. Going through menus with her, D'Arcy decided to do the cooking herself. Poppy was surprised and so was she but D'Arcy really wanted to cook for Max, who was himself a marvellous cook and gourmet. Food, like sex, was written in bold letters at the top of his life's priority list.

D'Arcy had a large and well-stocked larder, a room constructed from a small cave on one of the upper levels of her property behind the house. One entered it through a four-inch thick wooden door and was taken over by the luscious smells: drying herbs hung in bunches from hooks fixed in the stone ceiling along with Italian and French cheeses, and cured meats. The air was dry and always cool, perfect for keeping them. There were shelves upon shelves of peaches and pears and cherries, lemons and oranges, olives of several varieties, dried tomatoes in olive oil, and artichokes. A variety of pickles and radishes preserved in Kilner jars. Large clay storage pots of foodstuffs and under a brightly coloured kilim carpet, a large and deep freezer chest. D'Arcy's larder was the envy of everyone in Livakia, most of whom had been there at one time or another to borrow something, or begging space for something special of their own for a short period of time.

D'Arcy made her selection, placed it in her basket, retreated back to the kitchen and went to work preparing the meal for her guests: fresh pasta tossed in double cream with long slivers of smoked salmon, for a first course, followed by four-inch thick charcoal grilled fillet steaks, which she had brought back from Allen the butcher's in Mount Street in London and had had stored in her freezer. To go with them a sauce bearnaise, courgettes stir fried in the finest cold pressed extra virgin oil, potatoes done in the oven in oil, fresh rosemary and turmeric until they were crisp and a bright yellow brown. For pudding a tarte tartin which always looked with its caramelised apples as delicious as it tasted, and which she planned to serve with clotted cream.

When the men arrived D'Arcy's cooking was under control but she was not yet down. Poppy let them in and served them American martinis. 'Oh, it's going to be this kind of evening, is it?' D'Arcy heard Max remark as she looked down into the hall from the gallery.

'Yes, Max, it is going to be that kind of an evening,' she called down, and quickly descended the stairs to meet her guests.

D'Arcy had taken special care to dress for her evening at home. Several times she told herself, 'This is not like you, D'Arcy Montesque,' and it wasn't. She rarely dressed to impress but found she was doing that this evening, and was surprised to realise that it was Max she was dressing for, Max she wanted to please. What a curious thing, she thought, since she knew that there was no need to impress Max. They were close friends after all.

There was no missing the look on Max's face when he saw D'Arcy. He was quite dazzled. Not that Manoussos wasn't. He had rarely, if ever, seen D'Arcy as elegantly put together as she was for her two men that evening.

She wore her hair long and loose as she always did, but on her ears the Byzantine earrings and around her neck a collection of Byzantine gold necklaces and several strands of oriental pearls. There were ivory bracelets on her wrists and between them gold bangles. Her collection of Byzantine jewellery was set off by the simplicity of her clothes: a low-necked white silk blouse with huge balloon sleeves that were tight to the wrist, which fitted loosely but seductively, revealing a hint of nipple and the distinct shape of her breasts. Around her waist an emerald green belt of heavy silk satin shone like a jewel and below that a full-length skirt of deep purple velvet. She wore crimson silk slippers on her feet.

'You look like a royal celebration, I'm duly dazzled,' said Max.

'Well, it's about time,' she answered, a smile on her lips. She kissed first Manoussos and then Max. Oh, how good it was to have such men as friends and lovers. Well, one as a lover.

They spoke of many things which included her final break-up with Laurence. It hardly bothered her at all. They laughed a great deal. D'Arcy was up and down from the table to the kitchen to do the cooking and Poppy did the serving.

It was inevitable that the conversation should come round to Melina. D'Arcy was surprised when Max told them, 'I never felt good about my part in trapping that girl the way I did, but it had to be done. And, as usual, Manoussos, you were right to have handled the capture of her in the way we did. I cannot, however, say that the experience of being there has not affected me. It has, quite deeply. Kind of a life lesson you can live without, but once having lived it, I find it has in some strange way changed my perception of things.'

'I wasn't there but I know what you mean, Max. I feel exactly the same way. I think for me it was the untimely death of a friend, having to face my own mortality, and she was the instrument that made me do that. In a strange way I feel indebted to her. Melina was one of the reasons for my final break-up with Laurence.'

D'Arcy then told them what had happened, and asked the men, 'Do you think there'd be any advantage to the girl if I did go and see her? If there isn't I have no need to go.'

They discussed it and yet again D'Arcy was surprised at the degree of understanding Max showed about her wanting to do something constructive for the girl and yet still remain in the background. It was he who came up with the suggestion that D'Arcy should find one of her many Cretan friends who might have the time and the compassion to deal with it, his point being that Melina would be less resentful towards a fellow Greek than she might be to a foreigner and especially one who had been as close to Arnold as D'Arcy had been.

She felt it was a brilliant solution, Manoussos agreed, and they dropped the subject for more amusing ones and gossip. The evening went on until three in the morning. The men left together. That surprised D'Arcy because she'd thought that Manoussos might stay over. The signals for a sexual tryst had been there, or so she had thought.

It was late afternoon the following day. D'Arcy was in the drawing room reading when she heard a knock at her door. She opened it to a stream of giggling young boys, arms full of flowers, pushing past her to stand around her room. Dozens of red roses, white roses, arum lilies and her most favourite flower in the lily family, Casablanca, large and white, a mass of them. There were white daisies with egg yolk yellow centres, and sunflowers with huge black faces made up a glorious cut flower garden. She walked around the room of boys pretending to be vases, laughing and clapping her hands. There were more hothouse cut flowers in that room than she had ever seen in Livakia in all her life. Where did they come from? Who could have sent them? She touched them, bent her head to take in their scent, gloried in their beauty, and when she stopped in front of one of the smallest of the boys carrying sprays of perfect white moth orchids, she said,

'Yorgos, who gave you these flowers to bring to me?'
He refused to answer, merely turned to face the still
open door they had all filed through. And there framed
in it was Max, leaning against the door jamb, his smile
as bright as the sun, a twinkle in his eyes.

She tilted back her head and laughed because he
had caught her completely off guard, had surprised
and delighted her as she had never been before, and
because he knew it. She could see it in his face, his own
delight at having done it. Finally she composed herself
enough to ask, 'Max, however did you manage this?'

'I flew to Athens early this morning, raided the best
flower shops in Kolonaki, had lunch with a friend, loaded
the plane, and flew home. Just like anything else in
life, it's all quite simple when you really want to do
something.'

'They're absolutely gorgeous, spectacular! I'm overwhelmed by their beauty and their being here at all, and
of course by your gesture. Thank you, thank you. But
why would you do such an unbelievably touching thing
for me?'

'The word's romantic, D'Arcy, a romantic thing.
Because it's the best way I could think of to come
courting.' He gave her one of his sexy smiles then
added, 'I think this might be the right moment for an
exit. I'll call you later.'

When he turned to leave she saw Omboie and Ainsasha,
Max's two African housemen, faithful servants and
friends who had been with him ever since she first
met him. They were carrying large cardboard boxes
containing beautiful pottery vases she recognised as being

from Max's house. Since no one would have had enough containers for a planeload of fresh flowers, Max had thought of everything. The little boys left and Ainsasha and Omboie remained to help Poppy and D'Arcy arrange the flowers throughout the house.

The last vase was barely in place when the telephone rang. The telephone rarely rang in D'Arcy's house, few people had the number. She had no thoughts about who it might be, too dazzled by the Garden of Eden that Max had created for her and still too stunned by his announcement to think of anything else except being in a paradise, within a paradise: this floral garden, in her house, in Livakia.

She heard his voice and it brought an instant smile to her lips. 'What do you think, D'Arcy? Well, say something. Something like: "Well, it's about time you made up your mind to do something about me, Max."'

D'Arcy hesitated for a moment, sat down, then said, 'Max, are you sure that this is not just an extravagant thank-you note for dinner last night?'

'It was a very good dinner, I'll grant you that. And a great evening, I'll grant you that too, and it does deserve a thank-you note. I'll send one, if that'll make you understand that I've been blind to the fact I've been in love with you for a long time and have only come to that realisation in the last few months. Come and have dinner in my house tonight. I'll cook for you and we'll talk about it.'

'I don't know what to say, Max.'

'Yes will do.'

'Max, maybe it's just sex?'

'Well, we know that it's certainly that, sex has always

been something I've wanted with you, but now it's sex and more than that, those same things that you wanted from me and were afraid I couldn't give you. You were right to turn me down for all those years. I couldn't give you love with the sex then. Now I feel I can, and I want to.'

D'Arcy had felt her heart softening towards Max lately. She had always valued his honesty, and had been undeniably attracted to him, if wary of this in the past. Could it be true, were they falling in love? Were they in love? Had he too faced his own mortality and seen what was missing in his life, wondered what his legacy would be? She felt suddenly thrilled at the prospect of seeing him, loving him, having a sex life with him. She felt a great relief. If this were true, that Max was in love with her, that she might be in love with him after all these years of loving each other as friends, then the sexual attraction she had always felt towards him would no longer have to be put aside.

There was a great deal of cloud moving fast across the night sky and a huge white moon, very nearly full, kept playing hide and seek as did the millions of bright stars that also appeared and disappeared to lend the night mystery and romance – just what Max and D'Arcy needed as a backdrop to this special something that was happening to them.

She had given him the yes he so fervently wanted but asked him to pick her up so he could see the flowers arranged throughout the house. She was dressed and ready for him and standing by the window. For the moment the clouds were acting as a curtain to the heavens and it was pitch black outside. She saw the beam of a torch weaving its way up through the narrow lane to her property. Quite suddenly D'Arcy was overwhelmed by deeper feelings for Max, this new Max who was in love with her. She wanted him, it was as simple as that, she wanted him and no longer need hide that fact from herself, or him, or anyone else. She was not going to be a notch on his belt. There would never again be notches carved on his belt.

D'Arcy watched the torchlight coming closer, closer to the wall surrounding her house. There was a strong wind adding more excitement to the night. She flung open the front door and ran down the steps towards the wooden door in the wall just as he opened it. She called his name and, seeing her, he took the remaining steps separating them two at a time and they ran into each other's arms. They kissed – the kiss she'd wanted and been waiting to have from him all the years she had known him. The clouds raced away from the moon. It reappeared and its light turned the path and them and her house silver-white. They burned for each other, as hot as if it was the sun.

Their first night together was spent in his bed where they kissed and spoke to each other about their hopes and dreams, how they felt about each other in the past and present, and discovered each other's bodies: their scent, the feel of their skin, exploring their contours and their beauty, and falling in love with each other's nakedness. They had no need to keep sex at bay but they did, not intentionally but because it just didn't happen. They were too wrapped up in other aspects of their togetherness, knowing they had the rest of their lives for sex, erotic dreams and fantasies, all things sexual that two libertines in love would have as a natural part of their lives. They each of them intended to take this love affair slowly; it was after all going to last them a lifetime.

They did not intend to spend every minute together but their good intentions did rather go by the wayside since after only a few hours away from D'Arcy, Max would rapidly be courting her again with one romantic gesture or another. It did not take many days before everyone in Livakia could see the changes in them both and that their togetherness was more than merely momentary. People were glad for them, but suspicious also. Max had been too much of a womaniser for too long for his friends to be comfortable with the idea that there would ever be a lifetime love for him.

There were other concerns besides their love affair. D'Arcy was most definitely the sort of woman who when she believed it right to take on something would follow it to the end. In her newfound happiness with Max she did not forget Melina and went in search of the right person to help the girl, if Melina would allow herself to be helped. D'Arcy's friend Aliki did find someone she thought would be the right person, a twenty-year-old girl called Sophia who lived in Iraklion. She was the adopted daughter of Aliki's cook and worked on archaeological digs in Crete. Sophia had come through hard times, she was a girl with an understanding of what deep loneliness meant, and was willing to befriend Melina on D'Arcy's behalf.

Everyone concerned agreed it was worth a try. It was Manoussos who suggested to Max and D'Arcy that they keep what they were doing for Melina quiet in Livakia. Mark was drinking more and more and beginning to resemble Arnold in as much as his new lady love, Dorothy, or someone else would on occasion now have to see that he didn't slip from his chair, that he could get home safely. When in a seriously inebriated state he was more eloquent than ever but no more generous about Arnold and how he had caused the ruination of a young girl's life. It always brought people's hackles up. Max and D'Arcy took their police chief's advice and kept what D'Arcy was doing between themselves.

They went to meet Sophia twice to make certain taking on Melina was not going to be a negative in her life, and the more they saw her the more certain they were that Sophia might benefit from meeting someone who had gone all wrong where she had gone all right, since both girls started out in life in the worst possible circumstances. The next step was for Manoussos to go with D'Arcy to see Melina and talk to her, ask her if she would be willing to receive Sophia as a prison visitor, someone who would soon become her friend. Though Max was sympathetic to what D'Arcy and Manoussos were trying to do, he did not ever want to see Melina again, so his contribution was to fly them into Iraklion, and arrange a late lunch for them in an unusually good taverna where he was well known.

It was a very hot day and Iraklion was the madhouse of traffic and people it always was. Manoussos and D'Arcy gave Max their shopping lists and he was sent off while they took a taxi to the prison. Manoussos had fought hard to get Melina into this particular prison, believing she would behave better if she was inched into the harshness of the prison system slower rather than faster. Her age had helped. She was in a small prison, an old fortress high on a ridge overlooking the sea.

A police officer greeted Manoussos and D'Arcy in his office and then proceeded to take them to Melina. From the very moment the doors to the prison clanged closed behind her, D'Arcy felt uncomfortable.

She felt no better now. The stench was appalling, a combination of damp and heat and stale air. They walked down a narrow corridor passing prison cells with doors standing open. For the most part the cells were empty. A few prisoners were sitting on three-legged stools in the passage talking to one another.

They proceeded up a flight of old stone stairs that twisted and turned to the floor above. Here the passage widened and the rooms off it were much larger. All their doors were open and revealed administrative offices, sparsely furnished, with hardly an officer in sight.

At the end of that hall they went through another door that led to an open courtyard. The bright light blinded them for a few seconds. Hot sun poured over the stone yard. Three prisoners were sitting at a worn wooden table doing bead work – long, thin, beautifully made coloured glass bead snakes that were sold to the tourist shops in the town. It was close to midday and very hot, with not a breath of wind. There were a few birds singing somewhere in the shade of one of the trees outside the prison grounds. The sound of the waves crashing against the rocks five hundred feet below the cliff where the old prison perched. D'Arcy looked out to sea and then towards the city of Iraklion which had spread almost to the walls of the fortress prison. From a door on the opposite side of the courtyard entered a police officer followed by Melina. On seeing her D'Arcy felt suddenly very unwell. This was the first time she had seen the girl since she had been taken away from Livakia. She still had the same misgivings about Melina she had always had.

The officer somewhat harshly told Melina to sit down which she did at the far end of the table. Manoussos and D'Arcy joined her. She had that same cocky attitude she had always had, and D'Arcy felt herself foolish to have imagined her sentence might have softened her.

'Hello, Melina,' she said.

The girl ignored her. The officer now standing behind her chided her for having no manners and insisted she greet her visitors properly, but even a shove on her shoulder had no effect. Manoussos thanked him but said he would be grateful if the officer went off and had a smoke on the other side of yard. He offered him a packet of cigarettes after removing one for himself and lighting it.

They sat in momentary silence and then Manoussos asked, 'Are you well, Melina?'

'Yes.'

'I've come to talk to you because I want to know how you're getting on in prison.'

'I have nothing to say.'

'Nothing? Not about being here and how you're feeling and what you're going to do in the years you have to spend here?'

'No. What can I say? I wish I was free, I think

275

all the time of nothing but being free, that's all I can say.'

'And what do you think of then?'

'I think of the sea, of swimming in the sea, of being alone, of being free to walk where I want to, when I want to, of eating something good. You put me here, and you, a police chief, ask me what will I do in prison for years? You know what I'll do. Eat, sleep, make beaded things for cigarette money, learn to embroider for rich ladies.' At that she shot a dark look at D'Arcy then continued, 'Clean my cell, the prison, do my turn in the vegetable garden. I'll be like all the other prisoners watching the hours, days, months, years go by. That was a dumb question, Chief. What will you ask me next? I can guess. Do I ever feel remorse for killing Kirios Arnold?'

'Well, do you?'

She laughed at Manoussos and said, 'You see, I guessed right. No.'

'Nothing.'

'No. My feelings are mine, I don't have to tell them to you. Why have you come to see me? Why have you brought her? Why are you asking me all these questions?'

'Does it upset you that we've come to see you?'

'No, I'm not upset. I only ask why?'

'Because you've not been very clever in your life, but you're a survivor. I know that by the way you've lived in the past. You have fifteen years to become more clever in how you live when you leave here. You'll still be a young woman and can begin again but to do that you'll need a lot of help and you have no one to give it to you. You need a friend.'

'I don't want *her* for a friend.' Then she turned to gaze at D'Arcy for only the second time since they had been there. She spoke directly to her. 'You were never my friend. Only Kirios Mark was my friend. Only he understood me, you never can.'

It was then that D'Arcy found her tongue. She told Melina, 'You're right, I was not your friend and I cannot be your friend now, we don't much like each other. And Arnold was my very good friend. You killed him and don't even care that you did. But that does not stop me from feeling that you were born into miserable circumstances and were driven by them all your life. I know a girl, a Cretan girl, who has had as bad a time as you have had and a friend of mine extended the hand of friendship to her. Now she lives a full and happy life but has no friends that have suffered as she has, as you have. No one she can talk to who has in common with her the bad old times or knows what it's like to be an orphan. I told her about you and she thinks she would like to become a prison visitor in the hope that you might become friends and help each other.

'Look, let me be very honest with you, I believe that you are solely responsible for taking Arnold's life, that you acted alone but were influenced and manipulated by other people's actions and behaviour. Those things combined with your own darkness of soul, your ignorance, your vulnerability and obsessive attachment to Mark, made you kill my friend. I can never forgive you for that, but what I can do is hope that in these years when you are lost to the outside world, with a friend and help from the prison you might leave here with, at the very least, a vocation, hopefully an education of sorts, that will equip you to make a place for yourself in the world so you will never again want to take another man's life. I hope you'll allow Sophia to visit you because she's a special girl whom you might like. She'll have funds available for educational or vocational help by way of courses, books, a computer, tutors, even for the odd luxury you might earn through diligence. Have no doubts the prison system will allow such favours if you show willing and behave yourself. Don't be stupid, Melina, this is the time to get smart.'

'What do you get out of this?'

'Hopefully you'll never kill another friend of mine.'

With that D'Arcy rose and told the girl, 'We won't ever be seeing each other again. I think that would serve us both best. Be brave. Goodbye, Melina.'

She turned from the girl to face Manoussos and told him, 'If you don't mind, I think it's all been said. I'll meet you outside.'

Manoussos asked the officer who had brought Melina in to meet them to find someone to escort D'Arcy from the building. Then, after telling her he would only be a few minutes, he returned to Melina.

Under a tree, on a weatherworn wooden bench, just opposite the prison entrance D'Arcy sat and waited for Manoussos. Her hands were trembling and hot as the day was, she felt shivery – not the sort of tremor that comes with cold but the kind that comes with fear and anger. Her mouth was dry.

She'd had no idea that she was so angry over Arnold's death, not until she came face to face with Melina and her lack of remorse for what she had done. D'Arcy thought she had done with mourning Arnold months ago. Clearly she hadn't. She needed no psychiatrist to tell her that going to see Melina, doing what she was doing about her, saying what she had said to her, was her way of grieving for Arnold.

How had she not realised that she had never really done that for him or for herself? Tears began to trickle down her cheeks and then the sobbing came. After a short period of time, the pain of the loss of a close friend that she had kept so well buried within her began to slip away along with her hatred of Melina. She realised that she might never have resolved Arnold's death or how she felt about Melina unless she had made this trip. She had spoken up for Arnold, and now that someone had she hoped he could rest in peace. She knew that she could now live with the tragedy that had in so many ways woken her up.

She took a small mirror from her handbag and looked at herself, dabbed at her eyes with a handkerchief. Her colour was high and she was extremely hot, having dressed for colder late-October weather. Her hands still trembled. But she took stock of the face in the mirror, of the D'Arcy Montesque whose life was so changed by falling in love with an old friend. Had she and Max only been together four days? It seemed to D'Arcy as if they had been in love all their lives.

CRETE and
NEW ENGLAND

Chapter 13

'It's over, Max, I don't ever have to see her again. Going there was like a last lament for Arnold. It's done, it's over. Please, let's live.'

Those were D'Arcy's first words to him as he rose from his chair to greet her and Manoussos. The look in her eyes was for him and him alone when she had said, 'Let's live.' He had been waiting a very long time for her to want him as much as he had always wanted her. It was there for them now, the carnal side of D'Arcy Montesque. All resistance to him was gone, they were ready to discover the sexual side of each other's nature. The years of pent up lust they had had for each other, the fear of losing each other as friends had they consummated it, his insatiable promiscuity, were at last over.

Max swept her into his arms and held her there. He whispered in her ear, his heart racing, every fibre of his being hungering for her, 'I wish we were alone in a wood where I could take you in the most wild passionate sex, in all kinds of ways. But always remember that it's because of you, the way you excite me, who and what you are, and because I love you and am committed to you in love. We'll be all things sexual to each other – the brightest, the finest, the deepest, the darkest erotic pleasures will be part of our rich and full life together. Oh, yes, we'll live!'

Then he released her, still holding her hand, and gazed into her eyes. At the best of times D'Arcy and most everyone else could only see that Max de Bonn was a handsome, powerful and exciting man, one whom men admired and women hungered for. In love, and filled now with lustful desire for her, Max seemed to D'Arcy like thunder roaring in the sun.

She squeezed his hand and while gazing into his eyes, just before she kissed him, she whispered, 'Tonight.'

They were to have had a long and luscious lunch but it didn't happen that way. They had expected it to be a rather depressing affair after visiting the prison and Melina, but that didn't happen either. Max and D'Arcy's excitement over their togetherness, and for the night that awaited them, set them aflame and full of joy. It was infectious, and Manoussos, who adored them both and had insisted on relating how magnificent D'Arcy had been with Melina, got caught up in the sexual aura they were creating. The fun was back in their lives again.

It was Max who was first intrigued by an elegant woman on the far side of the room. She was beautiful but remote and she was dining alone. He had been watching her for some time before the others arrived and now that they had it was the woman who seemed intrigued. She kept stealing glances at Manoussos. Always the tease, Max was quick to point this out to his dining companions, who had fun with it. She might just steal Manoussos away and keep him for her pleasure for the rest of his life!

Joke as they might there was for Manoussos something

exciting about this woman who looked so out of place in the taverna. As there was little excitement about lunch and lingering over food for D'Arcy and Max, who clearly had other things in mind, Max decided to solve everything. He excused himself from the table and went first to the taverna keeper and spoke with him. D'Arcy and Manoussos were amused by the despair in the taverna keeper's face, the throwing up of his hands. Max's charm and a sum of money seemed to calm the man down. They were less amused when the waiters arrived to whisk away the platters of quail and roasted pheasant, a mound of buttered rice with the aroma of cardamom, cinnamon and lemon zest with sultanas and slivers of almond. A deep dish of peppers and aubergine and caramelised baby onions, a salad of flat-leafed parsley and diced tomatoes, spring onion and bulgur, a bowl of rich yoghurt flavoured with cucumber and garlic, a platter of small round freshly made peta bread vanished from sight. Before they realised what was happening even their plates had been removed with what little food they had managed to get on them, and D'Arcy and Manoussos were left with just the forks in their hand.

They watched with wonder as Max and the taverna keeper walked past their table to the lady sitting alone. No more than a few words between the three and Max was sitting with her. Both D'Arcy and Manoussos were amused. They could hardly stop laughing long enough for D'Arcy to ask, 'What's going on, Manoussos?' This was the old Max, doing what she had seen him do hundreds of times. She felt no jealousy, merely curiosity.

'I haven't the slightest idea. I don't mind him abandoning us but I do wish he had not taken the food with him.' Then they both began to laugh again.

Max was very quick. He could not have been away from their table more than three minutes when he rose from his chair, kissed the woman's hand and returned to D'Arcy and Manoussos.

'You weren't jealous?' he asked D'Arcy.

'No, not in the least.'

'You're so sure of me?'

'Yes, actually,' she answered, and beamed at him with a smile that made him melt, falling in love with her a little bit more.

'You trust me, would trust me with your life?'

'Without question.'

He rose from his chair and pulled D'Arcy slowly up from hers, wrapped his arms around her and kissed her. His kiss made her feel dizzy with loving, and she felt a rush of sexual pleasure. When he released her he told her, 'For that I'm going to make you the happiest woman alive for the rest of your life.' Then he turned to Manoussos and said, 'Her name is Chadwick Chase and she would like to invite you to lunch. Can you find your own way home or shall I come back for you in the morning?'

Manoussos stroked his moustache. There was a twinkle in his eye when he said, 'I could have managed that myself, Max, and yes, I think I'm old enough to find my own way home.'

A knowing smile passed between the two womanisers before Max said, 'I know that. But to be honest, I couldn't wait for you to get around to it, I so much want to take off with D'Arcy.'

The whole thing was quite wonderful and mad. A taxi had been called and all the food packed in containers and the containers packed in baskets and placed in the taxi and they were soon fighting their way through traffic to the dock where Max had moored the sea plane.

'Is life with you always going to be like this?' asked D'Arcy.

'Maybe not just like this but it will always be full of surprises. We just want each other too much to wait. Or am I wrong?'

'No, certainly not wrong,' she said, and slipped her hand beneath the belt around his waist and under his shirt to caress the firm flesh of his belly, run her fingers through the mass of curly pubic hair. He removed her hand, pulled her into his lap and told her in a voice husky with need, 'You're playing with fire there, D'Arcy.'

Once they had taken off the water they circled Iraklion and he flew over the little taverna on the outskirts of the town where he had left Manoussos. Max deliberately made a spluttering sound with the engine and seconds later Manoussos and Chadwick Chase appeared at the door and waved. Max dipped his wings and they flew off for Livakia.

He was clearly delighted to have D'Arcy next to him in the cockpit. 'Would you like to learn to fly?' he asked her.

'I must have been on the verge of asking you to teach me a dozen times or more.'

'Great! In time we can co-pilot each other. I want

to do so many things with you, take you to so many places, show you off to so many people. Tonight . . . I want tonight to be special for us so we're going to the hunting cabin I keep up in the mountains. I've never taken a woman there. You'd like that, wouldn't you? To have your first night of sex with me in a bed where no other woman has been?'

'Max – the other women . . .'

'Like the other men you've had in your life, they're all past tense.'

'Are you sure about that, Max? Because I am about any other men in mine.'

They were home by four o'clock. Max had radioed in for his house men to meet the plane and when D'Arcy jumped down on to the pontoon she was surprised to see the donkey boys ready to load up and haul the lunch baskets and them through town and up to the caves where they kept their cars.

'We'll take the 2CV, it needs a run. Now you're not going to play some macho game with me and insist on the jeep?'

'Wouldn't think of it.'

They stopped briefly at D'Arcy's house where she tossed a few things in a bag: warmer clothes, toothbrush, nightdress. Max gave her no time to change because of his concern for the time. They had at the very least a two-hour drive and more likely three to his hunting cabin.

They soon caught up with the donkeys and followed behind them, arms round each other's waist, and D'Arcy asked him, 'Max, how could I have been so blind to us?'

She stopped in her tracks and placed her arms around his neck and kissed him. He lifted her from the ground and held her tight in his arms, so tight she could feel his need for her and sex throbbing hard between them. He released her, aware of her hunger for him.

He cleared his voice before he spoke. 'Because timing is everything. You were smart enough to know that, when I didn't. I always did like and respect you for your cleverness.'

With that he swept her once again into his arms and raced ahead to one of the donkeys. He placed her on its back, and holding her hand, walked by her side as they made the last of the steep climb through the village to the clearing on the cliff.

Max watched D'Arcy walk away from him to back the 2CV from the cave. She was dressed in a mocha-coloured suede skirt that hung to the middle of her calves and was cut on the bias, a soft thin suede that moved sensuously with every step she took. Her jacket was short and finished tight to the waist with wide revers. He found her clothes sexy as hell. But then, he had to admit to himself that whatever she wore he had always found her sexy as hell. For years he had known that she was a foxy lady in and out of bed and had always admired her from afar for her lust and her bravery in enjoying sex to the fullest and without pretence. He realised now that he loved her for being the sexually free lady that she was, for the libertine that some claimed she was, for being the erotic adventuress that soon would be his.

He had always been attracted to D'Arcy because she, like Brett, like himself, was a romantic. Max had been one all his life and he knew from Manoussos that so had D'Arcy, ever since she had been a little girl. Does romance kill young girls or make them better? It was a subject that had often been discussed by Max and his men friends and he had always claimed that it made them infinitely better. D'Arcy was living proof of that. In all the years he had known her she had been happy in herself, sure of herself and her sexuality. She was like him in many ways. They were pleasure seekers, adventurers in life and lust, and now they would be together as partners in those same things.

He watched her back the car up towards him, and his mind wandered for a minute over the last few nights they had spent together, their sexual restraint, no more than discovering each other in nakedness, the odd kiss, the odd caress, but no sex. This had been a new kind of eroticism for them both. The power of the passion and lust they felt for each other came as much from what they didn't do as the things they did. He loved her, he loved their being together, for those nights of sexual restraint.

It had all come so naturally to him from the very moment he looked at her and realised that they were meant for each other and no one else. It just happened, this steady campaign to win her to him. His courting of D'Arcy had woken love for them both, and now lust. It had all happened in the right order because at this time of their lives that was what they needed. Fate had decreed it so.

He smiled as she popped out of the car and began pulling the roof down. Max went to help her. They smiled across the car at each other and she told him,

'I think I've never been so excited about life as I am now.'

He shouted over to the donkey boys to load the car and then, walking around it, he took D'Arcy by the hand and led her back into the cave and to the farthest wall where the light from the entrance just missed it. Max stood her in the shadows against the wall and raised her arms above her head. He held them together by her wrists with one hand and placed a very hungry, deep kiss upon her mouth. Their lips parted and tongue found tongue while their hearts raced with the intensity and intimacy of that kiss. Max raised her skirt above her waist and tucked it behind her. He tore the silk strings holding the triangle of silk between her legs and slid it ever so slowly, in the most sexy and tantalising way, to drop on to the stony ground. He felt her give in to his caresses. A man knows when he's setting a woman on edge for sex and orgasm, and Max knew his women, what seduced them to the god Eros, how to make them come with infinite pleasure.

He too was inflamed by the feel of her baby-smooth mound, and the long cleft beneath – so very sexy. Too dark to see her in the shadows of the cave in all her naked glory, he used memory of the nights they'd had together and grew more bold. He fingered that cleft, and separated her most intimate female lips. She was like silk velvet, warm, moist, slippery smooth in her lust. His thumb sought out that small bud that could bring women an orgasm other than penetrative. He hardly knew what he was doing when he used his fingers to explore deeper, as deep as he could, as his thumb teased open the floodgates of orgasm for D'Arcy. She never uttered a sound, she couldn't, for he never stopped kissing her. But her heart raced so fast, and beat so hard, he feared for her. She lost herself so completely in the pleasure he was giving her that she bit hard into his lips and struggled to free herself from him. Impossible. He held her fast, and felt the warm flow of her first orgasm with him. She was everything he had always thought she would be and this he told her in a whisper filled with love and passion for her erotic soul before he helped her to compose herself and they left the cave.

They drove off, D'Arcy at the wheel, through the wild terrain of mountainous Crete, the island they both loved so much that they had made it an important part of their lives. They talked with no embarrassment about what had happened in the cave. And as they drove through the rugged and thrilling stony landscape of the Lefka Ori range and the little 2CV climbed its peaks and took some of the flat upland basins in her stride, and they saw caves that seemed to create yet another landscape within a landscape and the sea become nothing but a thin ribbon of blue far off in the distance, Max entertained D'Arcy with stories of the erotic wonders he had seen and experienced in the Arab and African worlds he loved so much.

Exciting? Of course it was exciting to hear of such sexual happenings, of course it set the imagination and her fantasies going, and of course all that had been calculated by Max, not to frighten but to give D'Arcy a taste of what was to come, to prime the woman he loved for a sexual life that would keep them together. They knew they were experienced in the many and varied ways of sex, how important an adventurous sexual life was for them both. They had given themselves up to this new phase in their relationship back there in the cave and the more Max excited D'Arcy with his sexuality and seduced her with his erotic tales, the more she realised she was ready to follow him on any erotic road he would take her down, until death do them part.

They were driving now during those few minutes between dusk and nightfall. The dirt road had been winding and turning up the mountain towards its peak and several minutes before they arrived at the gate-keeper's one-room house it came into sight. Max took one of his shotguns from the back seat, and fired twice into the air.

'That will open the gate, so just drive straight through. If you stop the gatekeeper will talk us to death,' he explained.

The gate was a tree trunk stripped of its bark and a heavy stone tied with ropes at one end as a counterbalance crossing the dirt road. The gatekeeper, a tall young hulk of a man with a shotgun slung over his shoulder, had been quick because the makeshift road barrier was up by the time D'Arcy gunned the motor. They sped past him, waving a greeting, and Max called out, 'I'll come see you sometime late afternoon tomorrow, Petros. You can go home for the night.'

Looking in the rear-view mirror, D'Arcy saw Petros pull off his hat and wave back at them, a smile across his face and an arm raised, his hand making circles in the air, the expressive Greek gesture that meant something like approval, wonderment, admiration. Max had seen it too, from over his shoulder, and turned back to look at D'Arcy and tell her, 'Well, what do you think? Of course he's surprised. I did tell you I have never brought a woman here.'

They were on the peak of the mountain and still climbing the private dirt road. Old, twisted and windswept trees began to appear, at first sparsely and then more abundantly. The peak was capped by a small wood. It was an enchanting place and particularly in the last moments of daylight. A haze of pearly blue-grey light was coming down as the black of night was coming up. The headlights of the 2CV bumping along the rough dirt road were like small beams of sunlight, frightening the odd rabbit, surprising the last of the birds flying into the trees from their day of hunting. Then quite suddenly the climb was over, the road levelled out, and there in front of them stood Max's hunting 'cabin'. It was something marvellous, only Max could call his hunting lodge a cabin.

It was much more than that. It was several steps up to the huge covered porch where rustic rocking chairs stood to attention like sentinels. D'Arcy should have been exhausted from the two-and-a-half-hour drive but she wasn't, more excited by the place, the adventure, the prospect of a night with her lustful lover.

There was just enough time to unload the car and from the porch admire the spectacular, somewhat eerie view stretching out all around them before the last of the daylight vanished. With arms around each other they took a last look before Max opened the front door and led her inside. They had taken no more than a few steps into the huge room when he gazed into D'Arcy's eyes and told her, 'I never in my wildest dreams believed there would be a woman so essential to my life that she would be standing in this room with me as you are now. It has suddenly come home to me what I've done, and it's exciting, thrilling, but a little frightening.'

He took D'Arcy's hands in his and brought them to his lips. He kissed them several times, then told her, 'Don't move, let me light the lamps and the fire.'

There had been no sleep for them, just the odd moment to doze off in, and their passion and hunger for sex and all things sexual hardly left them time for even those few moments apart. While Max was stealing one of those odd moments, D'Arcy lay wrapped in his arms, listening to his heartbeat, admiring the beauty of the man she'd fallen in love with, this consummate lover of women who was giving her more sexual pleasure and adventurous sex than she had as yet known.

She listened to his even breathing and came to realise that it was for this moment in this man's arms that she had loved and left men, that she had gone on that extraordinary sexual odyssey with Brandon Ketheridge to experience sex as a libertine. Now she could not only understand Max as a sexual libertine but could share that part of his life with him as she might not have done had she not moulded herself into a woman who could enjoy her sexuality in the same way as he did his.

He was a master of the sexual seduction and corruption of women, she had always heard that and now she was experiencing it. He had infinite ways to reach into a woman's most secret sexual needs and desires, bringing them to the fore, drawing her out and making her erotic fantasies reality, to keep her constantly on the edge of orgasm and hold her off until she would kill, do anything he demanded, for that moment of intercourse where his penis took command and gave the most exquisite fucking. Max loved women, everything about women, what he could do to them sexually, the very many ways he could bring them to orgasm, the taste of a woman on his tongue, in his mouth. The night was over and their sex life had only just begun. D'Arcy was aware of that and that she would have laid down her life for more sex, an eternal erotic partnership with Max de Bonn.

Now it was suddenly very clear to her what she had been afraid of all these years: that she would indeed have been nothing but another notch on his belt, that he most certainly would have abandoned her as he had done all the other women he had had erotic affairs with, had he not come to love her first, wanted to make a life with her before they had entered into a night of such magnificent debauchery as he was giving her now.

They remained in the hunting lodge for three days and three nights. They walked in the woods, and Max hunted and fished in a rushing stream. The place was relatively well watered by a natural spring which created a narrow stream and even a small waterfall. They were alone with each other and nature at the top of the world and the views were staggeringly impressive, just like their three days of lust. Their sexual tryst never flagged. He took her in the woods, and on the bank of the stream, and in the lodge, in the most erotic and dramatic ways until he had mastered D'Arcy and her orgasms. Max delighted in making her come, by the mere touch of his hand, a look in his eye, the sexual games he played with her. She was out of control sexually, yearned for his commands, his ointments, his sexual toys, for his kisses, and thought of nothing but being riven by her lover.

They remained there until the food ran out. And then they packed up and drove down the mountain, D'Arcy at the wheel. They stopped in two villages where Max was well known, to leave as a gift the game he had killed, to drink ouzo with the men he usually hunted with, and to introduce them to D'Arcy. Every one of the men had heard about her as the brave driver of the 'tin can on wheels' – the curious Cretans with their endless stream of questions! She answered them all and waited for Max to declare their relationship to them, but he didn't.

All the way home they were happy. He touched her often, once even made her stop the car and open her jacket and blouse so he could kiss her breasts and suck on her nipples, so he could see her eyes when she came, and could bend her over the bonnet of the car, raise her skirts and enter her, taking her slowly but with deep thrusts that made her cry out and the sound of sex echo round the cliffs. They called out in sheer animal lust when they both came together in long and strong orgasms. They hugged each other for a long time, there in the road next to the 2CV.

It was still not enough for Max. He laid D'Arcy on the bonnet and drank their lust from her as if she were a golden vessel. When they kissed they could taste each other on their lips, in their mouths. Only then did Max sigh, and replete with pleasure ask, 'Would you like me to drive the rest of the way home?'

She agreed. They rode in silence for quite a long time, she resting her body against his. And then finally he said, 'I have grown to love this car, it's won a place in my heart.'

Their plan had been to be at the Kavouria for a late lunch, and they were. There were a few stragglers still at the table who greeted them. Mark was one, not quite drunk but well on the way. There was the usual banter as they agreed to join him and others at the table. D'Arcy and Max gazed into each other's eyes as they took their seats and he whispered, 'I get very excited thinking of you flushed with the warmth of our orgasms, all my sperm swimming round inside you. I'll think about that all through lunch, it's very sexy.'

They ordered food and their glasses were filled by Mark who said, 'And where's your lady friend?'

'This is my lady friend,' answered Max, and leaned over and gave D'Arcy a kiss, caressing her knee under the table.

'D'Arcy, be warned – once a womaniser, always a womaniser. No, Max, I mean the dark beauty Schawahan.'

'What are you going on about, Mark?'

'Your African beauty has been waiting two days now for your return.'

'Where is she?'

'Installed in your house.'

'D'Arcy, I don't know what this is about. I must find out. I'll see you later.'

D'Arcy took some teasing about the tall, slender, black

beauty whom they had all seen with Max many a time over the years. She had her lunch and lingered over it, waiting for his return. Then finally she left the restaurant and went home.

Several times she very nearly called Max and then thought better of it. He knew where she was. If he wanted to speak to her, he would be there or call. Hours passed. She missed him. Why wasn't he with her? His sudden running off to another woman made her more uneasy than she cared to admit. She bathed and changed and made ready for his arrival. He was certain to call and bring his lady friend with him. Surely he would know that D'Arcy would make Schawahan welcome, that she could and would be able to cope with all the ex-lovers Max had left behind?

She was dressing when she thought she heard the sound of engines, a plane flying over her house. The sun was low in the sky but the light was still good, the sky blue – good flying weather. She did not even bother to go out on to the terrace to look and see if she had been right, that she had heard a plane, because she dismissed the very idea. A man in love does not fly off without a word. She almost laughed at herself for being so silly.

Half an hour later Max's houseman arrived, not with a note but a message. Max had left Livakia. He would not be back for several days. He had to make the light or he would have come himself to explain.

D'Arcy was shattered by this news. He had done to her what she had always feared he would do: broken down her defences, wooed her to his bed, and seduced her to the extent of craving sex and more sex with him.

And then, having cleaved her to him, he flew away and left her behind. She felt seduced and abandoned yet again by love and sex, and yet – she knew he hadn't lied to her, that he was in love with her, that he wanted her as he had wanted no other woman. But was it enough for a libertine, a womaniser, like Max de Bonn?

For the next few hours, D'Arcy relived the courtship that Max had laid upon her. A lesser woman might have ranted and raved at the loss she was feeling. Not so D'Arcy. The initial shock of his leaving without a word passed and all that remained was the memory of the utter honesty he had shown in his courtship of her. They were what they were to each other, and D'Arcy was a woman who knew the power she had and did not have over men. She had no idea what was going to happen in this thrilling affair with Max but whatever it was she felt she had no option but to love him and get on with her life. She wasn't going to stop living because she had found Mr Right and her dream was going wrong.

Several days went by with no word from Max. D'Arcy missed him in a different way from the way she had missed every other man she had been involved with. The nights alone were the worst times for her, her libido would hardly let her rest in peace. She wanted sex and to feel on the edge of orgasm as he had kept her, she missed the excitement of her sexuality on a rampage, and just as much as those things, she missed his loving her, his adoration and respect for her, as he had put it, 'for catching me'.

For the first time in her life she felt a part of herself had left Livakia and she was only half there, so she left. She packed her bags and decided to go to Brett's birthday party. Every year on 8 November Brett celebrated her birthday by having a party in the house she had inherited from her parents. It was an open house affair, no invitations. Those who knew her birthday knew that the door would be open and all were welcome to come and stay the three days she would be there. It was all so typical of Brett, to allow people to be free to do as they liked about her birthday, appearing or not depending on what they felt like doing. D'Arcy left a message with Max's houseman. 'Tell him I've gone to a birthday party.' She liked the knowing smile on his face. It seemed to say, 'Well, here's one woman who's going to give him as good as she gets.' And she set off feeling quite happy.

New England was still relatively new to D'Arcy, but she had taken to it immediately. She had always known that that was where Brett had been born, a place she had never returned to because her parents had disowned her for being the black sheep of the family, unable to toe their line. It was therefore a surprise to them all that when the second of her parents had died, Brett announced that her father had left her his entire estate. Neither D'Arcy nor her sister or brothers knew what that meant – they had all assumed not much, since Brett and her children had lived a life of near penury until their fathers had each come into sums of money and everyone's lives were made easier.

None of the children had ever enquired about Brett's inheritance, it meant nothing to them, and so they were therefore surprised when she announced that she would use the house left to her in the Stockbridge Bowl for her birthday parties, and that all the children were welcome to use it whenever they chose to. They were to consider it their family home. That had been five years ago when D'Arcy, Abelard, Vronsky and Rhett, her sister, all turned up for the first birthday party.

D'Arcy had tried calling her siblings. She couldn't find Abelard or Rhett and Vronsky hadn't made up his mind whether he would or would not go to the party this year. It was never easy to root him out of his studio in Provence, and he saw Brett quite often anyway.

But then that was part of the fun of Brett's birthday parties: people arrived from all over the world, on the spur of the moment, taking off for a great party with nothing but fun on their minds.

The drive from Boston airport to Stockbridge and the Stockbridge Bowl was one D'Arcy enjoyed immensely. First the highway from Boston to Springfield and from there all secondary roads through the Connecticut River Valley, stopping off to lunch in Deerfield, one of its oldest towns. Possibly not the shortest way to get to Brett's place but it was a way to get cross-country and see this part of Massachusetts that she enjoyed discovering. She liked that combination of old New England with its small quaint villages and towns and the well laid out fields of corn, apples and peaches. She always made a stop over at the Memorial Hall Museum to look at the colonial furnishings and then the museum village and did every one of the thirteen historical homes open to the public.

That was the flat part of her drive. Now, only a few hours later, she was in the Berkshire Hills, or the Berkshires as Brett and most everyone else seemed to call them. How beautiful the scenery was, so different from Crete, so lush and green and full of the last of the coloured leaves. The sound and the sight of the rushing mountain streams along the side of the road as you climbed and climbed this southern extension of the Green Mountains of Vermont. The dappled light sending spots of colour and patches of shade over the road for D'Arcy to drive through, Nature's confetti.

It was always more fun to arrive at Brett's birthday party on the day and give her a better surprise, so when D'Arcy arrived in Lenox, only a matter of minutes from the house Falcon's Lair, she decided to remain the night there at the inn. It was seven in the evening when she checked in and reserved a table for dinner. The proprietor recognised her and made D'Arcy feel very much at home. One of the reasons she loved small towns was the lack of subtlety their residents showed. 'Here for the party, I guess?' he asked.

'Yes. Have any other of my mother's guests arrived?' The overflow usually stayed at the inn.

'Been very quiet so far, but you know what your mother's parties are like, we could have a full house yet. Charlotte over at The Flower Box says she's got at least two carloads of flower orders that have arrived already. Come from all over the world, they have. One way or another, looks to me like it's going to be a big birthday celebration this year, Miss Montesque,' Mr Peabody responded before handing her a key to a room.

The Montesques were a big name in the Lenox, Stockbridge area, having been one of the first settler families there when the town was incorporated in 1767.

Although having grown up there, Brett was practically a newcomer but her surname still carried weight. The daughter of Averill Montesque had always been a legend for having run away from home to Europe, never to return. Now that Falcon's Lair was hers, her eccentricities along with her generosity to the town were accepted as the norm. Legend is like fame – if it goes on long enough and is subtle enough for a New England town to handle it is always acceptable. It adds to its history.

No one was surprised that Brett had named her children after great romantic heroes of literary novels. They liked and respected her for it. They liked the eccentricity of it since in the nineteenth century Lenox had been a literary centre, home for a time to the American writers Nathaniel Hawthorne, Catharine Sedgwick, Edith Wharton, and others the townspeople still liked boasting about. They took Brett's ways in their stride with a certain degree of pride in the same way as they took having the estate of Tanglewood as the summer home of the Boston Symphony Orchestra. The concerts brought the town more renown and interesting visiting artists, and so did Brett Montesque and her children.

D'Arcy, on the visits she had made at various times of the year to Falcon's Lair, had found things here – a lost childhood, grandparents that never were, a family estate representing financial security and a certain stability – that she had never missed. It was always great fun for her to be here, like stepping into someone else's life for a few days or weeks. But the times she loved it most was when she was there with Brett and her fathers for Brett's birthday party.

In the morning she dressed in the same suede skirt and jacket that she had worn those last days she had spent with Max. She looked at herself in the mirror and was not displeased. The bloom of love for him was still in her face. The days and nights of sexual bliss in his arms were much more than memory – they were now a part of her life. And sexual fulfilment and love at the same time, no matter how brief it had been, had made her look and feel more beautiful than she could ever have imagined herself to be. That fate might deem it should never happen to her again on such a scale seemed to her out of the question. But where was Max?

She had a leisurely breakfast of sausages and pancakes dripping with home-made butter and the best Vermont maple syrup, black coffee, then unbelievably finished her repast with a chunky hot apple sauce with thick double cream. You never knew when you would get to eat at Brett's birthday parties, or what you would eat, only that the food would be sublime because Brett hadn't cooked it. She was a terrible cook, but she had a French chef who wasn't.

D'Arcy had the top of her rented car down and the radio turned on quite loud, Luciano Pavarotti singing *Don Giovanni*, as she slowly drove through the stunningly lush and beautiful terrain and past several great estates such as Shadowbrooke, the home the industrialist Andrew Carnegie had built at the turn of the century. Most of those robber baron estates were broken up or given over to educational institutions now but all kept their beauty and buildings pretty much intact.

Falcon's Lair was one of those estates, only it had

never been broken up, and had never been given over to any institution. It was strictly private and not very well kept up, which seemed to add to its charm. D'Arcy turned off the main road and through the open rusting gates hung on pillars topped with handsome stone urns draped in garlands of stone flowers. The sun was out and there was little wind, but enough to rustle the leaves on the trees. The scent of autumn was in the air. The road was rutted but had been cleared of broken branches and the fallen leaves spun up around the wheels of her car as she sped over it towards the house.

There it was, the first sight of Falcon's Lair, a great beautiful rambling white wooden house with turrets and bay windows and an enormous porch going all around it. Black louvred shutters stood open and pinned back on either side of each of the many windows and doors. Falcon's Lair sat on the top of a ridge and against the side of a hill overlooking a wooded terrain sparsely dotted with mansions and grand estates. It looked glorious, all forty-two rooms of it. The dirt road was now a gravel drive and wound up and up, past the tennis courts and the 1920s swimming pool flanked by stone lions. D'Arcy felt terribly excited to be there, even more so than usual.

She had already passed more than a dozen cars parked on the gravel but no one seemed to be in sight. She drove the car up to the main entrance to the house and honked her horn. She turned off the radio and cut the car's engine. She could hear music coming from the house, Chopin, someone was playing the piano. She closed her eyes and listened for a few minutes. Such passionate and romantic music. She was so lost in it she missed hearing footsteps on the gravel. Finally she opened her eyes.

He was standing next to her at the car door, watching her. Why wasn't she surprised? Because it felt so right that he should be there. She sighed, was so filled with emotion that tears came to her eyes. Max opened the car door and helped her out. He took her in his arms, and they kissed. He fumbled with her jacket and opened it, found her naked breasts and caressed and kissed them, then closed her jacket and found her lips and they kissed again. He stroked her hair and wiped the tears from her cheeks as he whispered to her, 'This is no time for tears. Every day away from you was a year of my life. I had to go. Schawahan's father was in trouble, he needed me, and I owed him. I knew you would be all right.'

'I love you, Max.'

'Well, that's a good thing because I've come to ask the family for your hand in marriage.' With those words he opened her hand and dropped a large square-cut diamond into its palm. 'A gift of love from me, and thanks and good wishes from Schawahan's father.'

They kissed again, several times, and when she finally recovered herself from being dazzled by the diamond and his intentions, she asked him, 'Max, don't you think you should ask me first?'

A look of fright came into his eyes, he actually paled for a few seconds. She saw his distress, that it had never occurred to him that she might say anything other than yes. She could hardly bear to see the look of anguish on his face. D'Arcy took his hands in hers and raised them to her lips to kiss them. She said, 'Yes, please marry me.'

The relief on his face was instant and a smile that warmed her soul appeared on his lips. They kissed once more and then started up the stairs to the front door.

They were all there, all the family: Brett, D'Arcy's fathers, Rhett, Vronsky, Abelard, several of her mother's friends. Everyone seemed to converge on them at once with greetings and kisses. D'Arcy needed no one to tell her that Max had arranged it all, had made sure they were all together. She looked at him and he smiled and shrugged his shoulders. Her first words to Brett after she had wished her a happy birthday were said, as D'Arcy opened her hand and displayed the magnificent gem lying in its palm: 'Brett, would you and the dads mind if I broke with the tradition of this family and got married – married Max?'

ROBERTA LATOW
HER HUNGRY HEART

'*A sunshine sizzler, packed with non-stop sex*'
People Magazine

He was handsome, tall and slender, with bedroom eyes
that devoured women. She was a tall willowy blonde
with the looks of a showgirl, wealthy, cultivated and
intelligent, an enchantress who knew how to tame men
and, once they were tamed, clever enough to keep them.
They met on New Year's Eve 1943 at a chic party in
New York's fashionable Stork Club. Their erotic
attraction was immediate and mutual. Their love affair
would last a lifetime. But Karel Stefanik was not free to
love Barbara Dunmellyn. He had Mimi, whom he had
abandoned in the cruel chaos of war, a child whose fate
becomes inextricably entangled with that of her father
and the woman he loves.

This, then, is the story of their hungry hearts, the lovers
that fuel their lives; and finally of their own all-
encompassing love.

'The first lady of hanky panky. Her books are solidly
about sex . . . it adds a frisson. It sets a hell of a standard'
The Sunday Times

'Naughty, certainly . . . the sex is larded with dollops of
exoticism and luxury' *Observer*

FICTION / GENERAL 0 7472 3884 7

OBJECTS OF DESIRE

Suppressed passions, secret cravings and erotic fulfilment come together in this sensational novel of desire

Roberta Latow

Married to a world-famous surgeon, and mother of twin boys, Anoushka Rivers seems to lead a perfect life. But her erotic nature is suppressed by a man who does not love her.

Page Cooper has spent a decade longing for a man she can never have. For three weeks of each year, they experience the sweet ecstasy of desire, knowing that it cannot last.

Sally Brown is a good-time girl looking for love. When she finds it in the arms of Jahangir, a darkly sensuous Indian prince, her sensuality is awakened as never before.

Drawn together, these dynamic women explore their true potential – mentally, physically and sexually. A liaison with a seductive stranger on board the QE2; an afternoon of erotic depravity in Paris; a lustful *ménage à trois* overlooking the Taj Mahal; endless nights and days of unbridled passion with men willing to submit to their every desire, exploring fantasies beyond belief. In their search for new horizons, they find within themselves a strength and peace of mind more satisfying than anything else. These women are truly – Objects of Desire.

FICTION / GENERAL 0 7472 4866 4

A selection of bestsellers from Headline

LAND OF YOUR POSSESSION	Wendy Robertson	£5.99 ☐
TRADERS	Andrew MacAllen	£5.99 ☐
SEASONS OF HER LIFE	Fern Michaels	£5.99 ☐
CHILD OF SHADOWS	Elizabeth Walker	£5.99 ☐
A RAGE TO LIVE	Roberta Latow	£5.99 ☐
GOING TOO FAR	Catherine Alliott	£5.99 ☐
HANNAH OF HOPE STREET	Dee Williams	£4.99 ☐
THE WILLOW GIRLS	Pamela Evans	£5.99 ☐
MORE THAN RICHES	Josephine Cox	£5.99 ☐
FOR MY DAUGHTERS	Barbara Delinsky	£4.99 ☐
BLISS	Claudia Crawford	£5.99 ☐
PLEASANT VICES	Laura Daniels	£5.99 ☐
QUEENIE	Harry Cole	£5.99 ☐

All Headline books are available at your local bookshop or newsagent, or can be ordered direct from the publisher. Just tick the titles you want and fill in the form below. Prices and availability subject to change without notice.

Headline Book Publishing, Cash Sales Department, Bookpoint, 39 Milton Park, Abingdon, OXON, OX14 4TD, UK. If you have a credit card you may order by telephone – 01235 400400.

Please enclose a cheque or postal order made payable to Bookpoint Ltd to the value of the cover price and allow the following for postage and packing:

UK & BFPO: £1.00 for the first book, 50p for the second book and 30p for each additional book ordered up to a maximum charge of £3.00.

OVERSEAS & EIRE: £2.00 for the first book, £1.00 for the second book and 50p for each additional book.

Name ....

Address ....

....

....

If you would prefer to pay by credit card, please complete:
Please debit my Visa/Access/Diner's Card/American Express (delete as applicable) card no:

Signature .... Expiry Date ....